PRAISE FOR *THE PERFECT CHILD*

"A mesmerizing, unbearably tense thriller that will have you looking over your shoulder and sleeping with one eye open. This creepy, serpentine tale explores the darkest corners of parenthood and the profoundly unsettling lengths one will go to to keep a family together—no matter the consequences. Electrifying and atmospheric, this dark gem of a novel is one I couldn't put down."

—Heather Gudenkauf, *New York Times* bestselling author

"A deep, dark, and dangerously addictive read. All-absorbing to the very end!"

—Minka Kent, *Washington Post* bestselling author

WHEN

SHE

RETURNED

ALSO BY LUCINDA BERRY

The Perfect Child

WHEN SHE RETURNED

LUCINDA BERRY

THOMAS & MERCER

Text copyright © 2019 by Heather Berry
All rights reserved.

No part of this book may be reproduced, or stored in a retrieval system, or transmitted in any form or by any means, electronic, mechanical, photocopying, recording, or otherwise, without express written permission of the publisher.

Published by Thomas & Mercer, Seattle
www.apub.com

Amazon, the Amazon logo, and Thomas & Mercer are trademarks of Amazon.com, Inc., or its affiliates.

ISBN-13: 9781542092920
ISBN-10: 1542092922

Cover design by Rex Bonomelli

Printed in the United States of America

WHEN

SHE

RETURNED

PROLOGUE

Shiloh's screams pierced the air. I hoisted my nightgown and sprinted through the darkness. She writhed against me, getting instantly worked up and letting out another wail. Fear thrummed through me. I slapped my hand over her mouth. Her tiny body jerked with silent sobs. I dropped to the ground and shoved my thumb in her mouth, hoping it'd pacify her. She quieted immediately.

Thank God.

My heart pounded in my chest, lungs burning. I furtively scanned the forest. It felt like I'd been running in circles for hours. There was no way to tell where I was, which way I was going, if I'd been there before, but it didn't matter. I just had to keep moving.

I glanced down at Shiloh. Her eyes were wide open, staring back at me while she sucked on my thumb. She always woke starved. I kissed the top of her forehead, reminding myself that she was my reason. I would do anything for her.

"Just hold on, baby girl; hold on," I whispered.

The forest wasn't quiet, and every sound made me jump. I was sure any minute one of them would reach out and grab me. Or worse, snatch Shiloh. They'd take her to him. What if they left me here?

I stood, cradling her tightly against me. We had to keep moving. I tucked her head underneath my wrap and took off again. Weeds and branches tore into my legs like barbed wire. No matter. I pushed forward. Rocks cut into my bare feet. I just wanted to rest, but I couldn't stop. It was only a matter of time before she fussed again, and this time my thumb wouldn't suffice. Her cries would lead them right to us. That couldn't happen. I wouldn't let it. I ran on, fighting through the exhaustion that came in waves throughout the night, making my head throb. Just when I thought I couldn't take another step, the trees thinned, and a wider space opened in front of us. My footsteps quickened, and adrenaline surged again, giving me the final burst of energy I needed to push through the clearing and make it to the road.

And then I saw it—the neon lights stretching into the sky.

I sprinted across the road to the gas station. Shiloh jerked awake and began crying, but it didn't matter anymore.

"You can scream now. Scream all you want," I cried.

Two gas pumps stood empty, but the lights inside the store were on. I rushed to the door, springing back when it didn't open. I pushed again.

Nothing.

It wouldn't budge. I smacked the glass.

"No!"

Shiloh's cries moved into terrified screams. I beat on the door, yelling wildly. All this way. I'd come all this way. Tears coursed down my cheeks. Snot dripped into my mouth. I crumpled into a pile in front of the store.

"Hey." A male voice startled me, making me jump. I gripped Shiloh closer to my chest and scuttled back against the wall. The man peered down at me through thick glasses. He reeked of smoke. His name tag said *Matt* underneath the Amoco logo.

"What are you doing out here?" he asked. "Are you okay?"

I scrambled to my feet and flung myself at him. "Please, please, you have to help me!" I clawed at his shirt. "Call the police! Please, you have to! I'm Kate Bennett."

ONE

ABBI

NOW

I nervously fingered the chain around my neck. The small locket held Mom's picture, and I'd been wearing it since she had disappeared. We had finally buried her five years ago, but it was hard to have a funeral when you didn't have a body. Dad had assured me it was okay and that families did it all the time, like there were other kids whose moms had gone shopping and had never come home. We had a beautiful memorial service instead of a formal funeral and had buried the important parts of her, like her violin and a video of her best performances, copies of letters she'd written to Dad, and pictures of the three of us together on vacations and other special occasions. Things like that. But now she'd come back to life. Nobody came back to life after they were dead. I still felt like I was at the end of a dream, waiting to wake up.

I stared at the back of Dad's head. The long hairs on his neck had curled from sweat, like they did when he worked out. Only this time it was nerves. He sat in the passenger seat while Meredith drove, nervously bouncing his right leg. She had insisted on driving, and normally Dad would've put up a fight, but he hadn't said anything. He hadn't said much since they'd broken the news to me.

I had known something was wrong from the minute they had walked into my room without knocking. Dad always knocked first. Meredith had been practically holding him up from behind and pushing him through the doorway. Her hands were shaking, and her face was pale, but she looked good in comparison to him. His pupils were huge, so big they had overtaken the green of his eyes, and he held them open like he'd forgotten how to blink. I'd never seen him so wrecked. I jumped up from my bed, where I'd been working on my science homework.

"Dad, what's wrong?" I stood in front of him, but he looked past me like he wasn't seeing me, and he gazed out the window behind my desk like there was something important outside that he needed to see. "Dad?"

"I . . . it's . . ." His Adam's apple moved up and down as he wrestled with his emotions. His face was ashen and slick with sweat. "If we . . ."

Was he having a heart attack? A stroke? Why were they wasting time talking to me if something was wrong with him?

"What's happening?" I turned to Meredith. "What's going on, Meredith?"

"We just received some very shocking news." Her voice caught as she spoke. "Why don't we all take a minute and sit down on your bed?"

Maybe it was Caleb. Or Thad. Wouldn't they have texted me, though? But Meredith would have been in worse shape if something had happened to one of her sons, and she had been the one helping Dad to the bed like he had been injured, so it had to be him. Something was wrong with Dad. My worst fear was coming true. It'd been my greatest fear since I'd lost Mom—losing Dad. Anxiety rushed through me. I tried to steady my breath, pressing my toes against my shoes to stay present, like my therapist had taught me all those years ago. I sat next to him, twisting my hands on my lap and waiting for one of them to speak.

"Scott, you need to let Abbi know what's going on." Meredith cut into my panic.

Dad turned to me, his pupils still huge. He worked his jaw as he spoke. "They found your mother."

Mom.

I flattened into the bed like a balloon losing all its air. My limbs felt like they were coming loose. "Is she . . . is she . . ."

"She's alive," Dad said.

I didn't catch much of what he said after—something about Montana—because my head was spinning with hamster-wheel thoughts. Now, as we sped down the highway, it was still spinning as I replayed my memories and tried to imagine how Dad felt. It'd been eleven years since Mom had gone missing from the Target parking lot. She'd disappeared like a ghost, with her keys in the ignition and her purse on the passenger seat—no sign of a struggle.

I was five when it happened, so most of my earliest memories were of going door to door in Arcata neighborhoods with Dad and handing out her missing person flyer. We knocked on every door, and if nobody answered, we left one for them, making sure we didn't skip a house. Dad taped elaborate maps on our living room walls, keeping a color-coded record of where we'd been and where we still had to go. People criticized him for taking me with him on his searches, but they would've criticized him no matter what, since they found fault with everything he did back then. No one cared that he'd passed the polygraph. They still saw him as a suspect.

We knocked on doors for almost two years. Every year, on the day she went missing, they ran her story, airing some of the original footage of Dad pleading for her return. They talked about the grim statistics of missing people—how the longer they were gone, the less likely you were to find them alive. But Dad didn't care about the statistics. He never had. Everyone said it was impossible that she was still alive. They obviously didn't know as much as they thought, because we were headed to the hospital to meet her.

I leaned forward in the car and put my hand on his shoulder, wishing I could crawl into his lap and stay there. He squeezed my hand without turning around. "You okay, Pumpkin?" he asked.

"I'm fine, Dad," I said.

Of course I wasn't fine. We both knew that, but what was I supposed to say? I was on my way to meet a mother whose mythical legend had framed my childhood. There weren't any words for that.

I didn't remember much about her, since I was so young when she had gone missing, but Dad was full of memories. He knew her almost as well as he knew himself, since they'd grown up together and been high school sweethearts. He shared his memories with me constantly, trying to make them my own. Over the years, she had become like my favorite character from a movie that I'd seen over ten times and studied until I knew every line by heart. I stared at her pictures until I'd memorized every inch of her face. Every curve. Each line. My favorite picture was in a yellow wooden frame on the nightstand next to my bed. She was standing underneath a sparkling waterfall and staring off into the distance, like she had a hilarious secret, a wide grin on her face and a twinkle in her eye. Dad always said she'd had an infectious laugh, and I could almost hear it when I looked at that picture. My heart quickened at the thought of hearing her laugh myself. Would she still laugh? A shiver went through me. The police had said she had a baby with her. That only meant one thing.

TWO

MEREDITH

NOW

Someone needed to say something. Anything. Scott hadn't spoken for over two hours. Not since we'd left California and crossed the Oregon state line. I had made some silly comment about how beautiful the mountains looked, but it had come out sounding like I was trying too hard, but I talked when I was upset. I couldn't help it. That was how I worked through problems. Usually Scott was the same way. It was one of the things I loved the most about him and what had drawn me to him at the bereavement support group where we'd met.

I'd been coming to the support group for over two months, and although I had expected it to be mostly women when I had gone the first time, I had been surprised to discover all the men in attendance too. They had an emotional depth that I'd never witnessed in other men, not even in my father, and he was an emotional man. Unfortunately, their emotional maturity had come at the expense of unimaginable heartache and loss. Most of the men had been in their late forties and had lost their wives to cancer, much like my own story.

I'd never expected to be a widow at such a young age. Nobody did. When I'd married my first husband, James, I'd had the same dream as everyone else—build a family together and grow old watching our grandchildren play, hopefully great-grandchildren, if we were lucky. Nobody was ever prepared to hear the word *cancer*, and it slapped us in the face, just like it had everyone else after James went in for his physical that year. I envied the men and women whose spouses died quickly and with dignity. Brain cancer was a slow, debilitating death that stripped every part of his former self. It had been awful to watch, and as hard as my sons prayed for James's healing, in the end they prayed just as hard for his death. They were the ones who suggested I find a support group for widows. Cancer hadn't just sucked the life out of James—it'd sucked the life out of me, too, so I went even though I'd never been to any kind of support group before.

I'd already started settling into my new reality when Scott had shown up. I immediately recognized him when he walked into the church basement. Most of us did. You couldn't live in Arcata and not know about him. His face had been all over the news and media outlets. In a town as small as ours, something like that affected us all. Some of us were part of the teams that had combed the surrounding woods and riverbanks looking for any sign of her.

His brown hair had grayed at the roots, but he looked better than he'd looked all those years ago on TV when he'd been ravaged by grief and resembled a madman as he begged for anyone with information on his wife to come forward. He'd put on weight, and it'd filled out his face, making him appear friendlier and more relaxed. His full lips were closed, and he didn't look at any of us as he slid into one of the aluminum chairs in the circle. He kept his gaze fixed on the floor in front of him.

He was like that for months and didn't even speak other than to introduce himself during the beginning of the meeting, but he slowly opened up over time. We became friends and were strictly platonic for years, because he refused to believe Kate wasn't coming back. We started playing chess online late at night, since chronic insomnia was another thing we had in common, and, much like the other, it began when we'd lost our spouses. We instant messaged back and forth while we played. He spoke more in our online chats than he did in group, but then again so did I. Communicating online gave me a brazenness I wished I had in my interactions in the real world.

Have you been out with anyone since Kate?

I'd recently stepped into the dating world again. Dating in my late forties was even worse than it was in my twenties, and I didn't like it then.

His response was immediate.

Absolutely not.

Kate had been missing for over four years, so I assumed he'd been on at least a few awful dates and that we could swap stories. There were two types of people in group—those who didn't like to speak about their lost loved ones and kept their memories close to them, like carefully guarded secrets, and those who couldn't stop talking about them. Scott fell into the latter category, and he shared so many stories about Kate that I felt like I knew her personally. I knew more about her than I did about some of my closest friends.

Have you thought about it?

His response wasn't so quick that time. I felt the weight of his guilt while he typed.

A couple times . . .

Over the next few months, Scott opened up more and more about the difficulties he had with moving on. I reassured him that it was okay again and again, gently nudging him in the direction of letting go. He was so young, too young to spend the rest of his life alone. Then one night I just finally came out and said it.

Maybe it would help you let Kate go if you had her declared dead.

It had been another two years before he had. Another year before our first date.

And now here we were.

Newlyweds.

It'd been ten months since we'd made it official down at the court-house, with our children as our witnesses—my two boys, Thad and Caleb, and Abbi. Both of us had already done it the traditional way and hadn't wanted to do it that way again. Besides, those spots were reserved for our lost spouses. We respected each other's memories in that way. Instead of a big reception, we had gone out to dinner to celebrate, but it hadn't been all that different from our monthly family dinners. Blending our families had always been important to us. It was why we moved in together long before we got married. We weren't fools. We knew it might not work out, and both of us were willing to walk away from our relationship if it didn't work with our children. They'd been through too much already.

The transition with Thad and Caleb went smoothly. Thad only had the summer before he left for college, and Caleb was starting his sophomore year at Drake, so they were too busy getting started with their own lives to care that much about our relationship. Abbi was a different story. She was almost thirteen when Scott and I started living together and had never shared her dad with anyone. She only knew a life with her and Scott, and she wasn't so willing to let it go. My boys were the ones who broke her down, because they adored her and doted on her constantly. It didn't take long for her to return the feelings. They had never missed a violin recital when they were home from college, and all her friends had swooned over them.

I glanced at Abbi in the rearview mirror. Her eyes were closed, but I doubted she was sleeping. She never slept when she was upset. She was the perfect combination of Scott's and Kate's genes. She had Kate's slender build, which, coupled with Scott's angles, gave her an athletic frame even though she hated sports. There was something wholesome and endearing about her despite everything she'd been through.

My head reeled as it replayed scenes from this morning. The knock at the door had surprised me, since we hadn't been expecting anyone. I had looked out the kitchen window and had called for Scott. I saw two police officers on our front steps. A loud sigh escaped his mouth when he spotted them as he came down the stairs into the foyer. He had been imagining the moment for years, and he couldn't hide his relief that it was finally over.

"Are you Scott Bennett?" the officer asked.

Scott nodded, too nervous to speak.

"Sir, Kate Bennett has been found alive in Rittsberg, Montana," his partner announced.

Scott stumbled backward like he was drunk. I guided him onto the bench lining the entryway wall.

"Lean forward and put your head between your knees," the officer said in the commanding way all service members spoke.

Scott's color was off. Pasty. Gray. His labored breathing made me nervous. He leaned over and put his head between his legs. I rubbed his back, trying to get his shoulders to relax. It took a few minutes before his breathing slowed, but it finally did.

"Told you it helps," the officer said, even though Scott hadn't said anything.

He must have been in lots of these situations before to be so arrogant. Did you have to get specialized training to shatter people's lives? Even though he was telling us Kate was alive, I felt the shock waves splinter our former existence. We'd forever live in a distinct before-and-after sequence now.

Questions had been chasing each other ever since. I couldn't turn them off. I rubbed my forehead, tired of the endless loop. I moved my neck from side to side, trying to release the tension that'd been building in my stress spot since this morning.

"How are you feeling?" I whispered to Scott, just in case Abbi really was asleep.

He shrugged.

I flicked my head backward, motioning to Abbi, and mouthed, *What about her?*

He shrugged again.

"Do you want me to turn on music?"

"Sure," he said. His voice was strained and hoarse, like it got after he'd been up all night or at the end of a baseball game. His color was still off.

I needed my phone to navigate, so I flicked on the radio. All my preprogrammed stations from back home were filled with static. I flipped through until I found something clear. Classic rock music filled the car. He shook his head. Country music was next, and he hated country.

"Sorry," I said, quickly trying to change it and accidentally turning up the volume instead. Abbi jolted awake.

"Jesus," she said.

Normally one of us would have said something about her swearing, but there was nothing normal about this day.

"Should I see if I can find anything on AM? Maybe I can find talk radio or something. Or give me your phone to navigate and you plug mine in, since yours doesn't work in the adapter. I—"

He interrupted me and laid his hand on my thigh. "Honey, I love you. But can we just be quiet?"

THREE

ABBI

I stared angrily at the closed door, holding back the urge to pound my fists on it until they let me in. She was my mom, and I deserved to be in there with them, but someone official looking had met us at the emergency room entrance this morning and whisked us through the hospital without ever introducing herself to me. She'd shooed me into the hallway and shut the door behind them before I had a chance to protest. Dad would've said something to her about treating me like a little kid, if he hadn't been in shock. It wasn't fair that Meredith got to be in there with him and I didn't. I'd counted every mile until we'd gotten to Montana and never expected to be shut out like this.

I hated being treated like a kid when it came to Mom's case. They weren't talking about anything behind their closed door that I hadn't already thought of. Probably twice. I'd played out every terrible thing that could've happened to her over the years, and there was nothing they could say that would surprise me, but it was too late now. I was stuck.

My stomach hurt. I had slept horribly last night, since I never slept well in hotels, and all I'd eaten today was a banana. I didn't want to, but Dad made me. He hadn't eaten since yesterday, either, so I had only agreed to eat one if he did. As much as it bothered me that Meredith had gone in the room while I had been left out, at least she was there to support him. He was a mess.

My phone buzzed in my pocket. It'd been vibrating against me since I had switched it back on. I'd turned it off last night because my best friend, Meaghan, had been texting me nonstop, asking how I was and what was going on, until I couldn't take it anymore. I would've left it off, but I wanted Dad to be able to text me from inside if he wanted to.

Was Mom in there too? She couldn't be, could she? Probably not. Dad had been speaking with an investigator named Marcos ever since we had found out about Mom, and he had said that Mom and the baby had needed to be hospitalized for their injuries, and the room they'd gone into wasn't a patient's room. It looked more like a regular office. But she was in the same building. We were officially breathing the same air.

I hadn't thought about Mom in a long time. Months. Maybe even close to a year. Guilt washed over me. In second grade, I had thought Mom's kidnappers would murder her if I didn't think about her every hour—like wherever they had her in the world, her survival depended on my thoughts. I had been obsessed with making sure I did it and had set my alarm at night to wake me up. I had developed a weird form of OCD, and it had gotten me sent back to the psychologist I'd only recently stopped seeing. It felt eerily similar now. Like if I didn't keep her in my awareness at all times, she'd disappear again.

I eyed the doors leading to the other parts of the hospital. If I wandered past her in the hallway, would she recognize me immediately? Or would it be more of a strange pull toward me without being able to figure out why? For a while after she went missing, I had insisted on getting my hair cut every few weeks so it would stay the same length, because I had been terrified she wouldn't recognize me if I looked different.

What did she look like now? Nobody had said anything to Dad about her appearance. They'd barely said anything at all. All Marcos would tell us was that she'd shown up at a gas station in northern Montana with a baby, screaming for help, and they'd hospitalized them. He had promised he'd answer all Dad's questions in person. I eyed the closed door again. It was taking them forever.

And why was nobody talking about the elephant in the room?

What was Mom going to think when she found out Dad was married again? It wasn't his fault he'd moved on. If he'd had his way, he'd still be stuck journaling to her every morning and laying out her nightgown on her side of the bed every night. He would've waited forever. He always said they had the kind of love that only came around once in a lifetime.

FOUR

MEREDITH

NOW

I gripped Scott's hand underneath the table. We sat in white plastic chairs at the head, like it was some strange formal dinner, and we were the important guests. Harsh fluorescent lighting cast a bluish-green hue across the run-down room, and floral-print wallpaper left over from the eighties peeled from the wall behind me. The lead investigator, Marcos, sat on the right side of the table. He was flanked by his partner on one side and a police officer on the other. An important executive from the hospital occupied the remaining chair, while other doctors lined the walls. There were too many people standing, and it made the small space feel even tinier.

"I just don't understand why you can't give me any answers." I'd never heard Scott sound so angry. He glared at Marcos. Scott had gone from being in a shocked stupor to releasing a series of rapid-fire questions from the moment they shut the door behind us:

"Where has she been?"

"Who took her?"

"How did she get to the gas station?"

"Why was she in Montana?"

Much like he'd been doing since we'd come in, Marcos held up his hand to stop Scott. "I told you—she's in a state of severe traumatization. We are not pushing her to answer any questions until she's been cleared by the medical director, but unfortunately she's been away at a conference and her plane doesn't get in until after eight."

"What time does she get in?"

I placed my hand gently on Scott's arm. "He said eight o'clock tonight, honey."

This was the third time we'd been around this circle. Scott needed rest. He said he'd slept last night, but I'd felt him tossing and turning next to me all night long. He had crept into the chair underneath the window sometime before three and never came back to bed. He'd barely eaten anything all day. It'd only been a little over twenty-four hours, but he already looked like he'd lost weight. Thankfully, Abbi had gotten him to eat a banana this morning.

"And what's being done before then?" he asked. His dark hair stuck out at random angles from running his hands through it so much.

Scott had always been convinced that there'd been a series of missteps with Kate's case from the beginning and that the police hadn't done their job right—starting with not filing a missing person report until after she'd already been missing for forty-eight hours. He said they had wasted valuable time focusing on him when they should've been out looking for her.

"Are you sure you want to be involved with a murder suspect?" my mom had asked me when she found out we were dating.

I had laughed her off. "That was years ago, and they ruled him out as a suspect almost immediately."

Everyone knew the spouse was always a suspect whenever their partner went missing. The FBI wouldn't have been doing their job if they hadn't put Scott through the wringer. He'd come up clean, even passed both polygraphs, but that wasn't good enough for some people.

Nothing ever would be. Thankfully my mom wasn't one of them, and she had grown to love Scott like one of her own. My brothers had too.

"We have a team on the ground gathering any evidence from the gas station and tracing the forest around it. They're searching the area for any clues." Marcos was dressed nicely in a well-cut suit. He had sandy hair and intelligent blue eyes that hadn't moved from Scott yet.

"When can we see her?" Scott asked.

My breath caught. This was really happening. Kate was alive, and we were going to see her. None of this had seemed real until now.

Marcos cracked his knuckles and kept his gaze steady. "We'd like to get you to see her as soon as possible. A familiar face might help coax her out of her shell." He cleared his throat. "We're hoping you'll work with us in sharing any information she provides you with during your visit. Anything, even if it seems insignificant."

Scott nodded his head eagerly. "Of course. I'll do anything that helps figure out who took her." He pointed at me. "Meredith will, too, and I'll be sure to let Abbi know."

"What about the baby? Is she okay?" I asked.

They'd told us the baby was a girl, but they didn't know much more than that. Nobody knew her name, and Kate wasn't talking. She hadn't said anything since they'd brought her into the hospital. They had sedated her in the ambulance because she had freaked out when they'd closed the ambulance doors and had tried to jump out. She'd been mute ever since. The medicine hadn't just calmed her down—it'd turned her off.

A doctor leaning against the wall stepped forward, as if on cue. "The baby has been thoroughly evaluated by our staff of qualified pediatricians, and except for minor dehydration and a few scratches, she appears totally healthy."

I breathed a sigh of relief. I glanced at Scott to see his reaction. So far, he hadn't mentioned the baby once. He didn't miss a beat.

"Can we see Kate now?" he asked.

Marcos nodded. "I want to warn you about her condition, though. We don't know what she went through yet, but her body tells us she's been through a lot. Her time away has aged her significantly. Wherever she lived and whatever she went through, it was rough."

Scott squeezed my hand underneath the table. "We can handle it," he said.

FIVE

ABBI

Dad knelt in front of me. He and Meredith had been the last ones to file out of the room. Everyone else had left, except for Marcos.

"Why don't you tell her about what we warned you about?" Marcos towered above us. He reminded me of the varsity football guys at my high school, with his broad shoulders and bulging chest. I could tell he didn't have kids by the way my presence made him uncomfortable.

Dad put his arm around my shoulders. His eyes were wet. "Mom has been through a lot, and it's going to take her some time to recover. She is going to look very different than you remember, so I want you to be prepared when you see her."

Dad knew more about me than most dads ever knew about their teenage daughters. Probably more than he wanted to, like my bra size and the brand of tampons I used, since I told him almost everything, but one thing I'd never told him was how little I remembered about Mom. It would break his heart worse than it'd already been broken, and I couldn't do that to him, but my childhood memories were filled with his face instead of hers. My memories of Mom were more of a feeling—a time in space, etched into me in a way that no amount of time could erase. But they were just pieces. Very small ones.

What I remembered most about Mom was how Dad's eyes shone with love whenever he talked about her. I had loved going through the things in her closet and listening to his stories about her as he fingered the fabric of her favorite dresses, like he was telling me the world's most important fairy tale—how they'd been best friends when they were kids and had thrilled everyone when they had gotten together as teenagers. I never wanted to dress up as Cinderella or Snow White, because Mom had been my favorite princess. Over the years, Dad had snapped hundreds of pictures of me in her dresses. Our favorite picture was the one where I stomped through the kitchen in her wedding dress, wearing too-big cowboy boots and balancing an Easter hat on my head. And then one day I just stopped wearing her clothes. Why did I quit wearing her clothes? Was it the same day I stopped believing in princesses and fairy tales?

Her clothes had been stuffed in boxes in the back of the garage for years. We needed to get them out for her. But she couldn't wear clothes that were that old, could she? What was she going to wear? Why hadn't anyone thought of that?

"We didn't bring her any clothes," I blurted out.

Dad raised his eyebrows. "What?"

"She doesn't have anything to wear." Emotions bubbled their way to the surface. It was something so stupid to cry over, but I couldn't help it.

Dad brought me to his chest and wrapped his arms tightly around me. "It's going to be okay. We'll find something for her to wear."

I giggled through my tears. Meredith handed me a tissue from her purse. I blew my nose and let out a deep breath.

"Everyone ready?" Marcos asked.

Nobody answered, but we stood and followed him out of the room, then down a few short hallways. The hospital was as tiny as the town.

Marcos stopped at room 28A. Our movements slowed behind him. He gave everyone a moment before knocking and pushing through the door.

I grabbed Dad's arm and hung on to his bicep. Her room was filled with people, and everyone moved against the walls, providing a path to the bed for us. My heart leaped in my chest. The air left my lungs.

And then there she was.

Mom.

Her hair wasn't blonde anymore, but a mousy gray with patches missing on top and long tattered strands falling down the middle of her back. Her radiant blue eyes, which had shone so brightly from her pictures, were sunken and shallow; her cheekbones were skeletal, like maybe there was cancer eating away at her insides. Angry scars marked the right side of her face.

That wasn't Mom. It couldn't be. We were in the wrong room.

I turned to Dad. He was staring at her, unmoving. She brought her hands to her face, covering her mouth with long, shaking fingers. She was smaller than me. How did that happen? She bore no resemblance to the woman whose picture I'd kept underneath my pillow until I was eight years old.

Nobody moved. For a second, nobody spoke, like we needed a moment of silence to recognize the significance of the moment, and then everyone talked at once, and activity swirled around me. Suddenly I was in front of her.

She reached out and stroked my face softly, like she couldn't believe I was real. "Abbi," she whispered, barely audible.

I hadn't heard her voice in years, but the second I heard it, something inside me recognized her. "Mom." My voice shook with emotion. Tears streamed down my face.

She pulled me close and wrapped her frail arms around me. I could feel each one of the bones in her back. Her ribs pressed against my chest. I was afraid I'd hurt her if I squeezed too hard. Her smell was unfamiliar. Nothing like the perfume she used to wear. She smelled like spoiled milk.

Dad did his best to be patient as he stood next to me. I could've stayed in her arms forever, but I stepped aside so they could have their time. He threw his arms around her, and her small frame disappeared inside his. Their shoulders shook with sobs, and they whispered things to each other that none of us could hear. The nurses looked away, not wanting to intrude on the sacred intimacy of the moment. Meredith moved away from the back wall and came to stand next to me. She put her arm around my shoulders and brought me close to her.

"Welcome home, Kate. We're glad you're safe," she said, wiping away tears.

SIX

MEREDITH

NOW

I glanced into the back seat of the car. This time Abbi really was asleep. She'd fallen asleep almost as soon as we'd left the hospital. Poor thing. She'd cried all the way through the hospital and into the parking lot. "I'm not going to go back to the hotel yet," I said to Scott. "I'm just going to keep driving around so she can sleep. I'm afraid she'll wake up if we stop and won't be able to fall back to sleep. She needs to rest." I used to do the same thing when my boys were babies and I couldn't get them to sleep. I'd drive around until they finally crashed and then park with the car running until they woke up.

"Good idea," he said, nodding.

I made a left on Main Street and slowly drove past the mom-and-pop stores lining each side. My heart ached for Scott and Abbi. Our visit had been cut short by the baby. Scott and Kate had been embracing when the nurses had brought the baby back into the room. Scott had leaped off the bed like it was on fire.

"Shiloh." Kate's face had lit up at the sight of her baby. The nurse had handed her to Kate. She had squirmed and rooted for Kate's breast. Kate had moved her off, but she had come right back. It had gotten uncomfortable fast, since it was clear Shiloh wanted to nurse. Scott had rushed us out of the room without Abbi getting a chance to hug Kate or say a proper goodbye.

"I know Marcos warned us about how different she would look, but he should've been more specific," I said. "I mean, he couldn't have said, 'Hey, by the way, she's going to look like an eighty-year-old woman'? I'm pretty sure that would've been helpful for everyone."

"Maybe he wanted us to be shocked."

"Really?"

He shrugged. "Maybe. Who knows. I have no idea why they do anything that they do. You're about to see what I told you about all those years ago."

I'd heard everything about Kate's case. I knew it as well as if she'd been my own wife—exactly how she'd disappeared from the Target parking lot that day, everything that had been on her list to buy, and where she had left her purse on the front seat of their Toyota. I knew every step of the investigation, each lead they'd discovered, then quickly dismissed. All the traditional and nontraditional things he'd done to find her or at least a promising lead—the psychics, the mystics, and all the weirdos who'd reached out to Scott over the years with stories about their own relatives who'd vanished. There was an entire group of people who believed in a mass abduction conspiracy by the government. They had talked about it on one of those forums Abbi was always on.

"The police and investigators never give you all the information they have. They've always got cards they're hiding underneath the table," he said as we drove, slowing at a stoplight. "But yet they want you to share everything with them. You're expected to be an open book."

"At least we have nothing to hide," I said.

"It doesn't matter. They still treat you like you do." His voice burned with anger, no doubt remembering the wringer they'd put him through.

Abbi murmured and stirred in the back seat. We hushed until she fell back to sleep.

"She was unrecognizable," I said. I'd been through all their photo albums and had watched the home videos with them numerous times.

He gazed solemnly out the window. "I don't know. I see her in there."

I'd looked in her eyes, too, but that was not what I'd seen. They had looked dead to me.

"What did she say when you were holding her?" I asked.

He blushed, mumbling something underneath his breath that I couldn't hear.

"What'd you say?"

"It doesn't matter," he said.

"Yes, it does. It could be important. Remember Marcos said to remember everything she said, even if it seemed insignificant?"

"She said . . . she kept saying, 'I'm so sorry, Scottie.'"

"Scottie?"

He nodded, looking away.

"You told me you hated being called Scottie."

Red crept up his neck. "I mean, it's just . . . you know . . . it's something stupid she used to call me when we were like ten."

That was the thing with the two of them. They had been best friends before they got together, so they had known everything about each other, because that's how it is with a best friend. Scott used to say they had known each other so well she was practically in his DNA.

"That's cute," I said, forcing a smile. I didn't doubt he loved me, but I'd never forgotten those years I'd spent listening to him describe how losing Kate had been like losing part of his body and that he was only half a person without her.

KATE

THEN

I fumbled in the bottom of my purse, digging for my grocery list. Instead, all I found was a Ziploc bag full of crushed Goldfish and the red lollipop Abbi had gotten from the birthday party she'd gone to last Saturday. I let out a frustrated sigh. I probably left it at home again. God, I hated grocery shopping on Friday afternoons. The store was always packed with people, and the shelves were half-empty, but our week had been too hectic to go earlier, and now I had no choice, since we were out of milk.

I jumped out of the car and slammed the door shut before hurrying inside. I only had an hour before I needed to pick up Abbi from preschool. I always told myself I was going to get so much done while she was at school, but the four hours flew by so fast, and now that I was getting more writing assignments from my editor, Leo, my time was even more crunched.

Things would be easier next year when Abbi went to kindergarten. I didn't know who decided to make preschool only a half day, but I was ready to drop Abbi off at eight and pick her up at three. Not that I wouldn't miss her being with me during the day, but we were both ready for it. Time apart would do us good.

I kept replaying my conversation with Leo this morning. He had been hesitant to assign me a new job because he was afraid I wouldn't have enough time for anything major, but I'd been telling him for months that I was ready to get my old assignments back. Besides, the person who called about the interview specifically asked for me, so he didn't have much choice. I'd taken a three-month maternity leave from my job as a writer at the *Forum* and never returned full-time. My job was the reason we'd moved to Arcata. I won a George Polk Award for a local investigative piece I did on elder abuse in two of the best nursing homes in Royal Heights. It gathered me all kinds of attention after they arrested two of the directors, and job offers came in from all over the country. It had always been my dream to move to Northern California, and it was like it was meant to be when we discovered Scott's sales company had an office located in the adjoining town.

We decided I would stay home with Abbi and only work part-time until she started school, since the first five years were so important. I was glad I did it, but there were times when the boredom of being at home without a real job nearly drove me mad. It was all worth it, though, to see how happy and well adjusted Abbi was turning out to be. I'd never met a kid who was more delightful. Everyone said it too. It wasn't just because I was her mom. She was happy and content, no matter where she was or what was going on around her. She was in good spirits if she took a nap and wouldn't fall apart if she didn't, like so many other children did. Even my best friend, Christina, who swore she was never going to have kids, joked that she'd have one if she got one as good as Abbi. I couldn't take any credit for her easygoing manner. She just came out that way.

Scott had been unsure about me transitioning back to work full-time when I suggested it, but I was bored with the trivial side stories I was assigned. I could only write about the local bake sales and watering-schedule issues so many times before I was ready to pull my hair out. I wanted to work on stories with substance again.

"It's good for Abbi to see her mother working. I want her to have an image of me that comprises both," I had said over dinner the other night, nearly gagging at how liberal and progressive I sounded. Really, I was just ready to go back to work. I loved being Abbi's mom, but I also loved my job.

Scott always agreed with me whenever we talked about parenting and childcare, but we were going to see if he meant it, because Leo made it sound like this next assignment was going to be tough. It was why he was so reluctant to give it to me. Big stories required lots of extra hours, and it'd been a long time since I had been able to do anything beyond the bare minimum, but I was ready to jump back in, especially after I heard it involved a potential cult that had moved into the area and was hanging around on campus.

Pierce College was the heart of Arcata, and people's lives revolved around it. Students came from all over the world to study in their chemical engineering program and English world literature specialization. But our cute college town came with the same host of problems as every other college campus across America—we battled the opioid epidemic, losing two students to overdoses last year. Recently, a religious group referring to themselves as Love International had been showing up on campus and helping kids get off drugs. They had a facility on the outskirts of town, and members of Love International had taken them into their facilities and helped them detox. They stayed with them around the clock until they were sober. They'd already been successful with over a dozen students. Stories of their miraculous recoveries were spreading like wildfire throughout the community. It wasn't as if their approach to carefully monitored detox and 24-7 care was all that different from other approaches to sobriety. There were hundreds of programs or sober coaches who provided the exact same services. The thing that set Love International apart was that they did it for free. All of it.

They were welcomed into the community with open arms even though nobody knew why they'd chosen us or where they'd been before. There hadn't been anything negative said about them until one of the students who'd recently gotten clean dropped out of school afterward to join their movement. He began working with them to help other college students get sober too. It wasn't long before he was followed by a few of the others they'd worked with. That started the tension. Parents wanted their kids sober, but they also wanted them in school.

In the past month, Love International's circle of influence had widened, and other students who didn't even struggle with addiction were dropping out of school and working with them. Parents were up in arms about it, and everyone was demanding to know more about them. The case garnered national media attention after the college newspaper ran a story about them, and it went viral. Their leader was a man named Ray Fischer, and he had refused to speak with any national media or give a formal interview until now. It was an interesting twist, since most of the time organizations like his thrived on publicity and actively sought it out. But he'd declined all offers from the press, even those that carried monetary compensation.

For some reason he was very rooted in the local community and had contacted Leo a few days ago to request an interview. He only wanted to do an interview if it was with someone local, and he asked for me by name, since he'd read one of my other pieces. Leo wasted no time in setting up an official interview, since the college newspaper beat us to the first story, and we needed to get a jump on it before our neighboring competitor, the *Sun*, got ahold of him.

Leo had wanted to do it with me, since we were the only two people who had any experience covering something this big. He came from a busy urban paper in Detroit, where he'd handled the crime section until working his way up to lead editor of the entire Lifestyle department. But his father was dying from a rare form of lung disease and in his final weeks. Leo was preparing to return home to be with him for it. Even with a dying father, the possibility of a big story was hard to turn down. Things just didn't happen in Arcata. It could be years before anything like this came across our desk again.

My interview with Ray was scheduled for Monday. I had researched him all morning but hadn't been able to find much before he started Love International, and even that material was scant. All I found was his birth record. He was born in Westin, New Jersey, in 1960, which meant he was forty-seven years old, but besides that—nothing. My luck wasn't much better with Love International. They didn't have a website and weren't listed in any business or nonprofit directory. Not any that I could find, anyway. Their only mention was in the comments sections of various religious books on Amazon and a few blog posts written by members. Like most blogs, the first few entries were enthusiastic and gung ho but slowly dwindled over the next few weeks until they expired. None of the blogs had been active for years.

"Doesn't that make you worried that you know nothing about these people?" Scott asked. He was my first call after I had hung up with Leo. I wasted no time filling him in on the opportunity.

I laughed. "Absolutely not. It only makes it more exciting."

I didn't want to admit it to Scott, but it'd been a long time since I'd been this worked up about something. I loved my family. I did, but most of my life was centered on caring for other people's needs. Becoming a mom felt like I had forfeited all my rights in favor of others. It was my own idealistic view of perfect motherhood that got in my way, but still it felt like I never stopped cleaning or picking up after someone. I longed to do something besides the mundane tasks that made up my to-do list. I never really settled in to the stay-at-home-mom gig, even though I'd never admit it. The pangs of jealousy I'd felt the first day Scott went back to work after Abbi had been born had never left me.

I hurriedly grabbed the sauce I needed for the chicken kiev I was making for dinner and rushed out of the store to go pick up Abbi, but there was a huge smile on my face. I couldn't wait for Monday.

SEVEN

ABBI

NOW

I picked at my orange chicken. It was covered in the perfect amount of sauce, just like I liked it, but I couldn't bring myself to eat it. I still wasn't hungry. Dad's hunger had returned with a vengeance, though. He'd wolfed down all his beef and broccoli and was working his way through Meredith's leftovers.

"Honey, you have to eat something," Meredith said. Her eyes filled with concern, and a frown tugged at the corners of her mouth.

"I'm sorry," I said. "I'm just not hungry. I don't have an appetite."

It was hard to eat when there was an armed police officer standing outside your hotel room. Someone from the hospital had leaked Mom's story, and the media was already swarming the hospital. Marcos had told Dad our security was only an extra precaution, but nobody believed him. Definitely not me. People didn't carry guns unless there was a reason.

All the excitement I'd felt earlier was gone. Things were even more confusing than before. I burst out crying. Meredith and Dad jumped up from their chairs and surrounded me, sandwiching me between them in a huge hug. The flood of emotions I'd been feeling all day rushed through me.

"It's okay. Let it out." They spoke on top of each other. "We love you. We're here."

I clung to Dad's shirt, burying my face in it. I couldn't remember the last time I had cried so hard. It felt like it wasn't going to end, and then suddenly it did—from out of nowhere the sobs just stopped. I disentangled myself, awkward and embarrassed by my outburst. For the second time today, Meredith handed me a tissue. Nobody had told me it would feel like this.

"What's going to happen?" I asked in a small voice.

Meredith opened her mouth to speak, then shut it quickly, allowing Dad to go first.

"I don't know, Pumpkin, but I wish I did." He wrestled with his emotions before continuing. "We're going to take things one step at a time, just like we did before. You probably don't remember this, but that's all I used to say back in the early days—'Scott, do what's in front of you.' I must've said it hundreds of times. Sometimes that's all you can do, and this is one of those times." He pointed to the food in front of me. "So right now, at this moment, you're going to do your best to get some food inside you so that your body has nutrients, and then all of us are going to try to sleep, because our minds need it." He patted me on the back. "That's it. We're not doing any more than that tonight. Got it?"

I nodded, picking up my fork. They went back to their seats, and for a moment we all ate in silence.

"I spoke with one of her doctors again tonight while you were in the shower," Dad said. He'd promised to fill me in on any new information he got about Mom, since he'd be the one everyone was talking to, and I wouldn't always be there when he did. "Your mother is pretty sick. All her tests and blood work are starting to come back from the lab, and none of them are normal. They're taking a bunch more and sending them out again."

"But it's just because she was dehydrated, right? There's nothing seriously wrong with her?" I asked.

His eyes flooded with concern. "Technically, yes, but it's complicated. Severe dehydration and malnutrition can really screw up your body's systems and organs over time. We have to wait and see what the follow-up test results show before we know anything more."

"How come the baby is so healthy?" I asked. I heard Meredith's sharp intake of breath behind me at the mention of the baby. Dad hadn't said anything about the baby, and I hadn't wanted to ask, but not because I didn't want to know. Everyone wanted to know about her.

"The baby is healthy because she was able to breastfeed, but your mother didn't have that option, so your mother is severely malnourished," he said without missing a beat.

"So the baby is hers?" I asked.

"Yes, the baby is hers. It looks like she gave birth seven weeks ago."

———

Dad held my hand as he led me into the hospital room with Marcos the next morning. Marcos motioned to one of the padded office chairs lining the wall. Bad jazz music played from a speaker somewhere, and soothing magazines filled a rack in the right corner. I stood, crossing my arms, like somehow if I didn't sit down, then they couldn't tell me whatever it was they were going to tell me, since this was clearly the room where they told people bad news. Dad, Meredith, and I stood in an odd semicircle.

Marcos's expression had been the same for two days; he never smiled, and there was nothing friendly about his eyes. The shirt underneath his jacket was red today. It darkened his skin.

"Why don't we sit?" He phrased it as a question, but it was more of a directive.

I gripped Dad's hand tighter as we sat in the chairs next to each other, so close our knees touched. It wasn't the first time an investigator had led us into chairs like this, but we'd never been here before. Someone in the hallway shut our door, and the air left the room immediately. Everything felt fluid. My head swirled with the motion.

"I wanted us to talk about the next steps with your mother," Marcos began, wasting no time getting down to business. He always referred to Mom as "your mother." He never said "your wife" to Dad or even mentioned her by name. It was weird. How did he refer to her when he and Dad talked alone? "The medical director from the hospital arrived last night as expected and was kind enough to come straight from the airport. After—"

"What did you find out?" Dad interrupted, unable to wait on a lengthy explanation.

"I wish I had more information to give you, but these types of investigations take time, and we have to make sure we do everything by the book. There's no room for mistakes. With that being said, the medical director cleared her for questioning, and normally we would be able to proceed with our investigation, but Kate failed the mental status exam, which puts us in a difficult position." He spoke quickly before Dad could interrupt him again. "Part of the reason she failed the mental status exam is because it asks basic questions like day of the week and year, and she can't answer those things correctly. But it's not because she's mentally incompetent—she's been isolated from society for years, so she has no idea how much time has passed."

"What do you mean by isolated?" Dad asked.

He shrugged. "We're not sure yet. It could be anything from being kept on the fringes of society to physically locked away somewhere."

"And you're sure that's why she doesn't know what day it is?" Meredith asked.

I turned to Meredith and raised my eyebrows at her. What was she trying to suggest? That Mom was crazy?

"Absolutely. There are other pieces of evidence too. For example, she hasn't received any kind of medical or dental care for at least five years. One of her back teeth was yanked out with an instrument, most likely pliers, from an infection that looks like it worked its way into her gums. She never received any care before or after delivery, so her body is pretty beat up from her pregnancy. The umbilical cord was cut with scissors or a knife. Things like that."

Meredith leaned forward in her seat next to me. She had a weak stomach. It was one of the things we teased her about all the time.

"One of our first priorities is to get her oriented to time and her surroundings. It's going to be nearly impossible to follow any kind of a timeline without her being grounded in the present at least somewhat. Thankfully, we have a team of experts arriving within the next few hours, and they're skilled in handling these types of delicate situations," he said.

Dad's hand relaxed in mine, and some of the tension left his body. He'd always complained about the police department's incompetency when Mom went missing. He said they weren't equipped to handle a crime of that magnitude, and that the FBI should've been called in long before they were. We had gotten Dean out of the deal when the FBI finally got involved, but we would always wonder what could've happened if he'd gotten there sooner. At least we were going to have the best people working with us from the beginning this time.

"We're still within the first seventy-two hours of the investigation, so our sole focus is on gathering as much evidence as we can from your mom and other sources. A few of our investigators stumbled across an old RV campground that had recently been abandoned, so our teams have expanded their search to the forests and canyons within a ten-mile radius of that campground as well as the gas station. The gas station attendant has already been interviewed, but he'll be interviewed again once the expert team arrives. A few truckers along the route have also been identified as potential witnesses, and those interviews are happening as we speak," Marcos said. "Drafting our media announcement is our first agenda item this morning."

What we were going to tell the media about Mom's case couldn't have been further from my mind. I didn't understand why we had to give them a daily update. "How is she doing?" I asked. Her case was important, but I wanted to know about her.

Marcos and Dad exchanged a look. Dad shifted in his seat.

"She's scared to death," Marcos said, taking a seat in the chair across from me. His big frame fit awkwardly underneath the David Hockney painting hanging on the wall. He leaned forward, his knees almost touching mine. "I know this must be difficult to understand, but when people are taken and treated poorly for a long period of time, their brains do weird things to keep them safe. Bad people can scare you quiet, and they can scare you quiet for a long time, even after help comes."

I fought the urge to cry like I had done yesterday. "How badly did they hurt her?"

Dad placed his hand on my arm. "The details aren't important."

I pushed it off. "Yes, they are. You of all people should know that. Details are everything."

He took a deep breath before nodding at Marcos, giving him permission to continue.

"It looks like she was systematically tortured over an extended period of time." Marcos maintained direct eye contact with me as he spoke, unflinching.

"What do you mean by systematically tortured?" I asked.

"She's been whipped with switches, and her body is covered in burns and other scars. It appears—"

Meredith interrupted him. "Please, stop. That's enough," she said.

It might be too much for her, but it was nothing compared to what Dad and I had been through. He'd had to view a dead corpse once to see if it was Mom. I leaned forward and tried to look nice while I said it, because I didn't want to hurt her feelings. "Sorry, Meredith, but if you can't handle it, then you're going to have to leave the room, because I want to know everything that happened to my mom."

KATE

THEN

My insides shook with nerves. It wasn't like I hadn't done big interviews before, but this was my first face-to-face interview postbaby—a step back into a part of my life I'd left behind after Abbi. I smoothed down the front of my skirt, grateful it was high waisted enough to cover the pooch I'd given up losing a long time ago. Maybe having to squeeze into something besides yoga pants would motivate me enough to lose the last nagging ten pounds. Once your child was five, it no longer qualified as pregnancy weight, did it?

What if I'd forgotten how to navigate in the professional world? But my confidence grew with each click of my new heels on the sidewalk. This was nothing. I'd done interviews in a prison before.

You got this, I reminded myself as I walked.

Love International's complex loomed in front of me. Their head-quarters were just past the edge of town, where the main road evolved into an old highway that was lined with a strange mix of houses and concrete buildings. They'd recently renovated an abandoned office building. They'd gone from meeting in parks and church basements to having a completed facility in only two months.

The sign on the front door read **WELCOME HOME**, and a woman swung it open right as I raised my hand to knock. She looked young—clean and fresh like soap—and her smile revealed a dimple in her left cheek. I'd imagined a New Age–looking space with woven tapestries of color hanging on the walls next to framed pictures of women in lotus positions, with their chakras lit up in different colors. Instead, the walls in the lobby were devoid of color. They were a muted beige, completely neutral.

"Welcome, I'm Bekah," she said breathlessly, like she might have run to the door. Her clothes matched the walls around her—a skirt that flowed past her knees paired with a plain T-shirt, all in various shades of beige. "There's no need to knock around here. Our doors are always open and unlocked."

"Thank you," I said, stepping inside. "I'm Kate."

She nodded. "I know. We've been expecting you."

"Thanks for taking the time to show me around today."

"No problem." She smiled. "It's my pleasure."

The set of double doors behind the lobby entrance opened into a wide, expansive room. Everything inside was minimalist, and the room gleamed with order and sterility. The smell of incense and burning candles that I'd expected was nowhere to be found. Instead, the fragrance of Pine-Sol filled the air. Dozens of aluminum chairs were stacked in the back, and a wooden podium stood at the front. There were three doors on the outer walls. Foldout tables dotted the room. Some had white plastic chairs. Others were empty. There was nothing warm or comfortable about the room. No personal touches, but something about it was still inviting.

"What's behind all the doors?" I asked.

She pointed at the first one on the left. "That one leads to the cafeteria. We serve three meals a day to anyone who shows up." She pointed to the one next to it. "And that is where all of our detox rooms are."

"Can I see one?" I asked.

"Sure," she said.

I hid my shock that she had said yes so quickly. I'd spent most of last night preparing my responses for the defensive and hostile attitude

I was sure I'd meet when I tried to dig deep. This was great. I smiled to myself. Leo was going to be so pleased.

She opened the door, revealing a long hallway lined with more doors. She tapped on the middle one on the right side, waiting for a response before stepping inside. I followed her into the cramped space. It wasn't much larger than my walk-in closet at home. Much like the rooms before, it was simple, clean, and orderly. There was a bed pushed against one wall and a small sink against the other.

"How do you detox people here?" I asked. Where was all the medical equipment? They at least had to be able to give people fluids, didn't they?

She pointed around the room like I was missing something. "We detox in this room."

"Like all of it? From beginning to end?" I asked, thinking about all the times I'd watched my mother writhe in agony on the bathroom floor as her favorite poison left her body.

She nodded.

"Isn't that dangerous?"

"Aren't drugs dangerous?" she asked with a smile.

She led me back into the main room and through a door on the other side. A maze of hallways lay in front of us, and she talked while we walked. I tried to peek into any slightly opened doors, but she walked too fast for me to get a good look. She slowed when she came to the end of the L-shaped hallway. "And this is Ray's area."

"He stays on-site with the members?" I asked.

She shook her head. "Oh, no, disciples don't stay on campus."

Interesting that she called it a campus. "There's a difference between the members and the disciples?"

"Yes."

"Who are the disciples besides Ray, and where do they stay?"

She smiled and motioned down the hallway and toward the door. "Come."

It wasn't lost on me that she hadn't answered my question.

She knocked on the door.

"Come in," a male voice responded.

She pushed open the door. A man rose from behind a desk in the center of the room and strode toward us wearing the same matching beige T-shirt as Bekah. I'd figured he would be handsome, since the college girls got all swoony eyed whenever they talked about him, but he was stunning. His curls were midnight black and swept away from his chiseled face. His eyes gleamed icy blue, and he smiled at me, revealing a crooked grin that, combined with the slight bend in his nose, marked his perfect looks in a way that only made him more attractive.

"I'm Ray Fischer," he said as he stuck out his hand to shake mine. "And you must be Kate."

"I am," I said, hoping my palm wasn't sweaty. Nerves always made me sweat. His handshake was firm, confident.

He pointed to the chair in front of his desk. "Have a seat." He turned to Bekah. "Thank you so much, Bekah. Will I be seeing you at dinner?"

"Of course." She nodded at him before turning to me. "I enjoyed meeting you, Kate. I hope to see you again soon," she said, shutting the door behind her before I had a chance to respond.

I pulled out my notebook and placed it on top of my lap while he sat back down. He leaned across the table and folded his hands together, resting his chin on top.

"What would you like to talk about today?" His eyes pierced me, immediately making me feel naked and exposed, like he could see right into my soul. It was unsettling.

I swept the room for any framed degrees or personal artifacts that might give me insight into him or the movement, but the walls were as blank as the rest of the place. They'd recently been coated in a layer of fresh beige, but that was it. "Maybe you could start by telling me a little bit about yourself?" I asked.

He burst out laughing. "Really? That's all you've got for me?" Heat rose in my cheeks. He didn't let me gain my composure before continuing. "How about you tell me about yourself?" His teasing smile lit up his face, and he waited for me to answer.

"I'm pretty boring," I said, flipping through my notebook like I was searching for something important, so I didn't have to look at him.

"I see that you're married," he commented, noticing the ring on my finger. It was hard not to. Scott had outdone himself on our tenth anniversary. We'd been so poor when he proposed that he'd only been able to get me a plain silver band. It'd never bothered me—still didn't—but it'd always bothered him, so he'd bought me the ring he'd wanted to back then. I nodded, still pretending to be buried deep in my notes. "How long?"

For a second, I considered lying to avoid the inevitable response, but I'd promised Scott a few years back that I'd stop lying about how long we'd been together. I'd only done it to avoid the comments about it, but Scott had flipped out when he'd overheard me, and we'd gotten into one of our biggest fights. He'd taken it way more personally than it had been—saying it hurt that I was embarrassed about our relationship. He was proud to have been together since we were teenagers and saw it as the most special thing about us. He hadn't said it that way at first. Initially, he'd thrown his immature, fourteen-year-old-boy tantrum by swearing and stomping around the house while he had yelled in my face about how coldhearted I could be. It had only been after a two-hour conversation that he had come around to talking about what was really bothering him.

"We've been married for seventeen years," I had said, bracing myself for whatever he'd have to say about it. Over the years I'd heard it all. There were people who thought it was the sweetest thing ever and others who asked if we'd *been with* anyone else, like people freely discussed their sexual history with strangers. Occasionally, I'd run across someone who thought it was gross after they'd found out that we used to have sleepovers together when we were kids.

"What's that been like for you?" Ray asked.

I shifted uncomfortably in my seat, pulling my skirt down. "It's been wonderful. Really wonderful. I feel blessed to have met my soul mate and best friend when I was nine."

He burst out laughing again.

"What?" I shrank back in my seat.

"I'm sorry, but you just sounded like a Hallmark card commercial. I couldn't help myself." His eyes danced with humor.

I couldn't help the smile from forming on my lips. "It is pretty cheesy," I said.

He gazed at me from across the desk, even though it was his turn to speak. It didn't take more than a few beats for me to realize he was content to sit in silence staring at each other. Not me. I looked out the window behind him, trying to focus. I had to control the interview. I couldn't let him walk away with it. "Why Arcata?"

He lifted his palms up. "Why not?"

"How long do you typically stay in one place?"

It was my polite way of asking whether or not they planned to take up permanent residence. As many people that were in favor of their presence, there was an equal number who didn't like how they'd infiltrated our community. Small towns were steeped in tradition and didn't take to change well, especially change that involved ideas they weren't familiar with, and strangers helping people for free certainly qualified as such.

"We never know."

"What's the longest you've stayed in a place?"

"Two years."

"And the shortest?"

"Three days." He smiled and reached for a stack of papers on the side of his desk. He riffled through them until he found what he was looking for and handed me a flyer. "This is a list of our meeting times. You won't get a better idea of what Love International is about until you attend one of our meetings. Why don't you come to one?"

I skimmed the paper and was surprised at how many classes were listed. Each day had at least three. Weekends were packed with different times for their gatherings.

He stood, indicating that our time had come to an end. I stood and stuck my hand out. "Thanks for taking the time to meet with me. I'll be in touch."

He led me toward his door, ushering me back out into the hallway. "Please do consider attending one of our meetings. I think you'll find them enjoyable, and I'd love to see you again." He shut his door quickly, without giving me a chance to respond.

I stared at the closed door. Leo wasn't going to be happy with me. I didn't know anything more about Love International than I had before the interview. Maybe getting back into the swing of things wasn't going to be as easy as I had thought.

EIGHT

MEREDITH

NOW

"Mom, you can't be serious—"

I cut in. "Keep your voice down, Thad."

I didn't want anyone to hear our phone conversation, and the hotel walls were paper thin. It didn't matter that I'd gone outside and was leaning against the railing at the end of the hallway. People used to say Thad had a grown man's voice in a little boy's body. He would've made a great preacher, but none of my children were religious, even though they'd gone to mass every Sunday when they were kids. They'd turned their backs on God after they had prayed for their dad to get healed and he had died.

He dropped his voice to a whisper. "You're actually thinking about bringing her back to California and living with you guys?"

I couldn't believe it either. The last forty-eight hours had been a whirlwind of activity. "The FBI is moving her case to California, since they have jurisdiction over it. There's some kind of safe house she could stay in—"

"Mom!" he shrieked, not even bothering to keep his voice down. "Are you listening to what you're saying? It's a safe house." He drew out the word *safe*. "They don't put you up in one of those unless you're in some kind of danger. And you're considering taking her into your home?"

"It would only be for a little while. Just until they get things figured out." I tried to sound optimistic.

"How are they planning on keeping you safe if they don't know what they're protecting you from?"

I eyed the police officer standing outside our hotel room door. He had been trying to pretend like he hadn't been watching me for our entire phone call. I still wasn't used to them following us around. "They're going to keep a security detail on us when we get home, like they're doing now. So far it doesn't look like anyone even knows where we are."

He snorted. "Because you're not home. All that's going to change once you get home and word gets out. It's only a matter of time."

That went without saying. It was one of the reasons I'd been hesitant to move in with Scott, because of the house's notoriety and strange following. He'd received his share of hate threats and messages, but at least those had been gone by the time we'd gotten together. Still. Every few months we'd find someone wandering slowly by the house, trying to pretend like they weren't taking a picture of our place.

"It's not permanent. It'd only be while they continue their investigation. Besides, Scott won't even consider letting her stay in the safe house. He's been talking about bringing her home with us since we drove to pick her up."

"And Kate? Any chance she's said anything about this?"

"No, but come on, Thad. You can't expect her to make any decisions in the state she's in."

We had no clue what she thought about everything going on around her. She hadn't spoken much since her first interaction with Scott, at least not to us or when we were in the room. She stayed huddled on her hospital bed with Shiloh pressed against her chest, her eyes darting back and forth across the room continuously. Even though her body was still, she was poised to run at any given moment. She jumped at the slightest noise.

"I can't even begin to tell you everything that's wrong with this plan." I could see him sticking out a finger as he listed each item on his list. He'd always been my logical and practical one. "You don't know where she's been or what she's been doing for eleven years. No clue. Nobody knows why she left. Still. She clearly hasn't been alone all this time." I could hear his eye roll. "Then she suddenly pops up out of the blue with a baby, but once she's rescued, she stops talking? Come on, Mom. You've got to admit, there's something weird about all of it."

I sighed. "Everything about this is weird."

"What about her family? Why aren't they there? How come they're not rejoicing that she's been found and coming in to swoop her up? Let her go live with them."

"I explained all this to you before," I said. "Kate was an only child. Her parents died in a car accident when she was a teenager. Most of her extended family lives in Sweden, and she was never close with any of them, because they were all wild and crazy."

"I'm sticking with my original judgment—this is a terrible idea." He huffed.

I would've had the same reaction if the situation were reversed, but I trusted Scott's judgment. He wouldn't do anything to put us in harm's way.

KATE

THEN

I hurried to make it on time to my second interview session with Ray. Leo was still annoyed about how things had gone before, but he couldn't get too upset, since I'd hit it out of the park with the other big story he'd assigned me—the girls' soccer coach who'd just been fired from Middleton High School for sending inappropriate pictures of himself to a girl on his team. I had uncovered a list of prior offenses before anyone else, and the article had quickly made national news. But it didn't make up for how terrible things had gone with this story, and I was determined to do better.

I walked in the front doors without knocking and quickly made my way through a meeting in progress, doing my best not to disturb them, and hurried down the rows of rooms until I reached Ray's at the end. His door was wide open, and he got up from his desk at the sight of me. He rushed toward me and threw his arms around me before I had a chance to protest. "Hi, Kate. It's so good to see you again." He quickly pulled away and motioned to the chair in front of his desk, where I'd sat before. "Have a seat. Let's get started."

He left the door open behind us, which felt strange. It shouldn't have, but something about it just didn't feel right.

"Does the door open make you uncomfortable?" he asked, instantly picking up on it.

I wasn't going to let him throw me off so easily this time. "I'm okay with it if you're okay with it."

He lifted both his hands, palms up like he was a magician showing me there wasn't anything up his sleeves. "I've got nothing to hide."

"Perfect. Then should we get to it?" I asked, not giving him any time to gain control of the questions. I pulled my tape recorder out of my purse and set it on the desk. "Do you mind if I record this?" I asked. He nodded his agreement before I continued. "What do you have to say to your critics who think you only get people clean so that they can work for you for free?"

He balked, taken off guard, but recovered quickly with a smile. "Okay, I see where you're going now. I don't have anything to say to my critics."

"Not even those who'd call you a cult?"

He burst out laughing. "We're not a cult."

"How would you describe yourself then?" I asked and quickly added, "In one sentence."

He rubbed his chin while he thought. "We're a social justice movement committed to spreading the love of Christ to all." He leaned across his desk. "Are you familiar with Matthew twenty-five?"

"Sorry, I'm not," I said.

"Matthew twenty-five, verses thirty-five and thirty-six, sums up our entire philosophy. Jesus said, 'I was hungry and you gave me something to eat, I was thirsty and you gave me something to drink, I was a stranger and you invited me in, I needed clothes and you clothed me, I was sick and you looked after me, I was in prison and you came to visit me . . . Whatever you did to the least of these, you did to me.' That's how we live our lives, and it's the closest thing we have to a creed."

It was hard to find fault with that. Not nearly as juicy as Leo and I might have secretly hoped. "So how does that work? Practically speaking." It sounded beautiful and poetic, but I wanted to know how that played out in day-to-day life.

He folded his hands on the top of the desk. "We live our lives as servants of Christ."

It still didn't tell me anything significant. Not anything that I couldn't read in one of the pamphlets stacked next to their front door. I shifted gears. "Were you always this into helping people?"

"Absolutely not. I stumbled upon it purely by mistake and divine intervention," he said.

I spent the next hour listening to him describe how he'd grown up extremely poor on a small farm in rural New Jersey. He started working when he was nine and never stopped, going on to become a successful stockbroker as an adult. He described how he was living the American dream until one day on his commute home he started questioning his happiness. It led him to go in search of greater meaning. It seemed a bit cliché to me, and my thoughts drifted as he continued explaining how he gave his money away to various charities. He had started with giving possessions to homeless people on the streets and had ended with allowing families from domestic violence shelters to move into the three houses he owned across the country.

"I've never looked back," he said after he finished.

"Not even once?"

He shook his head. "There was always a measure of unrest and emptiness in my soul. I spent my life ignoring it and pretending like it wasn't there. This way of life has not only taken away those feelings, but it's allowed me to stop living a lie and to step into a life of authenticity. The greatest riches in the world never gave me that," he said.

I did my best to keep a straight face and not show my annoyance. The only people who ever complained about having all kinds of money and not being happy were the ones who had it. One of the reasons I was so glad to be back at work was that Scott and I could stop fighting about money. We'd been arguing about money since Abbi was born, and we'd never been ones to fight about our finances. All that had changed when we had gone down to nearly a one-income family, but Scott refused to admit that was why we were struggling so hard. It was too big of a hit to his ego that he couldn't support us in the way we'd been used to on just his income alone.

Ray's voice jumped into my thoughts. "Boring you, huh?"

"Absolutely not," I said. Being a reporter meant I'd learned the art of feigning interest and pretending to listen when I didn't care all that much, and Ray's story was quickly losing me. It wasn't any different from that of so many of the other self-proclaimed spiritual leaders running around California. I motioned to the walls in our room, the facility surrounding us. "Who paid for this?"

"People give out of the generosity of their own hearts, and God always provides," he said.

Tomorrow I was interviewing the parents of a nineteen-year-old boy, Sean, who had been one of the first kids they'd helped get clean and had recently joined their movement. They'd given a $200,000 donation to Love International three weeks ago. It was hard to tell whether it was in support of the movement or a way to keep a roof over their son's head while he was with them.

"Have you had enough of this?" he asked, catching me off guard this time.

"What do you mean?"

He smiled at me. "Come on, Kate. I can tell when I'm boring someone to death."

I shook my head. "Not at all. I find this stuff fascinating," I said, hoping I sounded convincing.

"You don't lie to your husband like that, do you?"

I sat up in my chair. "Excuse me?"

"My apologies. I didn't mean to push any buttons."

"You didn't push any buttons," I snapped.

"I didn't?" He cocked his head to the side, eyeing me quizzically. "From where I'm standing, it looks like I did."

Was he like this with everyone? Or was it only with women?

"I'm not a liar," I said.

"We're all liars," he countered, eerily similar to the philosophy professor I'd had in college.

"What do you lie about?" I asked.

A wide smile stretched across his face, lighting up his eyes. "Now we're getting somewhere," he said.

———

It was my second meeting at the center, and I was so much more comfortable this time even though I was still bummed that Scott had refused to come.

"You know how I feel about organized religion," he had said.

But that wasn't the point. Religion wasn't my thing either. My parents hadn't even brought me to church on the holidays. I just thought it'd be fun, something different for us to do together, but he had no interest. Sometimes I didn't know why I even tried. He was a creature of habit. Always had been.

I poured myself a cup of coffee and grabbed two of the sugar cookies from the platter before taking a seat on one of the aluminum chairs. When I was a kid, I had loved how routine oriented Scott had been, since it had been so different from the chaos continually erupting at my house. His structure had grounded me. It had kept me sane through all those difficult years, especially after my parents had died, but lately it felt stifling, and I didn't know what to do about it. Guilt gnawed at me like it did whenever I let those kinds of thoughts creep in. I was lucky to have Scott. Period. I forced myself to pay attention to what was happening around me. The meeting would be a welcome distraction.

The aluminum chairs were arranged in a circle tonight. Last time I'd been in this room was for orientation, and they'd been in front of the podium. You couldn't attend any of the classes, lectures, or retreats until you'd completed their orientation. You weren't even allowed in the building unless you were registered to do it, and everyone wore name tags on lanyards around their necks once they were inside, so there was no mistaking who you were. There wasn't any official security, but you couldn't miss the large, bouncer-looking dudes roaming the hallways and peeking into their classrooms. They'd had to tighten up their open-door policy after they'd started receiving death threats from someone in the community.

"I'm not sure I want you going back there," Scott had said after he'd heard about it on the news.

I had dismissed him, not even entertaining the idea of not going back to their campus. None of the threats were serious. It was only talk.

"It's just the small-town mentality of people not liking change and being resistant to anything that doesn't fall within their traditional ideologies."

He had grabbed my waist and pulled me close, kissing me. "I love it when you get all smarty-pants on me."

I hadn't had the heart to tell him that sometimes I felt like I was describing him. Even though we'd both grown up in the same small town in Illinois—Castlerock, population all of three thousand people— I'd spent my childhood feeling like I never fit in and plotting ways to get out. Scott pretended to hate it as much as I had, but he would've gone back there after we finished college if I hadn't insisted on moving to Chicago.

I took my tablet out of my purse just as a van pulled up out front and a group of teenagers spilled out. They looked like the crew that went around town collecting donations from people's homes and thrift-store castaways. There were different crews responsible for doing things throughout the community, and everyone got to choose their crew based on how and who they wanted to serve. Everyone did their part. That's how things worked.

"So who cleans the toilets?" I'd asked Ray in one of our meetings. We'd met four times, and our talks were growing on me. His personality could be intoxicating, and I always came out of them feeling like I'd had two glasses of wine.

"You'd be surprised, but someone always selects bathroom duty. That's not even the worst job, though. Somebody has to clean out the grease pan underneath the industrial stove in our kitchen. Imagine how disgusting that must be, but people do it, and many do it with a smile on their face," he'd said in response.

The kids streamed through the rooms, sunburned, dirty, and tired, but with smiles on their faces. Some of them looked really young. We needed to get Abbi involved in service. She was old enough to do something. I made a mental note to talk to Scott about it when I got home.

Our room quickly filled with people, and it wasn't long before the seats were full. The disciples were dressed in their beige uniforms, making them stand out from the others. The women wore skirts down to their ankles, and the men wore khaki pants. They all had plain, matching T-shirts. Everyone else wore regular street clothes like me.

"Why the beige?" I'd emailed Ray. He was surprisingly responsive to email and almost always got back to me within twenty-four hours, even though he claimed they avoided technology unless absolutely necessary.

He'd explained one of their core beliefs was to eliminate all distractions and avoid any stimulus that might artificially create a spiritual experience where there was none. I had to admit, there was something inherently calming about it. Something about the nothingness quieted my mind.

I checked to make sure my phone was off for the third time. They had very strict phone rules. They weren't allowed at any gatherings, and you were asked to leave if it went off in a meeting or session. I still wasn't used to carrying the stupid thing. Who wanted people being able to get ahold of you all the time? Definitely not me, but Scott had insisted on it, and it wasn't worth the argument.

The door shut, and all the voices quieted instantly. A man in the far end of the circle began speaking. "Welcome, everyone. My name is Sol, and I'm so glad to have you here tonight." He had the glow of the newly converted, and there was no mistaking his zeal. "Before we get started, let's all just take a moment to center ourselves by taking a big deep breath." He closed his eyes, took a deep breath, and then dramatically let it all out before opening his eyes again. "There. Okay. Now let's get started." His eyes scanned the room. "Is this anyone's first time here?"

A few nervous hands went up around the room. I was glad they hadn't asked that at my first meeting, because the last thing I had wanted was to be singled out. My goal was to blend in.

"Whether this is your first meeting or your last, I hope that you will take something away from our time together that you can use to help you during your week. Remember, when you change yourself, you change the world around you." Those who could finished his sentence along with him: "Change yourself, change the world."

There was a group of people sitting on his right who weren't in good shape. Two of them lay curled on their sides in their chairs, with their legs hugged against their chests. Sweat dripped down the blonde woman's forehead. The man next to her shook and moaned every few seconds. I hadn't realized the ones being detoxed were allowed to come to the meetings. I figured you had to get sober first, but there they were, sweating it out. Each of them had a bucket at their feet. They wouldn't actually throw up in the meeting, would they?

And then there were others like me whose faces were as blank as the walls. What were they doing here? Were they new? Old? Trying to become members? I'd expected the others, but I hadn't expected so many normal-looking people. Most of them had jobs too. Like real jobs in the community. Yesterday I'd spoken with two lawyers and one of the chemical engineers down at Sumner. They'd been taking classes and attending gatherings for months. Their families had recently started coming with them, and they loved it too. I had to remember to get them to sign a release today. Leo would kill me if I didn't. He wanted to use one of the lawyers' statements from yesterday. What had he said?

Oh yeah, *"We are a community that feeds each other's souls."* It was a great line. I couldn't disagree with him on that, but it was useless unless he gave me permission to use it. He probably would. Most people loved seeing their name in print.

Someone cleared their throat next to me. A guy with half his face covered in tattoos. He looked irritated, like it'd been a while since he'd been trying to get my attention. He handed me a stack of papers.

"Take one and pass it on," he said.

So much for everyone being nice and friendly. I fumbled to grab a paper, realizing there were multiple papers stapled together, and it was a packet I was supposed to be taking. I took mine, placed it on top of my notebook, and passed the stack to the next person in line.

I stared at the heading on the paper:

Are You Happy?

NINE

ABBI

Mom scurried to the car, ducking her head and trying to keep Shiloh covered with a blanket in case any media had sneaked to the private entrance at the back of the hospital. She opened the back door and jumped inside, clutching Shiloh against her chest. Dad hurried behind her and motioned to the car seat he'd bought last night.

"Do you remember how to use it?"

She acted like she hadn't heard him. She was doing that thing where she went far away somewhere. She couldn't hear you when she was there and definitely didn't know what was going on around her. Yesterday one of the nurses had missed her vein when she had been switching her IV, sending blood spurting from Mom's arm, and Mom hadn't even flinched.

"Kate, you have to put the baby in the car seat," Dad said tenderly. "Here, let me help you. These things are so hard to mess with. They always have been. Remember how frustrated you used to get with Abbi's?" He moved toward her, and she jumped back, eyeing the car seat like it might attack Shiloh. She scrambled to the other side, crawling over the car seat in the middle and smacking her head on the roof. Her entire body trembled. Shiloh stirred within her arms. I held my breath, hoping she didn't wake up. We were trying to keep her asleep for as long as possible. Nobody wanted to deal with a screaming baby in the car.

Dad looked baffled at Mom's reaction to the car seat, but it wasn't about the car seat. It was about putting Shiloh down. She hadn't put her down yet, not even when she slept, and she'd only given her to the nurses because she had to, but I'd watched how hard it was for her every time she did.

I walked to the other side of the car and opened the door. I reached for the seat belt and pulled it across Mom and Shiloh. "I'm sure this is fine. There was a time when nobody rode in car seats, and they all survived."

Relief washed over Dad, and he took his spot in the driver's seat next to Meredith. He'd insisted on driving this time. At least that felt normal. I climbed into the back seat with Mom.

"Thank you," she said quietly.

"You're welcome," I said, trying to look at her without making direct eye contact. I didn't like looking at her directly because most of the time she started crying whenever I did. I'd never seen someone look so sad—grief carved into every line in her face. Or anxious. She always looked like she was getting ready to crawl out of her skin. Did they test her blood for drugs when they took it?

Drugs were always one of the possibilities discussed in her thread on the Vanished forum. I'd stumbled on the website in middle school, and it had been filled with missing person cases like Mom's—the kinds of cases where the person disappeared into thin air, and there was never any sign of foul play or anything amiss. They were just gone. Just like her.

There were hundreds of threads, and sometimes I browsed through them to read other people's stories, but mostly I focused on Mom. She had a huge fan club of people devoted to solving her case. Dad despised all of them—said they were all quacks—but I liked their postings. They really knew her. They discovered things about her that Dad didn't tell me, like how she'd gotten a misdemeanor for shoplifting when she was twenty or that she'd almost been held back in tenth grade because she failed advanced algebra. I'd always wondered why I sucked at math when Dad was so good at it and had secretly hoped it was something that I'd gotten from her. I never would've known that if I wasn't on the boards.

The members gave me new perspectives and went down roads Dad wasn't willing to go on. The consensus was that she'd had an affair and run off to be with her lover, which was why Dad felt the way he did about them. He was more likely to entertain the idea that she'd been abducted by aliens than he was that she'd been having an affair. He insisted she was happy, that their marriage was stable, and life was good. He always said the same thing whenever he was questioned. His story never wavered. Most people pitied him and took her happiness as the major piece of evidence proving she was having an affair, because no one believed anyone could be that happy with someone they'd been married to for that long.

Shiloh let out a whimper, and Mom pulled up her shirt and lifted her to her breast. She wasn't wearing a bra. I tried not to blush or act embarrassed, but it was hard. I'd never seen a woman's breast out in the open like that, so exposed. The only time I'd seen other women naked had been in locker rooms, and even then people had tried to cover themselves. Not that I minded breastfeeding. It was best for the baby. Everyone knew that. It was just weird.

She reached over and grabbed my hand while she nursed, which only made it odder—the three of us connected in this intimate moment in the back seat of the car. Was this too weird? I tried to catch Dad's eye in the rearview mirror, but he was too focused on driving. At least he'd have something to do during the fourteen hours stretching in front of us. I wished he'd installed TVs on the back of the seats like Meaghan's dad had. At least then we'd have something to look at. My phone was useless, because I got carsick if I read it in the car. I hated awkward silences, and so far that was pretty much all it had been when the five of us were together.

Dad had promised things would get easier after we got home. He was convinced a familiar environment would help Mom feel safe, but that was the thing—our house wasn't familiar any more. Three years ago? Yes, she could've walked into our house, and it would've been almost like she'd never been gone, since we kept our home as a shrine to her. But Meredith had ceremoniously changed things. The house wasn't hers anymore.

What if being at home was more traumatic for her? I'd tried to tell the investigators about my fear, but none of them were interested in what I had to say. I would be glad when we were home and Dean was involved. He had been out of the country on another case but was flying home to meet us tomorrow.

Dean was the lead FBI investigator on Mom's case. He'd stayed in our house during the weeks following Mom's disappearance. He'd worked with us for so long he'd become like family. I even jokingly called him "Uncle" sometimes. At least he knew how to smile. Marcos had been so stuffy and uptight he made me nervous, and I hadn't done anything wrong. No wonder Mom was so tight lipped.

My phone buzzed, startling Mom. She whimpered beside me. I rubbed her back with my other hand. Tears streamed down her cheeks. I wanted to help her but didn't know how. Her time in the hospital hadn't seemed to make her much better. All her blood work was slowly going back to normal, and her doctors expected it to continue improving, but she still seemed scared all the time, and the harder they pushed her to talk, the more she shut down. It was like she didn't know how to live away from wherever she'd been. Dean was bringing someone who specialized in getting people in Mom's situation to talk. I hoped they could help her, because I hated seeing her this way and wasn't nearly as confident as Dad that being home would make things any better.

TEN

MEREDITH

NOW

I raced through the house, trying to pick up the mess we'd made before we'd left. Everything was in disarray because we'd gone so quickly. We definitely weren't prepared for guests. The guest room was cluttered with things we wanted to sell in our garage sale, but they'd been stacked in the corner for the last two years. Scott was carrying them out to the garage while I made up the bed. I'd left Abbi and Kate sitting awkwardly on the couch next to each other downstairs. Kate had started crying almost every time she had tried talking to Abbi, and it was crushing to watch.

Where did I put the new pillows I had bought a few months back? I'd gotten two on sale at Target. Where were they? I was so scatter-brained. None of us had gotten any sleep since yesterday. Scott had insisted on driving through the night, convinced getting to California and back home was the key to getting Kate stable. Marcos and the other officers hadn't gotten anywhere with her for the last three days we'd spent in Montana. The doctors had diagnosed her with acute post-traumatic stress disorder with depressive features. Basically it meant she alternated between being agitated with fear and sobbing inconsolably. The goal was to help her feel safe by surrounding her with familiar things.

But I didn't know how any of us were supposed to feel safe when two unmarked squad cars sat in front of our house, and a team of FBI agents and officers were setting up their office in our dining room. Were they planning on staying up all night? Where would I put them to sleep if they weren't?

I gave up on finding the missing pillows and headed to our bedroom to grab the extra ones in my closet instead. The master bedroom had changed as much as the rest of the house. I hadn't wanted to erase Kate from the house, but there was no way I could go to bed every night with the framed photo of the two of them exchanging rings on their wedding day staring back at me, or the one above the dresser with Kate's naked body swollen in pregnancy and Scott behind her with his arms circled underneath her. Those were the first to go, followed by the rest of their professional wedding photos scattered around the house. I'd cleaned out her closet next because I needed a place for my clothes. We had packed her things in lined fabric boxes just like we'd filled her coffin with her violin, letters, and photos when we'd buried her. They'd been moved to the garage and hadn't been touched in years.

Other things followed from there. We updated the kitchen almost immediately after I moved in. They'd been planning on doing it right before Kate went missing, so it was in desperate need of help by then. I talked Scott into gutting the entire thing, and I'd gotten the kitchen of my dreams. But what would Kate think of it? It was a far cry from her traditional, farmhouse-style kitchen.

We'd all watched her when we'd walked through the front door even though we had tried to pretend we weren't; at least Abbi and I had. Scott's eyes were glued to her. He didn't bother to hide his eagerness at her reaction to their home. The desperation in his eyes at wanting something to spark her back to life was unmistakable, and so was the pain that followed when she reacted to it like she had to everything else around her—terrified.

I was glad to be home and out of the car, though. I couldn't have endured another moment of silence. Scott wasn't much of a talker on road trips, so we usually listened to music or audiobooks, but he had said something might trigger Kate, and we weren't equipped to handle her if she had an episode in the car. What did that even mean? And if we couldn't handle her episodes in the car, how would we handle them at home? Her psychiatrists kept referring to *episodes*, but they wouldn't come right out and say what that meant, and so far I hadn't seen one. Was she dangerous? Scott had assured me she wasn't, but how well did he really know her?

Kate coming home changed everything. That went without saying. But it changed my entire view of her as a person too. I had been sure she was dead. No part of me ever believed she was alive, no matter what Scott had said about it or how he had felt. Never. I had only seen him as a grieving man refusing to accept that his wife was dead from the first moment he'd shared his story in group. I had never told him, though, because it would've hurt him, and as time went on it was one of the things that drew me to him. I'd never seen a man so unapologetically in love with a woman even long after she was gone. James hadn't loved me that way, and he'd never once looked at me the way Scott looked when he said Kate's name.

How was it possible she'd been alive all this time? I'd always been as convinced of her love and devotion to Scott as he was, but was it possible he'd been mistaken? Maybe there was someone else. What if she'd gone willingly?

Don't be ridiculous, I admonished myself.

"Meredith?" Scott called from downstairs, interrupting my thoughts. "Where did you put the extra batteries?"

I hurried back downstairs to get them myself, since it would be easier than trying to direct him to them. I dug through the back of the junk drawer in the linen closet until I found them. He plopped them into the flashlight and handed it to me. "Give her this so she can find her way through the house at night if she needs to," he said. "I'll pick up a packet of night-lights tomorrow to put in the hallway and bathrooms, but it's too late to run out now. Everything is closed."

Abbi and Kate were in the same spot in the living room as they'd been when I'd left. Abbi tickled Shiloh's feet, sticking out from underneath her yellow blanket.

"Her toes are so tiny," Abbi squealed. Her dark, wavy hair was pulled into a long ponytail underneath the Dodgers cap she'd been wearing for days. "I've never seen anything so small."

Kate smiled hesitantly, unsure of herself. I cleared my throat, announcing my presence so I wouldn't startle her. I'd already made a mental note to make noise before I entered rooms, because she startled so easily.

"Abbi, why don't you go brush your teeth and get ready for bed? I'm going to show Kate the guest bedroom and bathroom upstairs." I felt like an idiot as soon as I said it because, obviously, she knew where the bedrooms were, but she got up and silently followed me upstairs. I pointed to the bathroom. "Still right through there," I said, trying to sound as normal as possible. The guest bedroom was next to it. She eyed the door leading to the master suite at the end of the hallway. Something passed through her eyes. Recognition? Sadness? Some kind of memory? Whatever it was, it was gone that quickly, and she shuffled into the guest bedroom. She perched on the edge of the bed. She kissed the top of Shiloh's head, nervously rocking back and forth.

I pointed to the lamp and the bottle of water I'd put on the nightstand. "There's water, but if you'd like something else, I can bring that up too."

She lowered her head. "Water is fine."

I gave her the flashlight. "Scott thought you might want this. It'll make things easier if you get up in the night."

"Thank you," she said softly, keeping her head down as she took it from me.

"I wish we had more things for the baby, but . . ." My sentence hung in the air awkwardly.

She searched for something to say. "Thank you," she repeated herself.

"You're welcome," I said. "Are you sure I can't get you anything else?"

I'd offered her a pair of my pajamas, but she had refused. She was wearing clothes that were donated to the hospital after no one picked them up from the lost and found. There was an entire storage room in the hospital filled with lost items that they recycled through to patients. Her gray sweatpants were two sizes too big, and she was wearing a faded shirt with a taco on the front. She shook her head.

I wanted to hug her. I couldn't help myself when she looked so fragile and frail, completely lost. What had they done to her? I had to go, because if I stayed in her room a minute longer, that was exactly what I'd do, and I knew it was the last thing she wanted.

"Good night," I said as I stood. "Please wake me up if you need anything."

KATE

THEN

"Are you seriously going to another retreat?" Christina threw her head back and laughed, her black hair spilling down her back. We'd already had too many drinks, and I'd pay for it in the morning, but I didn't care. I only got to see her twice a year since she'd moved back to Texas. "Haven't you already been to one?"

I drained the rest of my mojito and waved down our server for another. "Three, but this one is different."

"How different can they be?" she asked.

"Each one targets something else," I said. "The last one focused on forgiveness."

"You spent three days in the desert forgiving?" She smirked, trying not to crack a joke.

"Shut up." I playfully smacked her arm across the table. "It's not even like that. The whole purpose was to gain a new perspective on forgiveness. I didn't realize there were so many people I needed to forgive."

We'd gone into an abandoned house and spray-painted the names of everyone we'd ever resented on the walls. Then we'd taken turns beating them down with a bat. We destroyed every wall in the house, and the final ceremony was setting the house on fire while we chanted songs of release. It was one of the most powerful experiences of my life, but she'd never understand it because it was too irrational for her logical, pragmatic brain. That was one of the reasons she and Scott were such good friends and why both of them were amazing at their jobs. They'd met in English class during our freshman year at college. He'd brought her back to our apartment to study one night, and the three of us had been friends ever since.

"Are you working on a follow-up story?" she asked.

I shrugged. My story had gone to press over two weeks ago, and when I'd gone back to talk to Ray about all the backlash and what he thought about it, he'd invited me to become a member of Love International. I was considering his invitation but hadn't made up my mind yet, and writing another article would be the same as saying no.

"So what are you still doing there?"

"I just like being there, and you would, too, if you'd give it a try. Just come with me this weekend."

She shook her head, draining what was left in her glass. "No way. Jerry is coming into town this weekend, and you know there's no way I'm missing out on that good loving." It'd been less than a year since she'd divorced her husband, Rick, and she hadn't wasted any time getting back into the dating scene. She complained they hadn't had sex for the last two years, so she had to make up for lost time. I didn't know any guy could go that long without sex, but she swore she wasn't exaggerating. "Just promise me that you're not going to turn into Rita and get all born again, okay?" she asked.

I took the first bite out of the piece of chocolate cake in front of us. "That I can promise. This is completely different."

Rita was my oldest friend from high school, and I'd introduced the two of them over a decade ago. Rita had always liked to party, and after she had had her second child, she'd hit the pills hard too. So hard that coupled with the bottles of wine she drank every day, she had started showing up at preschool pickup smelling like booze. It wasn't long before her family had sent her to rehab. She'd started attending a born-again Christian church after she got out and had become so involved that her former self was almost unrecognizable.

"Too bad you couldn't just take Scott," she said.

I'd given up asking him to go with me, which was what always happened whenever I did anything new—he tolerated it from me but he didn't want any part of it.

"Are things getting any better for you?" she asked.

I'd spent our last two visits opening up to her about how much I was struggling in my marriage. I rarely talked about our relationship with anyone, but I hadn't been able to keep things in any longer, and talking with Scott about stuff had gotten me nowhere. He said the same thing whenever I brought up how stagnant I felt—"I love you. Every part of you. I want you to grow and change, experience new things. I support you."

But I wanted him to grow and change, experience new things too. His contentment with sameness was more maddening the older I got. How could we live our lives based on decisions we'd made when we were seventeen?

It wasn't like he hadn't tried to understand how I was feeling, but those discussions ended with his other favorite saying, "I just don't get it. Our lives are perfect."

That was just it. Our lives were perfect—too perfect. I'd explained it to Christina, and she'd understood. I didn't understand why he couldn't.

She was looking at me with hopeful eyes from across the table even though she tried to hide it and pretend like she didn't want me to answer a certain way. The problem with having a fairy-tale relationship story was how much other people were invested in keeping the fairy tale alive. It wasn't just our story—it was everyone's.

I shifted my gaze away from hers. "Things are getting better. Getting back to work has been a huge help. I'm interviewing one of the girls from my soccer-coach story next week, so I'm excited about that." I tried to sound convincing as I prattled on. "Scott and I are connecting again. All that weirdness between us is gone."

"See? I told you everything would be fine. You guys always work things out." Her smile lit up her face. "You always do. That's what happens when it's meant to be."

———

It was my first cleansing session with Ray, and I was more nervous than when I met him. He had refused to do a cleansing session with me while I was working on my article—said we'd be lacking the level of honesty that was necessary for it to be successful—but we didn't have to worry about that anymore. I wouldn't be doing any other articles on them. Not after the last angry letter we'd gotten in opposition to my defense of their movement. Leo wouldn't even consider it. We'd expected some opposition to covering such a controversial story, but never the magnitude we'd received. Whoever it was had been sending Ray hate mail too.

Our talks had changed since they were no longer on the record, and he was able to speak freely with me. But neither he nor anyone else talked about what happened in the cleansings. So much of the internal work at Love International was that way—deeply personal and private. Everyone shared the insights and lessons they'd taken away from their cleansing sessions, but there was never any mention of the process. Did it work the same way with everyone, or did he change his approach depending on the individual? What was his plan for me? People gushed about their spiritual breakthroughs afterward, but not all of them ended on a positive note. Some people came out of their cleansing emotionally wrecked. I hoped I wasn't the latter.

Cleansings were held in one of the detox rooms, which was less comfortable than his office, but I was pretty sure that was the point. I'd lost track of how many times we'd met together. It didn't matter, though, because my nerves still jumped every time. I was glad I wasn't alone. He had that effect on everyone. It wasn't just because of the way his eyes pierced into your soul. It was more about the way he cut straight to your core issues, stripping you raw within minutes.

"Hi, Kate." He rose from his position on the floor when I walked into the room. He hugged me before kneeling back on the floor. I sat across from him. I held back the urge to giggle as we sat cross-legged in front of each other, like we were back in elementary school about to have a shoe-tying race. "It's okay. You can laugh. Release any feeling that comes up," he said.

I blushed. "Sorry. I don't think it's funny. I j—"

He held up his hand. "Stop. Don't go any further with that statement. We do not justify or rationalize any of our emotional expressions during a cleansing." He looked at me sharply. He'd never been so serious.

"Got it." I nodded.

"The point of this cleansing is for you to get in touch with all those things you've pushed down and ignored. Those things that have been filling your heart and soul with cancer." The light in his eyes was gone, replaced with hawklike precision as he peered into my eyes. It took every ounce of willpower I had not to look away from his intense stare. "Why are you here?"

"I want to rid myself of my cancer," I recited, like I'd heard others do so many times before at retreats and in meetings.

"Bullshit." He shook his head in disgust. I'd never heard him swear. I pulled back, shifting away from him. "Why are you really here?" he asked. My mind drew a blank, his dramatic shift throwing me off. "Would you like me to help you?"

"You know what? I don't appreciate the way you're speaking to me right now," I said, straightening my back.

"Oh, I'm sorry. Would you prefer that I tiptoed around you?" he sneered.

"What's wrong with you today?" I'd never seen him act this way. He'd been confrontational before, but never like this, and certainly not mean.

"Were you expecting this to be easy?" Challenge filled his eyes.

"No, but I didn't think you'd act like this," I said.

"All I want is for you to be honest."

"I am being honest."

He shook his head. "Please. We both know you're lying."

"What are you talking about? I love my life." I scooted as far as I could until my back was pressed up against the door.

"Bullshit," he said again.

"You know what?" Anger surged through me, bringing me to my feet. "I didn't come here for this." I turned around and reached for the knob.

"If you leave out that door right now, don't plan on coming back." His voice was steady, calm.

I whipped back around. "What happened to 'You can come and go as you please'? I thought you weren't anybody's dictator?"

He remained seated. "Every individual who walks through these doors is unique."

"And I'm the one that you chose to be a controlling jerk with?" I glared at him. "Thanks. Truly flattered."

"Fear is ruling your heart right now. If you leave, you're letting fear win, and we can't have that here." His face was set in stone.

"I'm not afraid," I said, but I didn't believe myself any more than he did.

"Are you sure you want to leave?" he asked. I hesitated with my hand on the door, and he jumped on my uncertainty. "You're here because you're bored with your life and want more. The things you used to love are stifling you to the point where you feel like you can't breathe." I slowly slid down the wall onto the floor, crossing my arms on my chest to protect myself from his truths. "You are tied to the life you created when you were a teenage girl to survive, but that life no longer serves you. Yet you can't let go of it. Am I getting close?"

I stuck my chin out like a defiant toddler. "You don't know me."

He shook his head. "It's you, Kate, that refuses to know yourself."

Tears welled in my eyes. I brushed them away. I didn't want to cry because then he'd know he was right. My skin itched with the threat of exposure.

"What happened to make you feel so indebted to this life?" he asked.

It wasn't the life—it was the man. Images of how Scott had taken care of me after my parents died when I was seventeen passed through me in snippets—the hours he'd spent sitting with me at the hospital long after they'd been pronounced dead. He'd kept everyone away from me until I had been ready to leave. He'd been my emotional container for the fits of rage that I had unleashed for years as I had struggled to process how I'd been robbed of so much.

"He saved my life." I swallowed the tears in my throat before remembering that he'd instructed me not to hold back my emotions. I let go, and suddenly I was crying in a way I hadn't done since I was a kid. Ray didn't move from his spot. He didn't reach out to comfort me or say anything to make it better. The awkwardness of it all slowed my emotional outburst. "I don't know who I am without him. I've always wondered who I might be on my own. But I feel like the world's most terrible person for even having the thoughts."

I'd never admitted that to anyone before. Not Christina. Certainly not Scott. I'd barely acknowledged it to myself. What else would he pull out of me that I'd never told anyone?

ELEVEN

ABBI

NOW

My eyes burned. I stared at the coffeepot, wishing I could grab a cup like everyone else, but Dad hated me drinking coffee. He still believed the old wives' tale that it would stunt my growth. He didn't care that all my friends drank coffee when we went to Starbucks during open period. Sometimes I sneaked it anyway, and I was never going to make it through this day without some caffeine, since Shiloh's crying had kept me up most of the night.

My bedroom was next to theirs, and Mom had tried to soothe her all night, but nothing had worked. She hadn't stopped crying for longer than a few minutes. I had wanted to help Mom, but I didn't know anything about babies, and I didn't want to do anything to make the crying worse or embarrass Mom. I had ended up just lying in my bed, wishing them to sleep and scrolling through the older threads on the Vanished forums for anything I might have missed. Hopefully, Dad and Meredith had slept through the crying. They had been so exhausted last night Meredith almost fell asleep eating her pizza, barely making it through one slice. Mom had made up for Meredith's lack of appetite. I'd never seen someone eat the way she did. She had wolfed down an entire large pizza herself. She'd just kept shoveling it into her mouth, piece after piece, until suddenly it was the last piece and she'd looked mortified.

She was still upstairs getting ready. Meredith had tried to give her something of hers to wear again and Mom refused. I wished Meredith would stop offering her clothes, since she obviously didn't want them. Would I want to wear my husband's new wife's clothes? Probably not. Dad was going to drag a few of her boxes of old clothes out of the garage today, so at least she'd have something until we could go shopping.

Dean and his team of investigators would be here in an hour to interview her. The ones who stayed last night were in the dining room drinking their coffee. Their hushed whispers permeated the rooms downstairs. I didn't know how any of them planned to get anything out of Mom when she mostly said one-word phrases—yes, no, please, thank you. I'd barely heard her string more than two sentences together. Not sleeping wasn't going to help either. She'd fallen asleep at some point, though, because I had peeked in on them when I had woken up at six to use the bathroom. Everything on the bed had been untouched, and they had been curled up on the cold wooden floor, even though there was a rug in the center of the room. She hadn't even taken a pillow to sleep on. I had shut the door quietly and tiptoed back to bed, but I hadn't been able to fall back to sleep again because I couldn't get the image of them sleeping on the floor out of my head. Why would she sleep on the floor like that?

Dad's alarm had gone off at seven thirty, and Meredith had been running around the house all morning. She was determined to have breakfast on the table for everyone by nine, but I had a feeling people weren't going to eat much. But that was how she was. Any time we had company, no matter what the occasion or how long they were staying, she made sure to feed them. She was at the grocery store picking up a few things for the omelets.

"Dad, can I have a cup of coffee?" I asked, leaning against the counter.

He looked up from his phone. He'd been lost in his screen since I sat down, barely glancing up when Meredith left.

"You know—" He stopped himself. "Sure. Go ahead."

"What?" I asked in disbelief. The joke was always that I asked, he said no, and I begged until he promised me something sweet in return.

He shrugged before going back to his phone. I stood slowly and walked over to the refrigerator. Part of me wanted to cry. It wasn't about the coffee. I didn't care about the coffee. It wasn't even like it was the first cup of coffee I'd had in this house. He'd quit playing our game. Mom was back, and everything was going to change, even the parts of our life that I loved.

Some of my favorite traditions were when we celebrated Mom. Her birthday was one of my favorite days of the year, right behind Christmas. It was a vacation day whether we had obligations or not, and we spent most of the year planning it. One year we had gone on a hot-air-balloon ride and released balloons carrying messages we'd written to her after we were in the sky. Dad kept saying we were already halfway to heaven, so he was sure they'd make it there. Another year we went to Disneyland. They weren't always such huge deals. Sometimes they were smaller. Once we stayed in bed in our pajamas all day watching videos of her and eating chocolate ice cream. We picked out gifts for her at Christmas and included her name on our New Year's Eve lists. So much of our world had revolved around recognizing and remembering her. What would we do when she was here?

"Abbi, are you drinking coffee?" Meredith asked as she breezed into the kitchen. She didn't give me time to answer. "Everything in the living room is picked up. I just want to go through the bathroom down here one more time." She turned to Dad. "And can you make sure to empty all the trash cans?"

"Do you really think they're going to care about the trash cans being dirty?" he asked.

They'd been having the same argument since she'd moved in. Nothing ever changed. Dad knew Meredith was going to want the trash cans emptied in all the rooms before company arrived. She asked every time, and each time, without fail, he made some comment about it. Why not just empty the trash cans and avoid the drama? But before they got into their same old argument, there was a knock at the front door. We all froze even though we were expecting them.

Dad shot us an encouraging glance before getting up and heading to the door. We followed behind him as he opened it. Dean stood on the porch with a woman who I assumed must be the FBI expert Dad had told me about last night. She was almost as big as he was. Three men stood behind them holding equipment and various-size bags. Normally Dean would've rushed into the house and scooped me into a big hug, but he stayed in his spot, waiting for Dad to lead the way.

"Come in," Dad said, ushering them inside. "How are you?"

"I'm good, thank you," Dean said, shaking his hand.

"Hi, Uncle Dean," I said. All of this was so weird.

He tousled my hair. "Hey, you. Once all this is done, I'm taking you out for ice cream, okay?"

I smiled. Our relationship had started because of ice cream. Dad had to juggle being a grieving husband, father, and suspect all at the same time, so he had always been dragging me with him to important meetings and interviews. Not because there hadn't been people who'd volunteered to babysit me. There had been plenty of people who would've helped, but one of the downfalls of a recently disappeared parent was that you didn't let the other one out of your sight. And Dad had never pushed me to do anything I wasn't ready for. He had let me stay with him because he had understood how much it meant to me, but it had definitely made his life harder than it already was.

It was one of those days when something significant had happened in the case, and they had needed Dad alone. Dean finally talked me into leaving the police station and getting ice cream, but I refused to go unless he took me. His status meant nothing to me. He loved to tell the story of how I stomped down the sidewalk to get ice cream and ordered him to find my mommy or I was going to tell his mommy that he was a bad detective.

I gave him a quick hug. "Deal. But I want real ice cream this time. Not that gelato stuff you tried to convince me was good."

He laughed, but his laughter ended abruptly at the sound of Mom's footsteps descending the stairs. Everything stopped. It felt like nobody breathed. Mom kept her head down, avoiding eye contact like she always did. Dad reached out and helped guide her down the final step and into the entryway with everyone else.

"Kate, this is Dean Thompson." Dad pointed to Dean, and he stepped forward, reaching out his hand toward Mom. "He has been helping me search for you all these years. He's probably almost as relieved to have you home as we are."

Dean smiled. Mom tentatively shook his hand before tucking her arm back around Shiloh. The woman behind Dean stepped forward. Her dark hair was pulled straight back into a tight ponytail, making her wide forehead look even bigger. She wore a light-blue shirt buttoned all the way to the top.

"My name is Camille. I don't believe I've met anyone," she said, shaking Dad's hand first, followed by Mom's. She turned to me next. "And you must be Abbi?"

I nodded.

She pointed to the men behind her as an afterthought. "That's John, Carl, and Hernando. They're part of my team." They nodded their greetings in return. Camille eyed the house. "Why don't we move into a more comfortable place where we can sit down and get started?" she asked.

Meredith stepped forward. "Would you like some egg bake?"

"No, thanks. I'm fine," Camille dismissed her and walked into the living room. We all followed behind her. "Why don't you sit there, Kate?" She pointed to the couch on the opposite wall. Camille took a seat in one of the club chairs, perching on the end of it so she was as near to Mom as possible while still giving her enough space to handle Shiloh. John, Carl, and Hernando immediately went to work pulling weird-looking electrical equipment out of their bags and setting up their gear.

Dean sat in the opposite chair while Dad, Meredith, and I stood behind him awkwardly. Mom jiggled Shiloh against her, trying to keep her asleep. There had been more people in our living room before, but it had never felt so crowded. My chest tightened. Mom kept her eyes glued to the carpet as if she were mesmerized by the design.

"Are you ready to get started?" Camille asked.

Mom nodded.

Camille pulled out a device from her pocket and set it on the coffee table. "Do you mind if I record this interview?"

TWELVE

MEREDITH

NOW

"You guys were in there for over three hours—what do you mean she didn't say?" I asked Scott. Camille had wanted all of us there as witnesses when she got Kate's consent for the videotaped interview, but she'd asked us to leave after that. She'd asked Scott to leave, too, but Kate had grabbed his arm as he walked past her on the couch.

"Please, can he stay?" she'd begged, and she'd clung to his arm with so much fear that they'd relented.

Abbi and I went upstairs. I stopped at the landing, waiting for her to catch up as she walked much slower so she could keep her eyes on Kate for as long as possible. Abbi watched her constantly, like she might disappear again if she let her out of her sight.

"Do you want to come in my room while we wait?" I asked.

She shook her head. I reached out and cupped her chin with my hands. "It's going to be okay." She forced a smile for my benefit before going into her room and shutting the door behind her. I wasn't able to concentrate on anything. I gave up reading my novel after I realized I'd been rereading the same paragraph for over twenty minutes. I texted

Caleb and Thad, but they were both working, so they didn't text back. Finally, I lay down on the bed and fell asleep. Scott had woken me up ten minutes ago.

Kate still hadn't told them what happened the day that she went missing. It had been five days, and they still had no idea what had happened to her or where she'd been all this time. "You should see how traumatized she is, Meredith. Even basic questions like 'What did you eat?' make her sob uncontrollably. If anyone moves too quickly, she flinches, and every loud sound makes her jump. You'd think we lived in the middle of New York City for as many times as she got freaked out by the noises. We spent most of the time waiting for her to gather her composure between questions."

"How awful," I said. "Did they let you try to talk to her?"

"Are you kidding?" He snorted. "Camille wouldn't let me say anything. She wouldn't even let me comfort her when she was upset. I just had to sit there because she didn't want me to influence Kate in any way. It was actually pretty torturous."

I moved toward him and gave him a hug. I rested my head against his chest. His heart thumped wildly despite the fact that he was standing still. While he held me, I rubbed his back, trying to help him relax.

"I don't know what to say," I whispered. "I can't imagine how you feel right now." One of the worst things you could do to someone in the midst of tragedy was to give them a cliché, because the intensity of the loss was too big. I'd heard it all after James died. Sometimes it was better to say nothing.

He pulled away, sinking into his leather office chair and running his hands through his hair. "If they try to push her at all, then she starts saying 'You don't understand' over and over again or gibberish that makes no sense at all. She repeats things, too, and mumbles under her breath like she's talking to someone. It's so hard seeing her this way." His voice caught in his throat.

I'd seen her do the mumbling thing earlier this morning in the hallway upstairs, like she was talking to someone who wasn't there. I didn't know what to do and didn't want to embarrass her, so I'd turned around and gone back downstairs, pretending I'd forgotten something and hadn't seen her.

"I don't know what to do. How are we supposed to help her if we can't get her to talk? And it's not even just about helping her." He spoke at a frenzied pace. "I need to keep everyone safe. I can't do that if I don't know what's going on. I don't—"

I interrupted him before he could get any more worked up. "Honey, it's not your job to keep everyone safe."

He pointed downstairs. "You think they're going to stay forever?"

I laid my hand on his forearm. "We just got home. They're not going anywhere soon, and there's no way they're going to leave us alone while we're still in danger." He let out a frustrated sigh. "What if you got ahold of her old best friend—what was her name? Oh yeah, Christina. What if you arranged for her to come see Kate?" I couldn't help but think of my best friend, Lois, and all the secrets of mine she carried with her. There were things you told your best friend that you didn't tell anyone else.

"She refuses to talk to me."

"Why?" I asked.

"Let's just say she's not exactly on Team Scott."

"One of those?"

He nodded.

He'd told me about all the friends he'd lost after Kate went missing. Some of his closest friends had doubted his innocence and abandoned him, whereas others whom he'd barely known had stood by his side and become his closest allies.

"You don't think she'd make an exception after all these years? Especially if Kate's back? Besides, if she really does think you had something to do with it, then it's in her best interest to get Kate to talk so they can bust you."

He shrugged. "I guess I can try."

"Good." I pulled him up from the chair. "Let's go feed these people roaming around our house." He gave me a weak smile. "Besides, they're going to be interviewing her all afternoon. Who knows what they'll get out of her by the end of the day."

KATE

THEN

I threw my toiletry bag into my duffel bag and zipped it up, doing a final sweep of the small room before I left. It was my fifth retreat and the most powerful one I'd been to yet, even if Ray had managed to insult half the attendees last night.

I glanced at my roommate's untouched bed. Melissa hadn't come home last night after the campfire celebration that ended every retreat. She'd been flirting with one of the new members down by the river when I'd seen her last. I giggled at how self-conscious and embarrassed I'd been at my first campfire, when some of them had stripped naked and danced around the fire. I hadn't been able to take my eyes off them, but it wasn't because of their nakedness. It was the complete and utter abandon with which they had done it. I'd never seen anyone so uninhibited and free. I hadn't taken my clothes off. I wasn't there yet. I wanted to be, though. Maybe next retreat.

I'd fasted for the first twenty-four hours, and it'd been pretty awful, but I'd pushed myself past the point where I wanted to quit, and it'd been amazing, just like my mentor, Margo, had said it would be. I'd fasted before, but only cleansing diets that asked me to give up food or replace it with a weird powder. Love International didn't consider that fasting. A true fast meant giving up everything, even water. I'd omitted telling Scott I had planned on doing it this weekend. He hadn't liked when I'd drunk nothing but raw juice on a thirty-day cleanse once, so he definitely would've freaked out about this.

I plopped back down on the bed I'd just made. I wasn't in any hurry to get home to him. It was getting harder and harder each time, and last night had been especially powerful, which only made it more difficult to leave. Ray had given one of his best talks yet. He had spoken at the end of each day. We'd gathered around him on the grass, sprawled out on blankets.

"Let me ask you this." His booming voice carried throughout the crowd. "Would you die for what you believed in?" His eyes scanned the crowd. Nobody moved. "Would you?" His voice grew angrier, more intense.

Still nobody spoke. The silence grew. I welcomed it, invited it into my space. I focused on my breath as it left my body and the air that returned to fill it.

"Would you die for what you believed in?" People shifted uncomfortably. All my senses were alert, tuned in. I could feel the vibrations from the people on each side. We all hung there waiting for whatever came next, where all this had been leading. "This isn't a rhetorical question. Are there any of you out there who have that kind of faith?"

"Yes!" a man finally shouted from the back. I turned around. It was the guy who was going through a rough and bitter divorce. He'd shared his story at the opening gathering, eager to have people shoulder his pain as he walked through it. That'd been his goal for the retreat.

Ray searched through the crowd before spotting him. "You?" He pointed at him. The man nodded, and Ray motioned for him to come forward. The group parted, creating a pathway for him to the front. Ray put his arm around his shoulder when he reached him. The man's strawberry-blond hair was parted down the middle and tucked behind his ears with perfectly trimmed sideburns.

"What is your name, young man?" Ray asked, even though the man was obviously older than him.

"Kevin," he said. He puffed his chest out proudly as he stood next to Ray.

"Hi, Kevin, nice to meet you." He patted him on the back. "And what beliefs would you die for?"

He made a swooping motion across the crowd. "This."

"Tell me, how many retreats have you been on with Love International?"

"This is my first one." He beamed.

"Your first retreat? Really? So you've been with us for about thirty-six hours, and you are willing to die for our cause?"

"I know it sounds ridiculous, but that's just it—I feel like I've always been with you. Like this is my home and all my life I've been searching for it without knowing I was looking for it. Nothing has ever felt like it did the day I stepped on your campus." His gaze shifted from Ray and out into the group. "Most of you don't know me, but my life fell apart last year after my wife left me. She destroyed me and took everything I had. I couldn't stomach the idea of rebuilding it when all of it could come crumbling down again at any minute. That's where my happiness had been, and I refused to put it there. Not again." He was crying by the time he finished.

"I'm still having a hard time wrapping my head around how you could be so committed in such a short time," Ray said, unwilling to let it go. It was like that when he got fixated on something.

He shrugged. "What can I say? I was open to the message, and it filled me."

"Wow. That's pretty incredible." He rubbed his chin. "Do you think you could wait here for a minute?" Kevin nodded, and Ray hurried off to his cabin. A few of the others jumped up and surrounded Kevin, asking him more questions about his situation and how he'd found

Love International while we waited for Ray to return. It wasn't long before he did.

"Please sit," Ray said. He grabbed Kevin's arm as he moved to sit back down with the others. "Not you. We're not done."

"Oh, okay," Kevin said. He couldn't hide his excitement at getting to stay and keep working with Ray.

"Our entire philosophy is based on putting our beliefs into motion. We have to do more than say we believe in something. Our actions must support our words. We ask ourselves to prove our commitment to our beliefs in the same way that God asks us to prove ourselves." He threw his arm around Kevin's waist, bringing him closer to him. "And that's what I'm going to ask you to do tonight." He pulled out a bottle of pills from his pocket and waved them in the air for everyone to see. "You said you would die for Love International. These pills will shut down your internal organs." Ray unscrewed the bottle. "Open your hand." Kevin did as he was told. Ray dropped the pills into Kevin's palm. "Prove it."

Red flushed Kevin's face. He laughed nervously and searched the crowd, his eyes wide, hoping someone knew what to do. I had no idea what he was supposed to do. Ray's teaching methods were never conventional.

Ray snorted and rolled his eyes. "There you go, folks. This one lied. He's full of it."

"But Ray, I mean"—he closed his hand on the pills—"obviously I'm not going to kill myself in front of you all."

"Oh, it's our privacy that you're worried about? You are one with a full heart." I thought I'd seen all sides of Ray, but I'd never seen this one. I didn't like him. Not even a little.

"You can't be serious." His voice wavered with nerves.

"You were the one who was serious, my friend. The only person in the crowd tonight who raised his hand and assured us that he would die for our beliefs. You all heard him, didn't you?" Ray turned his attention to us, like he often did when he was working with someone. He depended on us to serve as his mirror, but this was uncharted territory. "There you go. So now what are you going to do? Did you mean it, or were you just blowing smoke up our ass to impress us?"

Kevin's face crumpled. I'd seen Ray reduce men to tears numerous times, but something about this one was especially crushing. Maybe it was because of the pure childlike hurt that filled Kevin's being at having displeased Ray.

Kevin stood rooted to his spot, his eyes downcast. "You're not going to do it, are you? You really aren't willing to die for your beliefs." Ray pushed him gently forward. "Go sit down."

Kevin hung his head as he walked back to his seat. We moved aside like we'd done before, but our words of encouragement were gone, and silence filled the space.

"Most of you have never felt that strongly about something, even if you say you have. Perhaps you may have felt it about your child or a loved one, but a belief?" He shook his head. "Not a chance. Guess what, though? Others are willing to die for their cause. They wear suicide vests and pull the trigger to blow themselves up. We look at them like they're crazy, just like everyone else in our society does, but, really, they believe so strongly in their God's purpose that they're willing to die for it." The world thrummed around him. Vibrant colors danced off him. "Have you ever been that committed to something? Had that much faith? Imagine how that would change your life if you did. That's the kind of faith that moves mountains, parts the Red Sea."

I'd never met anyone who had that kind of faith. Definitely not me.

"I don't know about you, but I'd like to have that kind of faith. I'd like to be so convinced of it that I was willing to blow myself up on account of it." There was movement in the masses. People stood up, trying to get out. "I see you leaving." He called out to them. "Every one of you. And you." He pointed to the man who had pledged to donate the inheritance he'd received to a charity organization working with children with rare endocrine cancers. Next he pointed to the group of yoga instructors holding on to each other as they tried not to step on anyone as they left. "And you. Lastly, you." His finger stopped on one of the only families to attend this retreat. Most children had stayed home. "This message is not for everyone. If there's anyone else who can't handle it, then please"—he made a rising motion with both hands—"get up. Don't stay. Follow them out." He waved. "Go. Please go. You are not the ones the Lord is searching for."

I sat in stunned silence. He'd never told people to leave before. They had to know he wasn't actually condoning terrorism. He was simply making a point—and a good one. I forced myself to keep my eyes forward even though I was dying to know who else was leaving. Where would they go? The buses weren't coming until tomorrow. That was part of the deal. Once you were here, there wasn't any way to leave. You had agreed to it when you signed the nondisclosure agreement and all the other waivers for the retreat. They had to have an emergency procedure, though, but how uncomfortable would that be for everyone? The moment seemed to last forever as more people shuffled out. Finally, Ray shifted his attention and focus back to those of us who remained.

"Family, you've witnessed something very important—real faith is not for the weak or scared, and I want to thank you for not being scared. I've got a question that might scare you even more. Are you ready?" He gave us a moment to gather ourselves and settle back into our seats after all the commotion. "What if we lived like the fate of the world was dependent on our love? What if we were the ones? Stay with me. Can you all stay with me? I know it's been a long day." He paused, inviting in the breath for a moment. We all followed suit. "Could we be the ones who bring the message of true love into the world in a way that's unparalleled to anything that's been seen before?"

"Yes!" a few voices shouted. They were quickly joined by others, myself included. "Yes!"

"Do you think you have the power to do that?"

"Yes!" We had been on our feet, cheering and stamping, excited to be the ones up for the challenge and feeling special because we'd withstood the tests from the evening.

I relived the excitement of the moment all over again, and for a second I considered throwing my bag down on the bed and putting my things back into the drawers. When you'd tasted the good life, how things were really meant to be and how you were designed to feel, it was impossible to go backward and pretend you didn't know how wonderful life could be. I was awake in a way I'd never been before. I'd been sleeping for so long, and the more awake I became, the more unsure I was about what I saw around me. I envied the disciples for being able to lead a life solely focused on serving God. It was the only way to come close to doing what Ray had talked about last night.

I was so curious about their lives, but everything about discipleship, including how they lived their daily lives, was kept a carefully guarded secret. Large parts of the community still considered them a cult, despite my article, but they were the only cult I knew who wasn't trying to recruit new disciples or add to their ranks. No one even hinted that it was a possibility. I had asked Margo about it once, and she had said, "We don't want people to join." She'd laughed afterward, but she had been serious. They didn't want to share what they had. It was special, and they wanted to keep it that way. I couldn't blame them, but sometimes I felt like I was sitting at the kids' table for dinner.

I set a thank-you note on the nightstand, like I always did at the end of every retreat, and shut the door behind me. There was no key, since they didn't believe in locks. I had a hard time getting used to unlocked doors. That one had been harder than the brazen nakedness around the fire at night. I gulped in the trees and beautiful skies one more time before heading down the main road to meet the others going back on the buses with me.

THIRTEEN

ABBI

NOW

My legs shook underneath our dining room table. They'd been that way since Camille had called everyone downstairs for a meeting, except she hadn't called it a meeting. She had called it a debrief and had said we'd be ending most days with them for a while. Meredith and Dad sat on each side of me, and normally it would've comforted me, but it made me feel wedged in. Maybe it was the investigators lining the walls behind us. They were like having ghosts in our house. They moved around without saying anything, drifting in and out of rooms while they did their jobs. One of their jobs was keeping the media out of our yard and respecting the perimeter they'd set up around our house. That guy was busier than all of them, since people were constantly trying to break the boundary or get to our door by pretending to be someone else. I'd be glad when everyone left us alone.

Camille stood at the head of the table, impatiently tapping her fingers on the wood as she waited for Dean and one of the other FBI specialists to settle into the seats on the other side of us. She'd dismissed Mom upstairs to rest with Shiloh before dinner, and Mom's face had melted in relief. "We've had our first break in the case today," she said once they finally sat down.

I reached for Dad's hand, clinging to it. His palms were sweaty.

"Are you familiar with an organization called Love International?" she asked.

I whipped around to see Dad's reaction. His first response would be my clue to how he felt, since he'd gotten so good at wearing a neutral face for me over the years.

"Yes, she wrote an amazing piece on them the year she went missing, and she was a member of their organization. Do they have something to do with this?" Confusion twisted his expression.

Camille nodded. "It appears that she's been with them since she went missing."

Nothing could erase the shock plastered on his face. "What? That's impossible." He rapidly shook his head back and forth. "How do you know? Did she tell you that?"

"She did." Camille's expression hadn't changed.

Over the years, I'd learned every person of interest on her case, and Love International had never made it on the list. Dad had been meticulous in his search. How had he missed them?

"But, but I . . . it just doesn't . . ." Dad dropped my hand and rubbed his forehead like the information had given him a headache. "They helped us look for her. They formed crews at base camp and organized searches. They plastered shopping malls and gas stations with flyers. I think they even held a candlelight vigil for her at their campus."

Camille interrupted him. "That could've been a diversion tactic all along. Maybe that was the point. Everyone would be too busy thinking of them as good guys to stop and consider that they might be the bad ones."

Dad wrinkled his face. "I just don't understand. She admitted she was with them?"

93

"Not right away, because as you're aware, communication with her is difficult, given what she's been through." She pointed to the walls around us. "She self-soothes by muttering phrases underneath her breath while she paces, and the living room is wired, so we've been analyzing all the audio for key phrases. She kept saying Love International over and over again when she talked. It didn't take us long to start putting things together once we had a name. You can thank my guys for how quick they work." She gave them an approving glance. "Are you familiar with their leader?"

"Ray Fischer?" Dad asked.

Camille nodded. "I asked her if she knew him, and for a second it was like I'd broken a spell. She confirmed that she's been with Ray and Love International."

"That doesn't make any sense. Why would they kidnap her? All of them loved her because of the article she wrote about them. They swore she was the only outsider who'd ever understood them. Everyone had such nice things to say about her." He shook his head, still unbelieving. "The police were more worried about her critics than they were them."

Camille raised his eyebrows. "Critics?"

"Yes," Dad said enthusiastically, grateful to give them information they didn't have. "Her article was followed up with angry letters to the editor and op-ed pieces by angry parents voicing their opposition to her. Some of them had really hateful things to say about her, and for a while the police suspected a group of her harshest critics. They even talked to Ray about the hate mail he'd received, too, and he gladly turned it over to them for their investigation. He was so helpful . . ." His voice trailed off.

"How about someone named Abner? Are you familiar with that name?"

"Abner?"

I'd never seen Dad look so bewildered.

"Yes. Abner." Camille enunciated it slowly, like maybe Dad hadn't understood before. "That was another name that came up over and over. At times it's as if she thinks she's speaking directly to him and he's responding to her."

She didn't need to tell me there was something wrong with that. What had they done to my Mom? Meredith must have sensed my pain, because she reached out to pull me close to her.

I jumped in while I had the chance. "How'd they take her?" I didn't give her time to answer before other questions tumbled out. "Where'd they keep her? Did she ever try to get away?"

Camille turned her attention to me. "We don't know any of those things yet, but I can tell you that this lead greatly narrows our search, and I expect to have more answers within the next forty-eight hours. I called in someone who specializes in deprogramming people who've been involved in cults to consult on her case. He's supposed to—"

Dad held up his hand. "So Love International is a cult?"

"She shows all the classic signs of someone who's been indoctrinated and brainwashed by a cult," Camille announced, like she was giving us a diagnosis.

KATE

THEN

Scott and I had a lovely evening with Abbi where we'd played all her favorite games—Sorry!, Chutes and Ladders, and her newest favorite, UNO. She had been exhausted by the time we were done and had fallen asleep while I read to her. Scott and I had just put on an independent movie and settled onto the couch. It was Saturday night, which meant halfway through Scott would put his arm around my shoulder and move closer to me on the couch. It wouldn't be long before he started rubbing my thigh in a way that only meant one thing. Then we'd work our way to the bedroom and fall asleep next to each other after we made love.

Nearly paralyzing claustrophobia assaulted me. Everything swirled around me like something terrible might happen, but nothing was wrong. Still. It made my skin crawl thinking about getting through another Saturday night and having to see the pained expression on Scott's face if I told him how I really felt.

"Are you okay?" Scott asked.

I jumped up. "I'm good. I think I just need some water. Do you want anything?"

He grabbed the remote, pausing the movie until I got back. "No, thanks."

I tried to act normal as I walked to the kitchen. My body was covered in sweat, and my heart raced. I turned on the sink and splashed water on my face.

This is it. Ray talked about this.

I slowly lifted my head and grabbed the towel to dry my face. He'd felt this too. It was what had pushed him to go in search of a higher meaning. He'd shared the story with me during our first meeting. I smiled at how long ago it seemed already. I was a different person.

I grabbed a water glass from the cupboard and filled it all the way to the top. I took a big gulp, hoping it'd help my throat stop feeling like it was closing up. This was it, wasn't it? The moment they'd all been talking about—the calling. A sudden peace filled my insides. The light was everywhere, making the kitchen shine brighter than I'd ever seen it. I set my water on the counter and dropped to my knees, hands folded against my chest.

"I'm here. Use me," I whispered.

I opened myself to the light around me, and it filled me.

"Kate?" Scott's voice called from the living room. "Are you okay in there?"

"Coming! I decided to sneak a cookie while I was in here."

My second lie of the night. That was what was wrong with my American dream. I couldn't tell the truth, and my soul needed to tell the truth. I stood slowly, savoring the knowing and the peace before heading back out to the living room to join Scott. The sounds from the TV seemed so meaningless. I went within to where I could dance like I wanted to. Scott's hand rubbing my thigh startled me back into the present. I took his hand and placed it back on his lap. "I'm sorry, honey. I have a bad headache tonight."

FOURTEEN

MEREDITH

NOW

Scott reminded me of Kate as he paced our bedroom. Camille had left and we'd all settled into our bedrooms for the night. "I still can't believe this. I wish you could've met Ray. The guy seemed so normal. I'm telling you. Completely normal. And Kate? I mean, she liked going to their meetings, and she was always going to those goofy retreats, but that was just Kate. She got bored easily. She liked to try new things. She was always flitting from one thing to another and was equally passionate about whatever thing it was she was doing. How was I supposed to know there was something off with this one?"

I didn't say anything. He didn't really want an answer anyway. I'd tried to interject when his rant started and quickly abandoned the idea after he snapped at me. I would wait until he tired himself out and try again. I stepped into the shower in our master bathroom while he leaned against the counter. I was only half listening as I turned on the water.

Today had been one of the hardest days yet. At least for me. My head had run an endless loop of scenarios, and each new piece of information had sent me spinning back to the beginning, trying to figure things out all over again. I was exhausted and had officially hit the wall. I stuck my head outside the shower curtain. "Do you think we could talk about something else?"

He stopped midsentence and flinched like I'd thrown ice water in his face. "What?"

"I mean . . . it's just, I'm sorry, honey—I don't want to make you mad, and I really don't want to be insensitive, but could we take a break from all the Kate drama? Just for a few minutes? I'm not even saying it has to be all night."

He pursed his lips together, eyes narrowing. "Sure, honey. What would you like to talk about? Do you want to talk about the Dodgers?"

"Scott, come on. Don't be like that. This has consumed every waking moment of the last week. It would do us both good to give it a rest."

He mumbled something underneath his breath before walking out of the bathroom. He didn't think I'd heard him, but I'd caught everything. He'd said, "You wouldn't be saying that if James came back from the dead."

But see, that was the thing. Our situations weren't the same. Not even close. James had never been my fairy-tale husband—Scott was. I'd never told him that, though, because how did you bring something like that up? Hey, by the way, I love you more than I did my first husband? I could never say that to him because he wouldn't be able to say it back, and I'd always been okay with that, but what would happen now?

I hurriedly finished washing and toweled myself off, wrapping up in my robe when I was done. I hoped Scott had made his way to bed, but he was sitting at his desk, staring blankly at his computer. I slid into his lap and put my arms around his neck. "Honey, please come to bed and don't be mad at me. You have to give it a rest. A good night's sleep will help things look differently in the morning."

"No. No, it won't." His face folded with the pressure of his pain. "I imagined this moment so many times and how I'd react when she came back. I prepared myself for it. I was so sure I'd be able to handle anything as long as she was alive and okay, and physically she is, but she's not the same person, Meredith. What if she doesn't come back?" He barely finished the question before breaking down into gut-wrenching sobs.

I wrapped my arms around him, and he clung to me, shoulders heaving. I rubbed his back and whispered, "It's going to be okay. You're going to be okay."

Traumatic grief was groundless, a free fall into space. Unless you'd been there before, you couldn't understand what it felt like. Scott tethered himself to me until the moment passed. He pulled away, wiping his face against his sleeve.

"It's all my fault." He choked on another sob.

I grabbed his face with both hands and peered at him. "You listen to me right now, you hear me? We are not going down this road again. None of this was your fault. You didn't do anything to cause this, and there's nothing you could've done to prevent it." He'd spent years in therapy weeding through his warped sense of responsibility. It'd been a while since it had reared its ugly head.

He took my hands and placed them back in my lap. "You might not say that if you knew the whole story."

My insides curled. "What do you mean the full story?" I asked.

He gave the same version of that day every time he was asked—he was perfectly happy, their marriage was great, and they loved their life. He'd kissed her goodbye in the shower before he left for work and that had been the last time he'd ever seen her.

He patted me on my thigh. "Never mind. I'm just being stupid." He moved me off his lap so we could stand. "You're right. I'm just really tired. Let's go to bed."

KATE

THEN

I tossed the toilet paper into my cart and scanned the aisle for our brand of paper towels. I wanted to get on the loudspeaker and announce that I'd been called for discipleship. I'd woken up like a giddy kid on Christmas morning and hadn't stopped smiling. Even my argument with Scott this morning and Abbi's ridiculous tantrum about her shirt hadn't bothered me.

This was what it was like, and all the disciples had been right—when you knew, you knew. It was inexplicable. But what did I do next? I quickly reminded myself that I didn't have to do anything. God would continue to reveal himself to me in the same way he'd done last night. Just like he had revealed himself to Ray and everyone else. I wanted to clap. I was officially part of them. I was all the way in.

The checkout lines were long, but I didn't care. I didn't know how I was going to make it until five, when I could see Ray. I had a huge deadline Friday, and it would take me all day to get the notes from my sources together. What would he say when I told him? He had to be expecting it. How many times had he said he could sense I was special?

What would I tell Leo? None of the disciples worked, since discipleship was your full-time job. That was a given. How would Scott react? And Abbi? My stomach clenched at the thought of her. How would it all work? There had to be some kind of transition period where they helped you sort out all your affairs. I'd get to know all the inside secrets. I couldn't wait for the day when we could all live together on campus.

Take a deep breath. One step at a time.

"Someone sure looks happy today," the cashier said as she scanned my items.

I gave her a huge smile. "I've had a great morning. How about you?"

"So far so good." She smiled back.

I walked to the parking lot, admonishing myself for being so worried and anxious. Where was my faith? The point was to make a blind leap. It wasn't a jump if I already knew everything that was going to happen afterward. The family piece just made it harder. They'd let me go home at night to sleep with them, wouldn't they? At least until they joined? What would I do if I couldn't sway Scott? Margo had said she'd known plenty of families who'd struggled with the concepts before aligning themselves with Love International. Scott would come around eventually.

But what if he didn't?

Would I still go?

Where was I really going?

My head swirled with the argument I'd been having all morning. Now that I'd received the call, my spirit was pulling me to take the next step. I'd sat in the living room until three in the morning, because I couldn't sleep last night, before tiptoeing back up to the bedroom, careful not to wake Scott.

Was I just supposed to go?

Move?

What had Ray said the last time I'd asked him? I threw the bags into the trunk and got into the driver's seat. And then I remembered how he'd quoted Matthew, *"Jesus said, 'Follow me, and let the dead bury their own dead.'"*

I froze. My keys slipped from my hands and fell on the seat. My pulse throbbed in my temples. Sweat trickled down my back. Scripture stirred inside me. *Take nothing for the journey—no walking stick, no bag, no bread, not a second cloak.* I slid my purse off my arm and set it on the passenger seat. Realization hit that this was the last piece of the puzzle.

"I get it," I said out loud, even though I was alone, and there was nobody there to hear me.

There was nothing left to do except go. I stepped out of the car, shutting the door behind me. My body burned with energy like I was on fire. I walked quickly, taking my first right out of the parking lot and then my next left. I couldn't contain my excitement and started running. I hadn't run since high school, but I felt like I could run for days. It wasn't long until I burst into a sprint and didn't stop until I reached Love International's campus. I plowed through the door, exhilarated and breathless, not bothering to say hello or talk to anyone as I made a beeline for Ray's office. I couldn't wait to tell him. He'd be so proud. I pounded on his door.

"Come in," he called from inside.

I pushed through. He glanced up from behind his desk, surprised to see me.

"Kate? I thought we were meeting later today?"

I would never need to make an appointment with him again. I could see him every day if I wanted to. A wide grin spread across my face. "I did it," I said, still out of breath. "I just left. What do I do now?"

FIFTEEN

MEREDITH

NOW

The exit counselor, Brian O'Donnell, arrived the next day and spent all afternoon with Kate. He asked to speak with me, Abbi, and Scott after he finished his session with her. We filed into the dining room, which was quickly becoming the spot for all meetings. He was unassuming and short, only slightly taller than me, which wasn't saying a lot. He was in his early forties, on the heavier side, and wore a cardigan tied over his shoulders, despite the heat in the room. He'd gone around the table and shaken hands with everyone before taking a seat in the middle. I'd offered him the head, but he'd quickly declined.

Brian's eyes moved around the room while he talked, making eye contact with each of us while he spoke. "Short of when Kate vanished, I'm sure this has been one of the most emotionally intense weeks of your lives. I want to take a moment and recognize everything you've been through."

I glanced at Scott out of the corner of my eye. Normally he hated anything hinting at mindfulness, but he was hanging on Brian's every word.

"In recognizing everything that you've been through, we also need to recognize everything that Kate has been through too. The world moves so much faster than what she's used to. It's almost like she's gone forward in time, so you can imagine how incredibly disorienting that would be for a person. Now take into consideration that she's spent the last decade immersed in a cult with an extremely charismatic leader whom she had very strong feelings for, punished whenever she thought for herself or did anything considered wrong, and isolated from any other viewpoints or thoughts that might tell her differently."

"She told you that?" I asked, shocked. I couldn't believe he'd gotten her to tell him all that in a few hours, and nobody had been able to get anything out of her for a week. He must have been fantastic at his job.

"Not in so many words, but in enough pieces to hint at similar truths. Besides, all cults are basically the same," Brian said. "Once she starts opening up, I'm certain her case will follow a similar progression as most cult survivors, and there are a few things that I want to talk about with you before we move any further." We nodded our heads in unison. "It's important that we don't ever approach Kate with any level of hostility toward them or their ideas. If we do, it will reinforce what Ray and the other members have drilled into her head for years—that you can't trust outsiders because they don't understand your beliefs or situation. If we come at her like we are the enemy, then all we've done is reinforce everything they taught her. It will make her second-guess leaving if that happens. Believe me—we learned this the hard way." The seriousness in his expression let me know he was telling the truth. "Victims tell their story in their own time and at their own pace. Eventually, it comes out, but sometimes it comes out very slowly. It usually takes about two years to deprogram a person who's been indoctrinated into a cult, and, from what I've seen and heard today, I expect her case will follow a similar timeline."

"How did they take her?" Scott asked. It was the question we were all dying to know.

"They didn't take her. Cults don't usually kidnap people. People leave their families and lives to follow cults voluntarily." Compassion filled his face. "I'm sorry."

Scott jumped up from the table. "No way." He shook his head rapidly. "Did she tell you that?"

"No, but Scott, it's highly unlikely that anyone from the cult kidnapped her." He kept his tone even.

Scott shook his head again. "Then, no, I'm not buying into your theory. I don't care if that's the way things normally work or how things usually go. There is not a chance that Kate left this family willingly. None." He looked over at Abbi, making sure she was listening, and pointed to the stairs, where Kate had retreated to the guest bedroom after their interview. "Now you get back up there and figure out how they got her."

Brian remained seated. His face was impassive, calm despite the anger radiating off Scott in his direction. "I'm sorry, Scott. I really am. I know this is hard to hear. It always is, but at some point you're going to have to accept that you might not have known Kate as well as you thought you did."

———

It'd been over two hours since Brian left, and Scott was still fuming over his suggestion that Kate had gone with Love International willingly. I had made up an excuse about being out of milk to get out of the house and away from all the tension. I chewed on my cheek while I walked down the dairy aisle at the grocery store, a nervous habit I hadn't done in years, but it was hard not to be anxious when everyone was staring at you. People tried to act like they weren't, but I felt their eyes drilling holes into my back as I shopped. Now I understood why

Scott had driven forty-five minutes away to do his errands after Kate went missing.

It would be devastating for him if Kate had left on her own, but once he was over the initial hurt, this could be a good thing for us. If they hadn't kidnapped her, maybe we didn't have to be afraid of them coming back to get her or trying to hurt us. Maybe she'd been able to come and go as she pleased all along. But that wouldn't explain her mangled body. There wasn't any confusion over whether or not she'd been tortured. Everyone agreed on that. None of this made sense. I had wanted to take my time, but it was so uncomfortable being watched that I hurriedly threw milk and eggs into my cart and headed to self-checkout.

I stalled on the drive home, hoping the night shift had replaced the day shift. The questions didn't stop until the day shift was gone, and I didn't have any energy left for more questions. I was surprised to find Scott and Kate sitting on the couch when I walked through the door. Normally he would've jumped up to help me, even though I only had one bag, but he didn't move from his spot.

"Hi, guys," I said, my voice one octave higher than usual. I'd clearly walked in on something. Should I stay? Run to the kitchen? I searched the living room walls like there was an invisible spot on them.

Scott cleared his throat. "We were just talking."

"Okay, okay . . ." Heat surged through me.

Scott pointed to the club chair in front of the couch. "You might as well be here for this." He waited for me to sit before turning his focus back to Kate. "I know I just said that this conversation is only between us, but, believe me, you can trust Meredith," he said.

She peeked up and gave me a tiny smile. I smiled back. There was no way to have a private conversation in a wired room, but I wasn't about to point that out.

"Kate, I hate doing this to you, but it's eating me up inside. I need to know what happened the day you went missing. Brian and Camille think that you left to join Love International willingly. I told them there was no way that was true, that there had to be some other explanation, and I know you don't want to talk about things, sweetie. I get that." He got off the couch and knelt on the floor in front of her. Their engagement photos flashed through my memory unbidden. I shoved them away as he stared at her with desperation written all over his face. "But please tell me what happened that day. You don't have to talk about anything else with me ever again, I promise. I just have to know—did they take you, or did you just leave?"

The room filled with the enormity of his question. I scooted forward in my chair, as eager for the truth as Scott.

"I left." Her voice was barely above a whisper.

"I don't get it." Confusion filled his eyes. "Why would you leave us? Why?"

Huge tears slipped down her cheeks as her lower lip quivered. "I'm so sorry, Scott."

He raised his hands and touched her face as softly as I was sure he'd touched Abbi's when she was a baby. "You went because you wanted to?"

"I did, Scottie. I did," she said. A heaving sob shook her body.

Scott's eyes never wavered from hers. He gazed at her with as much love as he had before he asked the question.

"Why, Kate? I just want to know why?" He was crying too. They'd forgotten I was there. Sadness washed over me.

Kate held Shiloh against her chest, rocking back and forth like she did when she got really upset. She muttered underneath her breath while she moved.

"Please, Kate." He sounded like a little boy.

"I waited for you to come," she said when she'd finally found her voice. "Why didn't you ever come?" Her question was engulfed by another sob.

KATE

THEN

Ray quickly ushered me into his office and shut the door behind us. "Are you sure you're ready?" he asked.

Short of marrying Scott, I had never been more sure of anything. "I'm ready."

He moved over to his desk, opened the bottom drawer, and dug through folders until he found whatever he was looking for. He grabbed it and slammed the drawer shut. "Wait here," he said, hurrying to the door. "I'll be right back."

Adrenaline coursed through my veins. I couldn't believe I'd done it. I was giddy in a way I hadn't experienced since I was a little girl. When would I start my training? There had to be some kind of training, since there was a class for everything. Was it the same for everyone? Questions tumbled on top of each other while I waited. Thankfully it wasn't long before Ray came back with Margo. She rushed into the room and threw her arms around me.

"I'm so happy for you," she squealed, jumping up and down. It was a side of her I'd never seen. She was always so stern and serious. Her husband, Will, was the same way. They were only in their thirties, but they carried themselves like they were much older. It didn't help that she always wore her hair in a tight bun.

"Thank you," I said, giggling with her as she twirled me around the room.

"Are you nervous?" she asked.

I nodded. There were too many different emotions swirling through me to focus.

"I was so scared I couldn't stop shaking. Mostly I was worried about how things would be when Will and I saw each other again, since it'd been almost six months."

Will was Love International's first disciple. He was one of the few disciples who'd known Ray before he'd given away all his possessions. Ray had found him passed out in an alley in Detroit, reeking of booze and vomit. Someone had stripped his body like a car, leaving him in his boxers and T-shirt. Ray had brought him to his apartment and nursed him back to health. He had walked him through early sobriety, and they'd been together ever since. Margo had met Will in his second year of sobriety, but I didn't know any more than that. I was hoping she'd tell me more of her story once my discipleship was official.

"What was it like?" I asked. I couldn't imagine being away from Scott for that long. We'd never been apart longer than a week.

"It was like being newly in love all over again, but even better because we were wiser versions of ourselves."

Margo had been a different faith before Love International, which was probably why it had taken her so long. At least Scott believed in God, so he would be more open to whatever process they had set up for him. He'd follow through with whatever they asked him to do, wouldn't he? My analytical mind was running wild again. I had to stay centered in the spiritual.

Ray interrupted our conversation. "I know we're excited, ladies, but there will be lots of time to talk. We need to get Kate settled as quickly as possible." He motioned to the door, and we followed him into the hallway. We took a left at the end and then another before arriving at a set of double doors. Ray punched in a code, and they opened to outside, revealing a large gravel lot. "This is where we keep our extra vans," he said.

The lot was empty except for a lone van in the far corner. It wasn't like the other beat-up white vans they drove on their volunteer outings, with rust eating away at the tire rims. This one was solid black and windowless, like a creepy child-molester van.

"Nice wheels," I joked to Ray.

Normally he would have laughed, but he ignored me as he fumbled with the latches on the back door. He gave them a sharp tug, and they came flying open. He pointed to the inside. "Hop in," he said to me.

I laughed and moved toward the front of the van. He grabbed my arm from behind.

"No, really. Hop in," he said.

"Oh, I didn't think you were serious," I stuttered, instantly embarrassed. "Where—" I stopped myself. Blind faith. That was what I was operating on now.

I climbed into the back and turned to help Margo get in, but she was gone. I could tell by Ray's expression that he wasn't joining me either. He gave me a strange smile as he shut the door, and I did my best to look brave. The latch clicked behind him, and panic washed over me. I forced myself to breathe and give my eyes a second to adjust to the light. It didn't take long, and as they did I saw that the van's seats had all been stripped out. Sleeping bags and pillows lined the cab's floor. The front doors slammed shut, and within seconds the ignition brought the van to life. I quickly plopped down, trying to arrange the pillows around me in a way that was comfortable and find something to hold on to. The van lurched forward, going slowly at first but quickly picking up speed, which meant we had to have jumped on the interstate.

Had anyone called Scott yet? I had no idea what his schedule was like today because we hadn't talked about it before he left for work this morning. All we'd done was get in that stupid fight. He was already mad at me and was only going to be more upset when he found out what I'd done. Hopefully he would answer their call, but he had a horrible habit of ignoring numbers he didn't recognize. What if he didn't listen to his voice mail until later this afternoon? I needed him to pick up Abbi from preschool. There was no way I was going to be done with this on time. How was any of this going to work? The magnitude of what I'd done engulfed me.

I needed to get a grip. They'd done this before. We weren't the only family with a complicated situation. I didn't need to figure everything out. Ray was always telling me that I had to release my control and allow life to naturally unfold in front of me. I forced myself to lie back on the blankets and focus on my breathing. I couldn't do any of this if I wasn't centered.

Listening to the thrum of the road calmed me, and it wasn't long before it lulled me to sleep. I drifted in and out, jostled awake by the bumps and turns before falling back to sleep. We drove for what felt like days, but it was probably only hours. Everything just seemed longer stuck back in the dark. Finally the van stopped. My eyes snapped open. Feet shuffled to the side of the van. The lock clicked, and Ray opened the door. Blinding light shone into my eyes, making me squint. He stuck out his hand, and I stepped outside into the sun. It took my eyes a while to adjust from being in the dark for so long.

We were parked in front of an old farmhouse. Large evergreen trees surrounded it on all sides. The roof sagged to the left, and faded yellow paint peeled off in chunks. Two of the stairs leading up to the porch were rotten. One of the windows was boarded up. The grass around it was long and unkept. The weeds had won the battle in the yard long ago. Ray walked around the house to the back, and I hurried along after him.

"Where's Margo?" I asked, struggling to keep up, still weak and disoriented from the long car ride.

"She stayed behind to take care of things," he said.

He immediately started clearing away a pile of brush leaned up against the back of the house. I moved to help, and we worked silently side by side as the sun lowered itself in the sky. The pile grew smaller, revealing two large cellar doors sealed together with an old padlock. Ray dug his keys out of his pocket and picked through them until he found the right one. He lifted open the doors. Dust filled my nose. Concrete steps led into darkness. Ray motioned to the steps. I ducked my head and stepped into the darkness, holding the railing on the left to steady my feet as I made my way down. I came to the bottom and turned to look up at Ray, waiting for him to follow me. But he didn't. He just stood there looking at me with a strange expression on his face. Then, without saying a word, he reached over and shut one of the doors. He wasn't coming with me?

"Ray?" I called up to him. He closed the other door. "Ray!" I yelled louder this time as I scrambled to the top of the stairs and pushed on the door. It didn't budge. I beat on it with my fists.

"What are you doing?" I screamed.

Nothing.

My ears buzzed with silence. What was happening? A surge of fear ran through my body. "Relax," I admonished myself. "This is all part of the process." I repeated it like a mantra until the fear began to subside and my thoughts slowed down.

I'd done fear exercises before. I'd stood naked in front of the entire group. All of us women had done it to release our unhealthy focus on our bodies. We'd all cried. I'd shaken through most of it. But I'd gotten through it and the next one, too, just like I'd get through this. I let out a deep breath, my muscles slowly untangling. I turned around and headed back into the cellar.

There weren't any windows, just four concrete walls. The paint had started chipping off in places, revealing rows of bricks underneath. Pieces had been gouged out like someone had tried to dig their way out. I shoved down the questions surging their way up the back of my throat and focused my attention on the other corner. There was a mattress with a thin blanket tossed on it. No pillow. The only other thing in the cellar was a bucket. I shuddered just thinking about what it might be for. All of this was so gross. I hadn't expected it to be so disgusting.

None of this was going like I'd imagined, but that was the point, wasn't it? Suddenly all I wanted to do was sleep. I'd never been so tired. I lay back on the mattress, resting my head on my arms. The mattress was so thin the weight of my body pressed me to the floor. The musty smell of the blanket made me want to gag—a mixture of body odor and urine. Had they forgotten to clean up after the last person had used this place?

I curled up on my side. How had things gone with Scott? Was he mad when Ray told him what I'd done? How did Ray help families outside of the membership understand the importance of discipleship? At least Scott understood commitment and sacrifice, even if he might not agree with what I'd done. Abbi wouldn't understand anything, but I would sit her down when she was older and explain all of it. She would be proud of me then. I rested my head on my arms, keeping the blanket away from my face, and closed my eyes, too tired to keep them open any longer.

———

I had no idea how much time had passed since Ray had put me in this room. It could be hours. It might have been days. I didn't know. There was a small overhead light bulb on at all times, so there was no way to tell if it was day or night. It stayed dim. It didn't help that it was stifling hot, like being cooked in a microwave. The bucket in the corner was for exactly what I'd thought it was. So far I'd only had to use it once, and there wasn't any toilet paper. The entire place smelled like urine.

My stomach gnawed at me. I hadn't had anything to eat or drink since the croissant with my coffee the morning I'd left, and I'd passed being starved a long time ago. Thankfully I'd been prepared for a fast. This part of the journey was familiar, and not eating would make it easier not to have to go to the bathroom.

I paced with built-up tension and energy but couldn't walk more than a few feet before I had to turn in the other direction. Seven steps to the door and seven steps back. Only five steps across. I'd had moments when the panic almost overtook me, but so far I'd managed to stay in control of my mind.

I had just slid down the brick wall onto the concrete floor when I heard it—a sound that didn't come from me. I sprang up. Was it coming from the doors? There it was again. There was no mistaking someone was at the door. I dashed up to the door just as one of the sides opened, and I plunged headlong into the sunshine. Ray pulled me back. I stumbled backward on the stairs, steadying myself against the wall.

"Move back," he ordered sternly. He grabbed my arm and twisted me around so I faced the cellar. Something about the way he gripped me let me know I didn't have a choice.

"What's happening? What's going on, Ray? I don't understand." My voice came out sounding like it had when I was a little girl. I tried not to cry as I stepped back into the cellar. I just wanted the sunlight.

He followed me down, taking in the space with one sweep before turning his gaze on me. I straightened up immediately, wiping underneath my eyes with my fingertips. I coughed nervously and tried to look alert. It was dark, but I could still see the disappointment in his eyes.

"What day is it?" I asked.

"Wednesday."

I had left Monday. I wanted to reach for him, but his arms were folded across his chest. His face was set in stone, impassive, the way he got when we were expected to feel our uncomfortable emotions without being comforted in any way. It was awful. I burst into tears, bubbling over with all the emotions I'd been through in the last few hours—days—I didn't even know. That was part of it. How was I supposed to get grounded when there was nothing to orient me to time and space? "Please tell me what's happening," I begged.

"You're going through your forty days in the desert, just like Jesus."

"Forty days? Nobody said anything about forty days. In here?"

He nodded.

"All alone?" My voice sounded so small.

"Right before Jesus was about to begin his ministry, he was taken into the desert alone and tempted by the devil for forty days. He brought everything he could against him, but Jesus withstood every single attack. He had to prove to God that he would withstand all tests against him. And he did. God expects the same of any of his disciples as they prepare for their ministry."

I shook my head. "I can't do this. I'm sorry. I can't," I cried. I felt like such a failure, but I couldn't take another minute.

"I understand if you don't have what it takes." His face broke into a tender smile. "It's okay, Kate. God loves you like he loves all his children. Nothing changes that." He pointed to the stairway behind him. "There's two doors at the top of those stairs, and they're wide open. Do you know how many people turn back at this point?"

"Really?"

He wrinkled his eyebrows in surprise. "Are you kidding me? Of course." He motioned to the brick walls surrounding us. "This is a pretty raw mirror of self." He laughed, and the sound of his laughter removed some of the tension twisting my insides. "I really thought you were one of us, though." He leaned forward and peeled the matted hair off my cheeks and tucked it behind my ears. I melted into his touch, like being enclosed in the womb. "I always saw you as having a warrior spirit. I'm usually not wrong about these things."

"I am a warrior," I said, instantly insulted. I pushed his hand away from my face. Didn't he know what I'd just done? All I'd been through? I'd walked away from my husband and daughter. I'd never been away from either of them for more than a few days at a time, and I'd left both of them, because I was committed to go to any lengths. Anything. And I loved them like they were a part of my body. If that wasn't being a warrior, then I didn't know what was.

He raised his eyebrows. "Really?"

"Yes."

"Then let me hear you say it," he said. He took a step toward me until we were standing chest to chest.

"I am a warrior."

"Louder."

"I am a warrior!"

"I want to hear you. That's not loud enough."

"I AM A WARRIOR!" I screamed until it cut my throat.

He grabbed me and twirled me around. "That's what I'm talking about—breakthrough." Dizziness made the walls move when he stopped. "The chains that bind you are being released now. In this moment, this very moment. I know you feel it too. It saddens me for you to leave it." He gazed into my eyes. "Once you leave, you will never have this moment again. It's gone."

I swallowed the terror in my throat and refused to break his stare. "I've changed my mind. I'm going to stay."

"I was hoping you'd say that." He reached into his backpack and handed me a paper bag. He tossed two bottles of water on the floor. "This is where you meet God for real."

SIXTEEN

ABBI

NOW

I hadn't gone to bed this early since I was ten, but things were so awkward downstairs that as soon as Mom said she had to put Shiloh to bed, we'd all pretended to be exhausted and jumped up, following her upstairs. It was impossible to chill in your living room when there was a video camera above the fireplace and detectives wandering around your kitchen reheating meals they'd brought from home.

None of us were sleeping. Dad's and Meredith's hushed whispers carried into my room, and Shiloh's cries reverberated throughout the house. She slept all day and was awake at night, like she came into the world upside down, which meant Mom would be awake most of the night again. The bags underneath her eyes were getting worse instead of better. How was she supposed to get through all this without any sleep?

I scrolled through my phone, catching up on what everyone was saying about us on social media. Our pictures were plastered everywhere. I was fine with the ones from when Mom went missing, because I'd seen them hundreds of times, so I'd gotten used to them, and besides, they were cute. They'd picked the most adorable pictures of me to pull at the heartstrings of Mom's attacker, but I hated my current one. It was my school picture from last year, and I looked terrible. I couldn't say anything about it, though, because I wasn't supposed to be paying any attention to the media. A quick scan told me nothing had changed, and everyone was still saying the same thing—Dad had something to do with it. That was what they always said.

Shiloh let out another wail, and I set my phone on the nightstand. Poor Mom. I had to help her. I couldn't do much with the baby, but at least she wouldn't have to be alone. I hated being up by myself in the middle of the night, because it was so lonely. That was what I hated the most about insomnia. Was she the same way? There was so much I wanted to know about her. I needed to stop being so afraid. I gave myself a final pep talk before getting up and tiptoeing over to her bedroom.

I knocked quietly. Mom cracked the door as she jiggled Shiloh in her other arm.

"I'm so sorry. I'm sorry," she whispered.

"It's okay," I said, smiling at her. "You didn't wake me up. It's still a little early for me to go to sleep."

She opened the door wider. "Come in?" Her voice wavered nervously.

"I mean, if it's okay with you. I don't want to bother you."

"It's okay," she said. Her eyes were downcast as we walked into her room. The bed was still untouched. I sat on the end and waited for her to sit next to me, but she shut the door behind us and stood in the center of the small room instead, swaying back and forth with Shiloh in her arms. Her eyes were wide open and fully alert as she stared up at Mom adoringly.

"Do you still sleep on the floor?" I asked.

She nodded.

I hated asking her questions when she had spent most of the day getting drilled with them, but there was so much I wanted to know about her. I played with one of the loose strings on the comforter, twisting it around my finger. "Can I ask why? You don't have to tell me if you don't want to. I mean, I know you're probably sick of everyone asking you questions."

"We don't sleep on beds," she said matter of factly.

"How come?" I couldn't imagine sleeping on a wooden floor. I hated sleeping on the floor even with our thick camping sleeping bags.

"We must put the flesh to death," she said in a creepy robot voice.

I'd never heard her talk like that before. I didn't want to ask any more questions about the bed. I eyed the room, taking in the dirty coffee-colored tone of the walls that Meredith and Dad swore they were going to tackle on their next home-improvement project. "What's your favorite color?" I asked.

"Color?" she asked, like I'd surprised her, and she let out a small giggle before quickly slapping a hand over her mouth. Maybe they weren't allowed to laugh either. "Red," she finally said. "Red." Almost like she had to say it a second time to reassure herself.

"Mine too," I said. I'd been secretly hoping that was what she'd say. I patted the spot next to me. "Sit."

She shook her head and turned the other direction so I couldn't see her face anymore.

"You sit on the couches downstairs. What's the difference?" I kept my voice as nonjudgmental as possible. "I really just want to know so I can understand. I want to know you, Mom." It was the first time I'd called her *Mom*, and the word hung between us.

She turned back around, her eyes wet. "You must hate me." Her voice trembled as she spoke.

"I could never hate you. You're my mom."

Tears slid down her cheeks. "And you're my other daughter."

Had she forgotten about me like she'd tried to forget about sleeping in beds? Or was there a part of her that had always felt me, too, in the same way I'd felt her all these years, like an impression that had never left, a dull ache for an unidentified need. Had she? What would she say if I asked? She would say yes, but what if I saw the lie in her eye? I kept quiet.

"Do you want to hold your sister?" she asked nervously.

"Really?" I couldn't believe she trusted me with the baby.

She smiled again. She'd never smiled twice in a conversation, and so far she'd only cried a little bit. Tonight was epic. Mom folded Shiloh into my arms, and she snuggled up against my chest immediately. "Oh my God, she's so little." Shiloh let out a tiny squeal at the sound of my voice, and my heart melted into my chest.

I had always wanted a sibling. Thad and Caleb didn't count, because they were practically adults by the time we'd met. I wanted someone in the house with me. Another kid who could help shoulder the responsibility with Dad. Sometimes it was hard being an only child, when all the expectations fell on you. I wouldn't have minded sharing the spotlight with someone else.

"Why don't you sit down?" I nodded toward the bed. I saw the longing pass through her eyes before she quickly returned to the stoic expression she wore most of the time. "I'm not saying lie down and sleep in the bed all night. Just come be next to us."

She considered my proposition for a second. It didn't make any sense that she had to think about it, as if I'd offered her some kind of plea bargain, but something bad must have happened to her while she was in a bed, or they'd told her something awful would happen to her if she used one. Either way, I couldn't help but be proud of myself when she finally took a seat next to me and Shiloh. She'd no sooner sat down than Shiloh stirred and started crying.

"Oh, she's hungry," Mom said.

I handed the baby back to her. She lifted her shirt, and Shiloh settled on her breast almost immediately. I was getting better about her breastfeeding in front of me, but I still never knew where to look when she did it. Was I supposed to look at her? Away from her? The baby?

This was one of the reasons you needed a mom when you were young. Someone to teach you these kinds of things.

"Does it hurt?" I asked.

"This?" She looked down at Shiloh. I nodded. "Not at all." We sat in silence for a few minutes before she spoke again. "You loved to nurse."

I gulped. This was all so intense. Part of me wanted to run back to my room just so I could gather myself and breathe, but the other part was glued to my spot, unable to move. This was really happening. I was in a room with my mom, and she was telling me stories about when I was young. I swallowed back the tears, afraid if I cried that she'd stop talking or start sobbing herself.

"You were the best baby. Content all the time. Barely ever cried, and even when you did your cries were these little whimpers that only made me feel even sorrier for you." She looked at Shiloh as she talked, but was she remembering my face as she spoke? Had I brought that same look of pure love and contentment back then? I burst into tears. She threw her other arm around me. "Oh, oh, I'm sorry. I'm so sorry. I didn't mean to hurt you," she stammered nervously.

I shook my head, too emotional to speak. She pulled me even closer, and I settled in next to her, leaning my head on her shoulder as she nursed Shiloh. I'd been here before. This spot was familiar. I could stay here forever.

KATE

THEN

"Hold me," I sobbed, throwing myself at Ray when he came downstairs, desperate for his touch, craving human contact. The starvation from human touch was worse than the hunger. He put his arms out and stiff-armed me back. "Please, Ray, no, please not this time."

Last visit he'd been so kind. He'd given me a sponge bath, and it was glorious. But it had been a long time since then. Much longer than he'd ever left me. I'd had all sorts of panicked thoughts, like something terrible had happened to him, and he'd never told anyone I was down here, so I would die in suffocating isolation. I almost drove myself crazy with worry.

"Do you know what happened the last time the devil visited Jesus?" he asked.

I knew the story by heart. I'd begged Ray to bring me something to read, because the only thing worse than the panic attacks was the mind-numbing boredom of being in a closed space with no interaction. He'd given me a Bible, and the temptation of Jesus was the first thing I had found. The story had been there in black and white, just like he'd said it would be. "He takes Jesus to the top of a mountain and shows him all the land below. He promises to give him all the souls in the world if he bows down and worships him. Jesus refuses, and that's when the devil finally leaves."

Ray grinned. I loved when he was pleased with me.

"Is this it? Am I close?" I asked.

He nodded. Excitement surged through me.

"You've denounced the world, much like Jesus. In the same way, you've curbed your earthly appetites and desires. The only thing left is to denounce the devil by putting the self to death." He gave me a second to gather my composure before ordering me to stand. I stood slowly.

"Take off your clothes," he said.

My clothes were the same ones I'd been wearing the day I left my life. I'd lost so much weight that my jeans hung on me, the waistband rolled over to keep them up. I stepped out of them and tossed them to the side. I stood in my sports bra and underwear, since I hadn't worn my T-shirt in a long time. I'd torn it into strips, one to hold my hair back and the others to use as cleaning rags. Cleaning my small space gave order to my days. Wiping my body down with the same rag day after day was pointless, but it made me feel like I was still a human being.

"All of it." His voice filled with threat.

I knew what he was asking me to do, but I couldn't get my arms to move. My body froze. I willed it to move, but it refused. The crack of his belt against my leg snapped me back into my body. I fumbled with my underwear, pulling it down to my knees. The mortification never got easier.

"Turn around."

I turned away from him, facing the brick. Shame burned my cheeks. I understood why Jesus wept blood in the garden of Gethsemane.

"The Lord says we must put to death the evil deeds of the body." His belt cracked against my bare skin, making me jump. "Let those who know the Lord renounce all wickedness."

Another smack. And another. Each one harder than the last. I bit the inside of my cheek to keep from crying out.

"Do you feel the sin leaving your body?"

I stumbled over my words, the pain making me stupid. The next hit almost knocked me to the ground. "I belong to the Lord so . . ."

It was gone. I couldn't remember. Where did it go?

"What does the word say?"

He barely gave me a chance to respond before smacking me again. My stomach heaved into my throat. Suddenly I remembered. "I belong to the Lord so crucify me," I blurted out.

He unleashed on me. I lost track of how many hits. Tears burned my eyes. My backside screamed in pain. I didn't recognize the sound of my cries.

"Please, please," I begged over and over. It was as if he couldn't hear me, or if he did, my words meant nothing. My knees buckled, and I crumpled to the floor before everything went black.

SEVENTEEN
MEREDITH

NOW

"And how long were you in the cellar?" Brian asked after Kate had finished describing what happened to her on the day she left and in the following days. We'd called Dean last night after our conversation with Kate, and he'd made arrangements to have everyone on the team here at eight to hear her disclosure. Brian and Camille were the only ones in the living room with Kate. The rest of us were watching the interview on monitors Dean had set up in the dining room. Abbi had been sleeping when people started arriving, and I'd told Scott he should wake her for it, but he'd insisted we let her sleep, since she'd been up most of the night with Kate.

"Forty days and forty nights, just like Jesus," Kate said while she played with Shiloh's fingers. It'd taken everything I had to sit through her descriptions of the cellar. For a second I thought I detected a hint of pride on her face at having survived down there for that long with no human contact besides Ray, but it was gone that quickly, leaving me doubting that I'd seen it at all.

"Refresh my memory, since it's been a long time since my Catholic school days—what exactly was Jesus doing in the desert?" Brian asked.

"While Jesus was being groomed and prepared for his ministry, he was taken into the wilderness, where he was tempted by the devil for forty days and forty nights." Her voice changed whenever she quoted scripture or anything else related to their theology. "His experience was actually much worse than mine. The devil was relentless in his pursuit."

Watching her talk about Love International would've been fascinating if it wasn't so disturbing. She was barely coherent, but the moment the conversation shifted into discussing Love International, she became an articulate and well-spoken individual. I had never studied psychology, but I didn't need to have a background in mental health to see she'd been brainwashed and indoctrinated with their propaganda. She'd obviously been coached. She was like an automaton trained to respond to certain trigger words.

I watched Camille during the interview as much as I watched Kate. She kept quiet, allowing Brian to ask all the questions, but her eyes were laser focused on Kate. I would've loved to get inside her head and see what she was thinking about all of this.

"Was the devil relentless in his pursuit of you?" Brian asked.

She nodded.

"That must have been awful." Was the concern in Brian's eyes genuine, or was he just trying to get her to talk? I couldn't tell. "What did you do to get through it?"

"I read."

"What did you read?"

"The Bible. I read to Abbi. That helped."

"Did you do anything else?"

She took a minute before answering, either working to gather her thoughts or trying to decide if she should tell us. "I put myself places," she finally said.

Brian looked interested. "You did? What does that mean?"

Her eyes filled with tears, and for a second she almost broke down, but she pulled herself back together. "I traveled outside of myself a lot."

"Where did you go when you traveled outside yourself?" Brian asked like it was normal to believe you could leave your body and take little trips around the city. I couldn't wait for the interview to be over. It was making my skin crawl.

She paused. "Home."

"And what did you do at home?"

Her gaze shifted upstairs. "I watched them sleep." She smiled like she was watching them now, or maybe it was the memory. "Not Scott. Abbi slept. He walked. I counted his miles." Scott burst out laughing. Kate let out a small giggle when she heard him from the other room.

He told me his insomnia started after Kate left, but that couldn't be right because how else would she know that he was up pacing, unable to sleep from stress? Why would he lie about that?

"Doesn't it say something about how the angels attended to him after he was taken out of the desert?" Brian asked.

"It does."

"Did the angels attend to you when you were let out?"

"They welcomed me."

"The angels being the other disciples?"

She nodded.

"What kind of ceremony did they have for you?" he asked. He never let time lapse between questions, as a way to keep her talking.

"A welcome-home one," she said.

"Welcome home . . . hmm." He made an exaggerated production of looking around the room, taking in the framed picture of Abbi, Scott, and Kate displayed on the mantel above the fireplace. "But I thought this was your home?"

———

Scott sat at his desk in the corner, trying to catch up on his emails from work. He was struggling to stay on top of things even though he hadn't complained about it. His supervisors were completely understanding about our situation and told him to work from home for as long as he needed, but commercial sales wasn't a job that was easily done from the desk in our bedroom.

He typed while he talked. "I keep trying to put myself in her situation, picture myself there, and I just can't wrap my brain around what it must have been like to be thrown in a cell and kept in complete isolation for that long. Prisoners go crazy when they're kept in seclusion rooms, and those guys are hardened criminals. Kate isn't a wimp, but she's hardly someone that you'd think could survive in those conditions."

"When are you going to tell Abbi what's going on?" I asked. She'd slept until after ten, and Kate's interview was already over by then. Camille had spent the rest of the afternoon with Kate, so Scott had had plenty of time to fill Abbi in on the details she'd missed since last night, but he hadn't. He'd spent hours going over yesterday's videos with Dean instead.

He wrinkled his forehead. "She knows everything that's going on."

Was he avoiding telling her? She would find out about it at our next debriefing session anyway, so what was the point? There was no way to shield her from the hurt.

I placed my hand on top of his, forcing him to stop typing and pay attention to me. "We knew this would be hard, but you're only prolonging the inevitable by not telling her. She would much rather hear it from you than a bunch of stiff FBI agents. Besides, you can frame it for her in a way that will mean more and might help lessen the blow."

"Meredith, come on, you saw how Kate was in there today. Nothing about her joining Love International was voluntary. That man completely brainwashed her while she was down there." He shook his head in disbelief and astonishment. "The crazy part is how he played with her and worked his way into her head without her even knowing he was doing it."

Brian had said something similar during one of our coffee breaks this morning. He'd said if you wanted to brainwash someone, you used language specifically designed to draw them in, coupled with mind-control tricks. He had sworn people didn't stand a chance over time when the practices were grounded in the so-called purpose and will of God.

"Did you hear how many times he told her that he liked it when she smiled? He knew that would only make her want to work harder to please him." His eyes were on fire. "He knew her so well, right into her psyche. It's how he made her into his slave. Think about what it must have been like for her. You're all alone in a dark space, and he becomes the only contact with the outside world. Christ, she depends on him for food and water; her entire survival depends on him. It's genius. It bonds her to him in a way that wouldn't be possible any other way."

"Scott, can we get back to my original question?" He would have gone on forever if I hadn't stopped him.

"That's what I'm talking about, honey. This gets to your original question. It's too complicated and convoluted to tell Abbi that her mom abandoned us. It's not that simple." He eyed me pointedly.

He was avoiding it like it wasn't going to be real until he told Abbi, so he was putting it off for as long as possible. But even that didn't explain his behavior. Worry seeped into my thoughts. He'd made that strange comment last night about me not knowing the full story—even if he'd laughed it off like it was because he was tired, he'd still said it—and now this.

"I love you, Scott, and I know how unbelievably difficult this must be for you." I was beat from the stress, and mine paled in comparison to his. "All I'm saying is that I think you shouldn't waste any more time before bringing Abbi up to speed."

He pulled his hand away from mine and shoved the keyboard aside. "I don't want to argue about this anymore. It's not your call to make."

His words stung. I raised my hand to my cheek, like they'd left a physical mark. We were supposed to be on the same team. "I'm going downstairs to get myself something to eat." He didn't wait for me to respond before leaving the bedroom and heading to the kitchen.

I wasn't going to let him avoid the conversation. Someone had to think rationally about our situation, and I had to be the one to do it, since he was too emotional. I quickly followed him downstairs.

EIGHTEEN

ABBI

NOW

I rushed around the corner and into the kitchen just as Meredith said to Dad, "I think you should tell her right now. She—" She stopped as soon as she saw me.

"Tell me what?" I asked, since they were obviously talking about me.

They both froze. I was supposed to be upstairs doing my homework, but I'd forgotten my math book on the table and couldn't finish without it. They turned to each other, trying to communicate with their eyes, like married couples do, but I wasn't going to give them a chance to get their story straight. "Tell me what?" I asked again, more direct and forceful this time. I'd walked in on something, and I wasn't leaving until they told me.

"Is your mom still resting?" Dad asked.

I nodded. She'd been lying down since after dinner. She'd gotten one of her horrible headaches after her session with Camille this afternoon. Those sessions wiped her out more than the others. I wouldn't want to be interviewed by Camille either. Everything she said came out sounding like she was mad at you.

"This is probably a great time to have that conversation we've been talking about." Meredith eyed Dad, their exchange barbed with hidden meaning. He glared at her.

"Do you want to sit?" Dad asked me. He pointed to the table, where my math book lay splayed open, just like I'd left it.

"What? Just tell me—what's going on?" Dad never made me sit. It must be really bad news. Why did people always make you sit down for bad news? I stayed standing.

Meredith tried to appear relaxed, but her anxiety peeked out from behind her smile. Dad's anger boiled beneath the surface, like he was only keeping it together because I was in the room. His temple throbbed every time he looked at Meredith. He was a teddy bear until you pushed him too far.

"It's your mother," Dad finally said after a few more beats had passed.

I nodded. Obviously. I waited for him to say more, but he stayed quiet.

Meredith cocked her head to the side. "Scott?" she prompted.

"What is she talking about, Dad?" A knot of anxiety balled in my stomach.

"I told you I wasn't sure about this." He struggled to control his voice. Meredith put her hand on his back and pushed him toward me, like getting him closer would make it easier for him to talk. "Your mother wasn't taken from the Target parking lot . . ."

I waited for him to go on, but he didn't. "Where did they take her from?" I asked.

"She left from Target." Sweat dotted his forehead.

"You just said they didn't take her from Target." I sneaked a glance at Meredith. She looked fine. Was Dad in some kind of shock again? This was starting to freak me out.

He sensed my fear and quickly spoke. "Your mom wanted to become a disciple of Love International, so she left everything in her car to join them and walked to their campus. When she got there, she agreed to let them take her in a van—"

"Wait? What? Slow down." He was talking too fast for my brain to process. Mom left? That's what he was trying to get at?

"Your mother joined Love International because she wanted to. It was voluntary," Meredith said. "Nobody kidnapped her."

I turned to Dad. "I don't understand. What's she talking about? Are you saying Mom left us?"

His face contorted like he was in physical pain. "Yes."

My brain couldn't wrap itself around his words. "No, she wouldn't leave us. You said she would never leave us. Dad?"

Tears streamed down his cheeks. Meredith stepped toward me. "She told us last night and confirmed it again this morning—"

"You found out last night, and you're just now telling me?" I shrieked. "What happened this morning? What else haven't you told me?"

"I'm sorry, Abbi—you were sleeping this morning, and I didn't want to wake you," Dad said, reaching out to hug me.

"Seriously? That's your excuse?" I pulled away. My head swam. Mom had left us, and I'd missed the moment she'd told us why.

"I know this must be so hard for you to process right now on top of everything else," Meredith said. "We just thought—"

"Stop talking. I don't want to hear it." No more. Not from her. Not from them. Not from anyone. They were too close to me. I had to move. I couldn't process this with them staring at me. I needed to think. I turned on my heels and headed back through the house.

The two of them followed behind me.

"Abbi, stop. Talk to us," Meredith called out to me.

I hated when she referred to the three of us as a unit. Always had.

"I'm sorry," Dad said. He'd already apologized. I wished he'd stop apologizing. "Where are you going? What are you doing?" he asked as I opened the front door of the house.

I didn't know what I was doing. I took off running as soon as my feet hit the pavement.

NINETEEN
MEREDITH

NOW

"I couldn't find her anywhere." Scott's voice shook. He'd just gotten back home after driving around for almost an hour searching for Abbi. He'd bolted after her as soon as she'd left, but she must have zigzagged through backyards, because he hadn't found her. "Did you get ahold of Meaghan?"

"Yes, and she hasn't heard from her." Abbi had left so fast she'd forgotten her phone. I'd gone through all her contacts and texted all her friends. Nobody had seen her, and she hadn't gotten in touch with anyone yet from someone else's phone.

"What's going on?" Kate interrupted from the top of the stairs.

"Everything's fine," I said, hoping I sounded convincing.

"Oh, now you want to be quiet?" Scott snapped. I'd never seen him this angry. Abbi joked he had a temper, but I'd never seen it.

"What happened?" she asked with her hands on her hips. It caught me off guard how closely she resembled Abbi in that moment. Abbi's forehead had been set in the same stubborn line as hers earlier tonight, and her eyes had narrowed in the identical pattern.

"Abbi took off, and we can't find her," Scott said.

Kate's eyes filled with panic. "Why did she do that?" She rushed down the stairs, joining us in the entryway.

"She was upset," I said. "You know how teenagers can get." Scott glared at me, but I didn't think it was a good idea to add more to her plate. She wasn't in any kind of state to deal with Abbi.

"Why was she upset? What happened?" Kate asked.

Scott refused to meet her stare. "We told her what happened on the day you went missing." He paused, working up the courage to say the words. "She knows that you weren't kidnapped and that you chose to leave."

The color drained from Kate's face. "She does?"

Scott nodded, hanging his head like a puppy hung his tail between his legs when he'd been caught peeing on the floor. Kate sank to the floor at the base of the stairs. She pulled her knees up to her chest and burst into tears. Scott rushed to her side and wrapped his arms around her.

"I'm so sorry," he said. "I'm so sorry." He rocked her back and forth like she was a small child.

He touched her the same way he talked about her—with such tender adoration, as if she were an expensive piece of china that might break if he pressed too hard. Tears sprang to my eyes. I wanted to put my arms around them both, and for a second I almost moved in their direction, but instead I stood there awkwardly until the intimacy of the moment became too much, and I had to look away. I moved around them into the kitchen, waiting in the doorway for a few minutes to see if he'd notice I was gone. The tears in my eyes found their way down my cheeks when he didn't.

TWENTY

ABBI

I'd never been in the park this late before. I had no idea what time it was, but I wasn't ready to go home. It'd taken me over ten minutes to get my lungs to stop burning—that was how fast I'd run. Dad had to be worried sick; that was a given, but I couldn't bring myself to go home. Not yet.

"Hey, kiddo," a voice broke into the night.

I turned around. "Dean?"

He walked through the shelter and up to the picnic table, where I'd been sitting for the past few hours. "I figured this is where I'd find you, but I don't ever want you here at this time of night again. There are too many weirdos out for you to be alone in a park after dark. You understand?" I nodded. "Now come here and give me a hug." He put his arms around me, and I sank into his chest.

"Did Dad call you?" I asked.

"No, I just happened to be going out for a midnight stroll." He smiled at me and brushed the dirt off the bench before sitting down next to me.

"Shut up." I punched his thigh. I didn't need to ask how he knew where to find me. For years, it'd been my secret spot—the one me and Mom used to go to on Sundays whenever we were letting Dad sleep in. I'd never told Dad about it because it was the only place where I had a memory of Mom that was all mine. All his memories were of the two of us or him watching her while she interacted with me. The one thing he couldn't give me was what it was like when it was just the two of us. It was only a piece, a sliver, really—just a flash of me on the swing with the sky above me and the feel of her hand on my back for a brief second—but it was something, and it was where I came to feel close to her. I'd shared my spot with Dean after he'd lost his brother in a motorcycle accident, hoping it'd bring him the same peace and comfort it'd brought me.

"Did he tell you what happened?" I asked.

"He said that all of you were arguing and you'd gotten upset and left. Why don't you tell me what happened?"

I shrugged, exhausted and spent from the day. "I found out Mom abandoned us, and Dad's been keeping it a secret from me all day. That's pretty much it."

"Sounds like a lot to me," he said.

Dad was supposed to be my rock through all of this. How was I supposed to deal with any of it if I couldn't trust him? I didn't have any experience with not being able to trust him. He had never come close to betraying me. It was one of the things I liked best about our relationship. "Dad promised to always tell me any information he had on Mom."

"Promise not to bite my head off when I say this?"

I cocked my head to the side. "That depends."

"You're not going to like it, but you might have to cut him a break on this one. It's not like he waited weeks to tell you. I mean, you didn't even give him a day. Those are pretty high standards, don't you think?" He squeezed my arm, pretending he was going to pinch me until I couldn't help but giggle. "My two cents?" I nodded. "Maybe you're mad at your dad because you got left out of an important moment this morning? I totally get that, and, honestly, I don't know why I didn't think to wake you up. I should have, so if you're going to be mad at him, then you're going to have to be mad at me too." He smiled at me while he shrugged. "Sorry."

"Did I miss anything else?" I asked.

"No, and we recorded the entire thing. I'm pretty sure I can get Camille to let you watch it."

"Really?"

"Of course. It's not like anything on there is a secret."

I let out a deep sigh. "If Mom left because she wanted to, does this mean nobody is going to get arrested?"

He wrinkled his forehead. "We can't make an arrest if there hasn't been a crime, and she hasn't revealed any."

"But at the hospital they said it looked like she'd been tortured— that's a crime."

"It's not illegal if it's done with your consent."

"She allowed herself to be tortured?"

He nodded like he wished it wasn't true. "At least during the first month she was with them. It's all on the video."

"But she had marks on her back like she'd been whipped. She said that was okay too?"

"She did."

"She admitted this?" He nodded again, but no matter how many times he said it, I couldn't wrap my brain around how someone would let themselves be treated so awful. And if whipping was okay, then how bad did things have to get before she said enough was enough?

"Now that doesn't mean we won't find out other crimes were committed during her time with them, because there's an entire decade we don't know about yet. Our investigation is far from complete, but we are no longer looking at kidnapping charges, which shifts the FBI's involvement when it's not a crime that crossed multiple state lines. It changes the threat level and the amount of manpower we devote when the danger is no longer immediate. I know it's a huge dagger in the heart, but it brings us a step closer to solving the puzzle."

I raised my eyebrows. "Really?"

"Okay, well, the case is moving painstakingly slow, but it at least gives us more important pieces, and those pieces are enough for me to sleep better at night about your safety."

"What do you think happened to make her leave us?" I asked. It hurt to say the words, but that was what she'd done. I might as well get used to it.

"It's not a crime for people to go missing. It happens all the time. More than you'd think. Remember when I told you that all those years ago?"

I nodded. It was shortly after I'd stumbled on the Vanished forums. I had been thirteen, and up until then I'd never considered any other possibilities about Mom's disappearance other than the ones Dad had given me. We had been working on our genealogies in history class, and it had stirred up all these questions and emotions inside me, so I'd googled Mom. Vanished had been my first hit.

The things I had read shook me to my core, and Dad wouldn't consider anything they wrote. He wouldn't even talk about it with me. Eventually, I'd gone to Dean for help processing everything, and unlike Dad, he had been willing to admit there was a possibility that Mom may have decided to leave on her own. I had told him how they talked about the possibility that she might have committed suicide, and he had shocked me when he had told me that they'd already ruled it out. It was one of the things I loved the most about Dean. He was refreshingly honest. Always had been.

"And then she just suddenly decided to come back? Why would she do that after all this time?" I asked.

"Your guess is as good as mine." He took his arm off my shoulder and cracked his knuckles. "But I'm going to do my best to figure this mess out."

"Thanks, Dean." He had a way of always making me feel better. "All of this is just happening so fast. It's like every time I get my feet on solid ground, something happens and I'm falling all over the place again. Tonight was just like bam—bam—bam."

"It must be hard for you to see your mom this way," Dean said.

I shook my head. "That's the thing nobody understands. It's really not."

His eyes grew in curiosity. "It's not hard seeing her so wrecked?"

"It's hard to see her in pain, yes, but I would hate seeing anyone in pain. That's not what I'm talking about. Dad has before-and-after versions of her, but I don't. My only version of Mom has always been through his eyes, but it was never mine. She was never real to me from experience. It was always his version. You know what I mean?" He nodded, signaling me to continue. "It's easier for me in a way because I didn't know her, and all I want to do is get to know her. I don't care who she is—I just want to know her. Even if she turns out to be totally damaged from whatever she went through, or she's a completely different person than I thought. It doesn't matter. Not to me. It's different for me than Dad."

He tousled my hair with his other hand. "You're a smart kid, you know that?"

I smiled. "Dad's totally freaking out, huh?"

"Yep, but this time I can't blame him." Over the years, Dad had freaked out many times and called the police or Dean to check up on me somewhere. It was one of the reasons why I'd never had a boyfriend. I was sure he'd follow our every move, and I'd die of embarrassment. "I texted him when I spotted you sitting here, but he's probably climbing the walls waiting for us to get back."

"We should go?"

He nodded. "We'll do this thing one step at a time, kiddo. One step at a time." He reached out his hand to help me up, and I smiled at how much he sounded like Dad.

KATE

THEN

I moaned with ecstasy as the hot water spilled over my head. I couldn't remember the last time it'd been hot. Even the water they'd used to bathe me with after I came out of the cellar had been cold. It felt so good it didn't matter that I wasn't in a real tub. I sat cross-legged in a hollowed-out tin while Margo bathed me in preparation for Scott's visit. I was glad they'd allowed her to be the one. I'd still be mortified when she moved her way down to my private areas, but it'd be less awkward and embarrassing if it was her.

Her fingers massaged my scalp as she lathered my hair with shampoo. "Fill me in on how things are going," she said, since I hadn't seen her since the day I left the center.

I'd been secluded at a remote cabin in the woods with another recently converted disciple, Willow. New disciples were always paired up and served as each other's mirror while undergoing their Phase One training.

"I really miss my family, but it's a relief not to be living with one foot in both worlds," I said. That had been the easiest part of settling into discipleship, not having to be in conflict all the time. "How long have I been gone?" I asked. Coming out of the cellar had been almost as disorienting as going in, since they'd taken us straight to the cabin and left us without any cues to time or the outside world, just like it'd been down there.

She shook her head. "Letting go of time takes a long time," she said, laughing as she realized her play on words.

I smiled back. It was nice to see her, even if she wouldn't give me any hints to help ground me. Willow and I got along well enough, but she was twenty-four and had been raised to be a free spirit, since her parents were retired hippies from the sixties. The only thing we had in common was Love International, which was fine, but sometimes it was nice to talk about other things, and that was where our commonality ended. Margo was closer to my age and understood sacrifice, since she'd given up a successful law practice to join. It wasn't the same as my family, but it was something.

"I missed you," I said.

"I missed you too." She squeezed my shoulders. "How are your caretakers?"

I shrugged. "They're all right."

The only other people at the cabin were two women whose sole purpose was to tend to our needs so we could focus solely on our spiritual growth and development. They cooked and cleaned for us, speaking to us like children while they did it. We weren't even allowed to bathe ourselves. I didn't like being reduced to such an infantile state and hadn't gotten used to it. Probably wouldn't.

Margo grabbed my hand and scrubbed underneath my fingernails, but it didn't matter how hard she scrubbed, the dirt buried underneath them from the hours we spent scrubbing the floors on our knees was never coming out. Not that Scott would mind. He wouldn't be paying attention to my hands. My cheeks flushed at the thought of seeing him again.

"I still can't believe Ray is letting you see Scott."

"It's important for my spiritual growth," I said. It was the same thing I had said to Ray each time I pleaded my case to him, and I'd asked so many times before he'd finally agreed that I'd lost count. Phase One of discipleship focused on letting go of our worldly attachments, and I couldn't do that without having a chance to explain things to Scott myself. Ray had tried speaking with him on numerous occasions, but he was too furious about what I'd done to listen to him. I was hoping he would understand if it came from me.

She wrung her washcloth out in one of the basins she was using before dipping it into the other one filled with warm, sudsy water.

"Lean forward and let's see what we can do about those," she said, referring to the broken skin on my back.

I grabbed the edge of the basin and clenched my jaw as she tenderly worked the washcloth across my latest lashes. I'd done my best to avoid any reckonings before the visit, but Ray didn't like the haughty eyes I'd given him three days ago. I'd begged him to just let it go that one time, but he'd refused. Thankfully I was going to be covered, because there was no way Scott would understand this part of the practice.

"It's going to be okay," Margo said, like she could sense I was about to spin off.

I sank back into the tub of water. She was right. I needed to relax and enjoy this moment. Who knew when I'd get warm water again, and besides, none of my worrying would change anything. I sank into the bubbles, inhaling the smell of soap. It didn't matter that it was cheap. My senses missed stimulation so much it hurt.

She let me lie in the tub until the water ran cold and then quickly scrubbed all my private parts while my cheeks burned with shame. I appreciated how fast she finished. I stepped out into the towels she held out in front of me. My skin filled with goose bumps immediately. She stopped me when I reached for my gown.

"Wait here," she said before turning and hurrying out of the room. She came back within seconds and held up a beautiful red sundress. "Put this on," she said as she handed it to me.

My eyes grew big. "Are you serious? I can't wear that. What about the modesty guidelines?"

"Ray approved it."

"He did?"

She nodded. I couldn't believe it. The dress even had straps instead of sleeves. Why would he ever let me wear something so revealing?

"Well, are you just going to stand there and stare at it, or are you going to put it on?" Margo asked.

I took it from her and raised my arms, sliding it over my head and smoothing it over my body. What would he think about all the weight I'd lost? Hopefully he wouldn't think I was too skinny. He hated when I lost my curvy hips. I slipped my underwear on underneath. I was more nervous than I'd been before I walked down the aisle on our wedding day.

"You look beautiful," Margo said.

I blushed. "Thanks. Do you think he's here yet?"

"He should be. I heard the door a few minutes ago."

"Oh my God." I stepped backward, reaching for something to steady me against the wave of emotions surging through my body.

Margo gave me her hand, and I gripped it, following her out of the bathroom and into the common area. My eyes took in the room in one sweep—the worn hardwood floors, wrought iron stove in the center, chipped coffee table, and outdated couch, sagging in the middle. Ray sat in one of the wooden chairs from the kitchen table. I scanned the kitchen area, searching for Scott. He wasn't there either. Was he still outside? Why had Ray left him out there?

Ray rose and moved toward me. "You look so pretty, dear." He bent to kiss my cheeks, and I pulled away.

"Where's Scott?" I asked.

"Why don't you sit?"

I shook my head. "I don't want to sit."

I wanted Scott. My insides crumbled. I turned my head so he wouldn't see the tears sliding down my cheeks.

"He showed up to meet me at our designated spot, but I'm so sorry, Kate. He didn't want to see you. He is under the impression that we had an affair, and nothing I said could convince him otherwise. He said that he wants nothing to do with you. I'm so sorry."

"No." An involuntary sob escaped.

"Let me hold you." He reached for me, and I slapped his hand.

"Get away from me. I don't want you to touch me." This wasn't happening. It couldn't be. They were supposed to come. I was supposed to be able to make things right. "What about Abbi?"

Margo put her hand on my back.

"He said that you are the definition of an unfit mother by abandoning her the way you did, and he doesn't want you anywhere near her," Ray said.

"But I didn't abandon her," I cried. "Did you tell him that?"

"I tried everything I could think of to make him understand, but he refuses to see things differently." He shook his head. "Unfortunately the courts will probably agree with him. The world has a hard time understanding our methods and training practices." I sank to the floor in defeat. Margo knelt next to me, and Ray sat on the other side. He put his arm around me, and this time I didn't fight him off. "This may be the Lord's way of doing for you what you couldn't do for yourself."

"Losing my husband and daughter?" I could barely speak through my sobs. "What kind of God requires that kind of sacrifice?"

"The same one that sacrificed his own son," Ray said.

———

I buried my face in my pillow, trying to stifle my cries, but it was no use. Willow had amazing hearing and was at my cot within seconds. She knelt next to my bed with her face inches from mine.

"I can't even imagine how much this hurts," she whispered, even though we were the only two in the cabin, and there was no one around to hear us. "Remember that you're giving up so much more than most of us, so think about how much more you will gain as a result."

She'd been saying the same thing for the last two days. It didn't help. The pain of losing my family felt like it would never end.

"Move over," she said, and I lifted the blanket so she could slide underneath. She pulled me next to her, wrapping her arms tightly around me. "Shh . . . shhhh . . . you're okay," she said over and over again in the same voice you'd use to soothe a crying baby. I clung to her, sobbing into her chest.

"I can't do this without them. I can't," I cried.

"Yes, you can." She ran her hands through my hair. "You've been doing this without them. For months probably. You're stronger than you know."

I shook my head. "I'm weak, so weak." Their faces were my last images before falling asleep each night and my first thought each morning. That would never leave. How could it? Knowing I'd be with them again had gotten me through so many difficult moments during my training.

"No matter how hard this might be, it's your last step in letting go of your worldly attachments, and you have no idea how much freedom you'll experience once you're on the other side of this," she said.

Her words pierced me like knives. Scott and Abbi were more than earthly attachments. They were my heart living and breathing outside of my body, and I didn't know how I was supposed to exist in any kind of world that didn't include them. I wished discipleship had asked me to give up my physical life. That would have been easier than this.

TWENTY-ONE
MEREDITH

NOW

Kate sprang out of the chair and raced toward Abbi after she came through the door with Dean. Her shoulders shook with sobs. She kept pushing Abbi out to arm's length, like she was checking to make sure she was unharmed before pulling her back into a tight hug. Scott walked up to them and made sure Abbi wasn't still mad at him before circling his arms around them.

"Abbi, please don't do that again. We were terrified." Kate spoke to her like a mother for the first time. I glanced at Scott to see if he'd noticed. He'd caught it too. He was staring at her with such intense longing that I had to look away. Within seconds, Kate was crying again. "I'm sorry, Abbi. I'm so sorry for hurting you."

"It's okay, Mom." Abbi's voice wavered as she tried to be strong for her.

"No, it's not. I hurt you, and I'm sorry." Kate's voice trembled as she spoke. "Nobody forced me to go anywhere. I left you and your dad to become a disciple of Love International." The pain of her decision carved deep lines in her face, but I'd never heard her sound so real and authentic. "God called me, and I went because I believed in them. I thought I was joining a movement that would change the world, and eventually you would join me." She hung her head as she continued, too embarrassed to make eye contact with anyone. "You must think I'm so stupid. But I waited for you to come. Both you and your dad."

Scott frowned. "How could we? We didn't have any idea you were with them."

"You should've talked to Ray," she said with a hint of anger. "He would've explained things to you if you'd have let him."

"Talked to Ray? I talked to him all the time."

Something passed through Kate—a memory, recognition, something—and then it was gone.

"I don't understand." Her voice slowed. "You talked to Ray?"

"And Margo and Bekah and some other guy that was always with him. There were a lot of them who came out, and I can't remember their names after all these years. But, yeah, a bunch of people came out from Love International and helped with your search."

She stared at Scott with a blank expression, like he was speaking a foreign language. "But why didn't he tell you where I was or what was going on?"

The reality slowly registered on Scott's face. "Kate, he helped us look for you. He organized search parties and led teams trying to find you."

———

I'd watched Kate's world crumble after Scott had told her about Ray. His brain had been spinning almost as fast as hers.

"How could he do that? I mean, what kind of a man helps look for the woman he's keeping in a locked cellar? It's sadistic," he'd said. He'd called Ray all kinds of names when Kate told him the story. Abbi's eyes had grown huge at the things that came out of his mouth tonight.

She'd only ever heard him use the soft cuss words, and he'd taken it to another level.

It was a horrible deception. There was no denying that, but something about it didn't sit right with me. She'd still made a choice. Once she'd heard that Scott wasn't coming because he thought she'd been unfaithful, she could have decided right then that her family was more important than Love International and gone back to them. She could have at least tried to explain things to Scott herself. There was no way I would let James think I was having an affair if I wasn't, and we could barely stand each other at the end. And what about Abbi? Short of being tied up, there was nothing in this world that could keep me away from my boys for eleven years. But I didn't dare say any of it to Scott. I hadn't said a word since they came back with Abbi. Not like it mattered or anyone was interested in my opinion, anyway.

I'd never felt so much like an outsider as I had tonight. Not even when Scott and I had started dating and Abbi would fake an illness or injury whenever we went out, and, like clockwork, Scott would drop whatever we were doing and go to her. He had left in the middle of a play once to help her get something out of her eye. It wasn't just that he had skipped out on our plans—he had never taken me with him when he went, even after we'd been dating for over a year. But that didn't compare to how I felt now. I was still trying not to cry, and Scott hadn't even noticed, which only made it hurt more.

Kate had given up valuable information when she'd told Scott how Ray had led her to believe he'd told Scott her whereabouts. Dean had been quietly listening, but he had jumped into the conversation then, latching on to the new lead.

"Wait." He held up his hand to stop her. "Are you saying that Ray told you Scott knew where you were?" She nodded. "And he asked if Scott wanted to see you, and he said no?"

"Yes," she answered in a weak voice.

Dean wanted to keep going with his questioning, but Shiloh woke up and needed to be fed. Everyone else was grateful for the distraction, too spent to do any more, and it was the middle of the night. Dean scurried away, quickly tapping out a message on his phone as he left. Probably to Camille. I needed to go to sleep. Even though Dean had been up half the night with us, he'd be here at eight before anyone else to help me make coffee.

I stretched out in our bed, pulling the covers up to my chest. Scott still wasn't close to coming to bed. He sat in his office chair with the computer turned on, but he was staring at our bedroom door instead of the screen, fingers unmoving on the keyboard. He hadn't gotten out of his clothes or brushed his teeth.

"Come to bed," I said for what felt like the tenth time. I was exhausted and wouldn't be able to fall asleep until he did, because his movements would startle me awake if he got into bed after me. "There's nothing you can do about any of this tonight."

"Really?" he asked like he wasn't sure. "I don't know how you can even think about sleeping. Shouldn't we keep her talking? I mean, just look at everything she gave us tonight. We're finally getting somewhere. I don't think we should stop."

"It's probably not a good idea for you to talk to her by yourself." They still recorded all her interviews and reviewed the footage afterward. It was what the night shift spent most of their time doing—deciphering her videos for clues. It was how they'd figured out that the abandoned RV campground had been their camp.

"Why can't I talk to her by myself?" He turned his nose up like he smelled something foul.

I sighed. "That's not what I meant. Scott, I'm tired. Can we please go to bed?"

"I'm not tired," he snapped, raising his voice.

I put my finger to my lips. "Shh, you're going to wake everybody up."

"Why do you suddenly care so much what everybody else thinks?"

"What? How is that even related?" He was being ridiculous. I rolled over on my side, trying to keep from getting riled up. If I got upset, it'd be hours before I could sleep, and I didn't want to do another day on four hours of sleep. "I just want to go to bed."

He scowled. "Oh, here we go again. Back to how inconvenient all of this is for you."

"You are impossible to deal with right now. I can deal with logic; I can't deal with whatever nonsense you keep throwing at me." His over-the-top reactions only proved he was as tired as I was.

"I don't care. I'm going over there to talk to her." He moved toward the door. I flung the covers off and leaped out of bed. I grabbed his arm and pulled him away from the door. "Stop! She's asleep in there with the baby. What are you thinking?"

"I can do whatever I want." He ripped his arm away from me. "This is my house, and she's my w—" He stopped himself, but it didn't matter.

There it was. She was his wife.

At least he'd admitted what I'd always known. I was his second-place wife. But now that she was back, I wasn't even that. I didn't know what I was. He had always assumed we were the same, and even though I'd tried to set him straight over the years, he had refused to hear it. But that was the thing. Scott was my first-place husband. I'd fallen for Scott in a way I'd never fallen for James, but Scott loved me because of our shared pain. In the beginning of our relationship, I had understood that was why he loved me, not because he'd stopped loving Kate, but part of me had hoped that he would grow to love me the same way he'd once loved her after enough time had passed. Those dreams had died when the police had knocked at our door.

He turned around. "Come on, Meredith. You know I didn't mean that. You of all people have to know how confusing and weird all of this is." But he wouldn't look me directly in the eyes while he talked. "This is super complicated. You'd feel the same way if things were reversed. Can you just please admit that?"

But I couldn't. It wouldn't be the same. Not even close.

"I went to meet with a divorce lawyer two weeks before James's cancer diagnosis," I blurted out.

His eyes widened. "What?"

I nodded, swallowing hard, my mouth dry. "I did."

The weight of my secret forced him to sit. He sank into his office chair. "Why would you do that?"

"I was going to divorce him." It felt good to finally say it. It was never supposed to be a secret.

"What happened?" he asked.

"We got married young because I was pregnant, and it was the right thing to do. We had Caleb and fell in love with being parents. We didn't waste any time getting pregnant again with Thad. And, honestly, we were a good team. Our lives revolved around them, but then they grew up and didn't need us as much. You know how it is. Anyway, we were strangers and ones who didn't really even like each other. And then he got cancer. I couldn't divorce a man with brain cancer. Nobody is that evil."

"So everything was a lie?" I could see his head swimming with questions.

"The work I did in group wasn't a lie. I loved him once. More than anything. I'd been grieving his ghost for years." I'd spent most of Caleb's freshman year of high school crying in secret, because I knew our marriage was dead and had no idea what to do about it. "And I tried to tell you. I did, but you wouldn't listen to me."

I couldn't count the number of times I'd started the conversation, but he'd always stopped me. "We don't need to talk about it. I get it," he'd say. "You still love James, and I still love Kate, so it feels like we're doing something wrong. I know someone will always have part of your heart, just like someone will always have part of mine." The conversation always ended there.

He remembered. I saw it in his eyes. He rose slowly and walked over to the bed. He plopped down next to me. "Can we just go to bed tonight and pretend these last five minutes never happened?"

"Sure." I forced a smile for his benefit, but not because I would ever forget.

KATE

THEN

Willow was right—leaving California was what I'd needed to let go of my life there, even though I'd fought against it with everything in me right up until the day we left. Being physically near my family made me feel close to them even if they wanted nothing to do with me. The new physical space created new emotional space within me. It was exciting to live somewhere besides California, since I'd been there since I was three. But my guilt wouldn't allow me to enjoy it. Happiness felt too disrespectful to my family's memory.

Twenty-three of us had piled into vans and headed to Oregon after Ray received a prophecy that we were to separate ourselves from the rest of the world to prepare for the next part of our journey. A sense of camaraderie had grown up among us as we had created our new home. I'd never worked with my hands before, but all we had done was work in the forest clearing trees and digging in the dirt, and it had been some of the most satisfying work I'd done. Things would have been almost perfect if we hadn't been starving. Our meals had dwindled down to beans and rice while we waited for our crops to grow. All we'd had for dinner tonight was bread and water. We'd been nervously waiting around the campfire for Ray to return ever since.

He'd disappeared by himself after lunch, promising to have food when he returned, without any mention of how he planned to get it, and he'd refused to let anyone join him. It wasn't unusual for him to go off by himself, but it was getting dark, and he still wasn't back yet. We were almost ready to go to bed when someone spotted him coming through the clearing behind the spice garden. Something dangled in his left hand, but it was too hard to see what it was in the dark. As he got closer to the fire, he raised his arm up, dangling two rabbits upside down, eyes bulging out of their sockets.

"Are they dead?" Phil's eyes widened in horror. Most of the disciples were vegetarian. He was one of them.

"I think so," Bekah said, fixated on Ray.

Ray proudly waved them for everyone to see. Red stained their necks. There was no mistaking they were dead. Ray grinned. "Who is hungry?" he asked.

We all stared back at him, too stunned to speak. Phil turned to Will, waiting for him to say something, since he was usually the one who stood up to Ray, but Will was still eyeing Ray in disbelief. Phil was too angry to wait on Will.

"That's not funny," he spat. "Where did you find them?"

"What do you mean, 'Where did I find them?'" The goofy grin was still on Ray's face. "I went hunting for them."

Silence again.

Ray wanted us to pull it out of him. Something about the exchange pleased him, almost like he was playing some kind of a game. I hated when he acted like this.

Phil put his hand over his mouth and breathed deeply, working his jaw as he tried to get the breath past his chest and down into his stomach, where it could do some good. "How did you hunt them?"

"What do you mean?"

Phil narrowed his eyes to slits. "You know exactly what I mean."

Ray feigned innocence. "Is there another way to hunt animals besides killing them that I don't know about?"

Phil took a step closer to him. His chest puffed forward with challenge. "How did you kill them?"

Ray took a few steps forward and set the rabbits down on one of the chairs around the fire. He reached into the back of his pants and pulled out a handgun. "I shot them with this."

Will jumped up, waving his arms around. "Put that thing away! What are you doing?" he shouted.

"Being completely transparent," Ray said as he set the gun down next to the two rabbits. He raised his hands in a peaceful gesture. "Please allow me to explain myself." He gave Phil a second to respond before continuing. Phil looked like he wanted to explode, but he allowed Ray to speak. "I promised to protect you and care for you when we left California. As you know, things have been much more difficult with farming than we'd expected, and our food supplies have dwindled down to almost nothing. Most of you are starving." His face filled with concern. "I couldn't let God's people starve. I just couldn't." He waved his hand around at all of us. "Before anyone gets riled up again, I want you to know that I didn't tell anyone about my plans to hunt, because I knew there would be those of you who would stop me." He looked at Phil. I didn't know him well enough yet to read him, but he seemed less angry. His shoulders had relaxed since Ray had started talking. "I had to find a way for us to eat." He pointed to the rabbits. "And I did. In a minute, I'm going to cook these over the fire, and anyone is welcome to the meat. Please don't partake if it makes you uncomfortable. I will be giving up my portion of beans going forward to anyone who doesn't eat meat."

Will pushed his way through the crowd and stood in front of Ray. "You had a gun, Ray, and nobody knew about it. As far as I'm concerned, that's a much bigger problem than who's going to eat these stupid rabbits."

Ray nodded. "I can see why that would concern you, Will. I stumbled on the gun the other day when I was checking one of the tire springs in the back, and it was tucked underneath the tire jack." We had a strict no-violence policy, and it went without saying that guns qualified. "One of our old drivers used to take this van on mission trips to the south side. He got robbed three times at gunpoint and started carrying a weapon for his safety. I guess he forgot it was back there, and nobody ever thought to look." He shrugged, then raised his head to the sky. "Perhaps it was God's way of doing for us what we couldn't do for ourselves."

Will wasn't convinced, but I eyed the rest of the circle to see the others' reactions. Doubt shone on most of their faces too. I turned to Margo, like I did for most things. She'd grown to be my voice of reason. She appeared unmoved, waiting on Ray with an expectant look on her face. Maybe this was some kind of test that she'd already figured out. If she wasn't shocked or surprised about Ray having a gun, then I wasn't either. After all, she knew him better than I did.

TWENTY-TWO

ABBI

NOW

I quietly knocked on Mom's door. It had been two nights since I'd been
in her room. I didn't know what to say to her after everything that
had happened. I still didn't, but I missed talking to her at night. Our
interactions weren't the same when we were around everyone else. She
relaxed with me in ways she didn't with them. Mom opened the door,
and Shiloh smiled when she saw me.

"Oh my gosh, Mom!" I squealed. "She smiled at me, like really
smiled at me."

"You're her sister," Mom said. She gave me a quick hug before moving to the side so I could get through the doorway. I scooped Shiloh
from her arms and brought her to me. I sniffed the top of her bald head.
She always smelled so good after she came out of a bath.

"I wonder when people start stinking?" I asked.

Mom laughed. It was different than how Dad described her laugh,
but most things about her were. There wasn't much of anything he'd
said that was true about her anymore, but you couldn't go through
what she'd gone through and not become a changed person. Dad had

always said her laugh was loud and boisterous, like an old fat man's. Not anymore. It was quiet and gentle, tinged with guilt, like she wasn't supposed to find things funny anymore or enjoy life.

"I can't remember when it happened with you. One day you had the new-baby smell, and the next day you smelled like the food you'd smeared all over your face." She smiled at the memory.

I climbed on her bed with Shiloh, laying her on her back while I rested on my elbow above her. She kicked and flailed her arms wildly. I giggled as I stroked her cheeks. Mom sat behind me and rubbed my back.

Her eyes misted. "I'm sorry for all this. Everything. Leaving. Not coming back."

"Please stop saying you're sorry, Mom." My words hung in the air. Hanging out with Mom had forced me to get comfortable with silence. It was amazing how long she could go without saying anything. I wasn't there yet. "What made you stay with them for so long?"

"I followed the word of God. It says, 'I was a stranger and you invited me in. I was hungry and you fed me. I—'"

I put my arm on hers to interrupt her. None of her scripture ever made sense. Maybe it did to the others, but I just thought she sounded like a robot. It creeped me out, and I didn't like it. "What was it like for you besides all the God stuff?"

She took a moment to think about her answer this time. "It was beautiful. Their purpose. The way they lived. Spoke. All of it. I'd never felt anything like it before, and it bonded us together. We felt like we belonged together, and Ray said he was responsible for us, that he'd never let anything bad happen to us." Her eyes lit up when she said his name. They always did. "It was like falling in love. Everything else fell to the wayside."

It hurt to be the "everything else," but I'd asked her to tell me the truth, so I had to be open to hearing what she had to say even if I didn't like it. "And Ray? What was he like?" I asked tentatively, not wanting to push too hard.

"He was charismatic." She giggled nervously. "But it was more than that. He had this huge presence." She spread her arms out wide. "It filled every space he went into. Being with him felt like a gift he bestowed upon you. Somehow he did it without being arrogant." Her forehead crinkled in thought. "I don't know how he did that."

"Everyone loves the guy," I said.

"Huh?" Her forehead wrinkled in confusion.

People had been fascinated with Ray since the story broke that Mom had been with Love International. They'd created Facebook and Instagram profiles in support of him. Countless of his followers had pledged their support of him, swearing there wasn't any way he'd hurt Mom even if she'd been with them all this time, but I couldn't tell any of that to Mom, since I wasn't supposed to be looking at it. But I didn't want to lie to her either. I eyed her bedroom door, which I'd made sure to shut behind me so that nobody could hear us if they happened to get up.

"I've seen Ray," I whispered.

She grabbed me. "What? Where?" Her eyes skirted the room, like I might have hidden him in the closet or underneath the bed.

"On social media," I said quickly, before she could get any more worked up.

"Social media? That's the stuff on the internet?" she asked.

I smiled. Sometimes I forgot how little she knew about technology. "Basically."

"And they had his picture?"

I nodded.

"Can I see?"

I froze. If I wasn't supposed to be looking at any of this stuff, she definitely wasn't supposed to be looking at any of it.

"Please, Abbi?" she asked when I still hadn't responded.

It was only a picture, and it wasn't like she didn't know what he looked like anyway. I wouldn't show her any of the articles or things they'd said about her. I grabbed my phone from my back pocket and quickly scrolled through the images on Google until I found the one that had gone viral. Everyone made comments about how gorgeous he was, but I didn't think so. He reminded me of Tom Cruise—too pretty. I enlarged the picture and handed her my phone.

She stared at it like she was seeing a ghost. Her hands shook, and her eyes instantly filled with tears. Anxiety tightened my chest.

"Hey, Mom, you know what? That's probably not the best idea. I don't know what I was thinking." I reached for my phone. She sprang off the bed and clutched it against her.

"No!" Her eyes were wild. The muscles in her neck stretched taut.

I inched my way off the bed. I could scream for Dad if I needed to, but he'd be furious that I'd set her off. She hadn't gotten scared like this since we'd gotten home. "It's okay, Mom. You can have my phone. I won't take it from you."

It took a second, but my words startled her back to herself. The color drained from her face. "I feel sick."

I rushed toward her and put my arm around her waist. "Here, why don't you just sit back down on the bed?" I helped her to it and set her down delicately. She still hadn't let go of my phone, but at least she wasn't looking at it anymore. Her body was rigid, stiff. The muscles in her neck hadn't relaxed. Shiloh was asleep at the top of the bed, and I brought her to Mom without waking her up, hoping she'd snap her out of it. At first she held her robotically, like she was on autopilot, but as Shiloh settled against her, Mom slowly relaxed her body into hers. I breathed a sigh of relief.

I wasn't doing that again.

TWENTY-THREE
MEREDITH

NOW

The restaurant was packed with people. I scanned the crowd and spotted Caleb at a table by himself in the corner. I hurried past the hostess, and he rose to meet me. He gave me the hug I'd been waiting for all day. I hadn't seen him in almost seven months. It was the longest we'd ever been apart, but he was buried in his internship at one of the law firms downtown and barely had time to breathe. We didn't usually go out for dinner when he visited, since he preferred my cooking, but there was no way I was having him over to the house tonight. We had all been walking on eggshells around each other, and having an awkward sit-down dinner with everyone was the last thing I wanted to do.

"You look tired," he said, pulling out my chair.

I laughed. "Thanks so much, son."

He lifted his palms up. "Well, at least I'm honest."

He had ordered me a glass of merlot, and his sat in front of him half-empty. A brush with alcoholism in his teens had terrified me, and I had kept an eye on his drinking ever since. It'd scared him bad enough to keep him sober for a decade, but in recent years he'd started drinking again. He swore it was only socially and he didn't have a problem. Only time would tell.

"You need a haircut," I said, taking a sip of my wine. I didn't like when he wore his hair long. It made his nose look too big for his face.

"I'm growing it out." He smirked at me, knowing how I felt about his long hair.

"Have you talked to Thad?" I asked. I'd barely spoken to him all week.

"Mom, please, can we just get to the good stuff? We can talk about Thad any time."

"I don't even know where to start," I said. Not to mention I couldn't remember what I'd told him and what I'd told his brother. I took another sip of my wine.

"Are they out of your house yet?" he asked, referring to the FBI's command center.

"Not yet. Monday. That's when everything changes," I said.

There'd been a huge shift in how the FBI was going to handle Kate's case going forward, since she'd revealed that she hadn't been kidnapped. Camille felt confident that it was safe enough for her to start doing her forensic interviews at the police station and her deprogramming work with Brian at one of the local counseling centers downtown. Brian had spent most of our debriefing session yesterday stressing how important it was for all of us to start getting back into our daily routines to help us feel a sense of normalcy again, since it'd been almost two weeks since our world had flipped upside down. He said it would help Kate feel more secure too. On Monday, Scott was going back to work, and Abbi was going back to school, even though neither of them wanted to.

"Are you going to be the one driving Kate to all her appointments?" Caleb asked.

I nodded.

"And they're sure all of this is safe?"

"More so than they were before, but we can't stay quarantined forever." He waved down the server, and he quickly placed our order, not bothering to ask what I wanted, since I always had the caramelized pork chop with a spinach salad. "Have they found Love International yet?"

"I told you they found their camp, right?"

"Yes, and that it had been abandoned, but they were pretty sure that's where she'd been living for at least the past few years."

I nodded before continuing. "They haven't found Ray or any of the other people they're looking for, but members and disciples of Love International have come out of the woodwork."

"Really?" He raised his eyebrows. "What's that like?"

"Bizarre and nothing like I expected. Most of them are regular people. Some of them are super successful people too."

He shook his head. "No way."

"Seriously. You'd be surprised. I had no idea. And most of them are in support of him. They swear he changed their lives." I tried to stay away from watching any of the footage, but it was almost impossible. *Dateline* had interviewed six former members last night, and nothing could've kept me from the program. All of them spoke in favor of Ray and the movement, except for a set of parents who'd lost their twenty-four-year-old daughter to Love International. They'd always been convinced they had something to do with her disappearance and described their hunt to find her.

"Well, they definitely changed Kate's. How's she doing? Any better?"

"It's hard to say. She doesn't mumble nearly as much, or at least not around other people anymore. She still seems pretty spacey and out of it most of the time, though, but she gets lively and interactive with Shiloh and Abbi. You can tell she cares about them."

"At least you're getting your house back soon," he said. "It's not going to be as comfortable for Kate down at the station, but it's going to be so much less invasive for all of you."

"Yeah, I suppose, but I have no idea what we're going to do with ourselves the rest of the time, when everyone else is gone. It's going to be so weird. We've only been alone together one time, and that was the first night she got here. I don't know how to even talk to her," I said, fighting back the urge to cry. I tried not to cry in front of them, since it made them so upset, and I hated upsetting them. It was about more than being alone with Kate. I could feel Scott slipping through my fingers, and there was nothing I could do to stop it.

"I really want to meet her," he said. He'd texted me something similar a few days ago, but I wasn't going to let anyone treat her like she was some circus freak, not even my son. I shook my head. "Come on, Mom. It's not like I'm not going to meet her eventually. She's part of the family."

"She's not part of the family," I snapped without thinking. Except that she was. A bigger part than I'd ever been, and my part only became smaller the more time went on. That was what hurt the most.

KATE

THEN

"Our pain is only there to tell us something. Listen to what it has to say," Ray had instructed us before he left for another one of his thirty-day soul journeys. Last time he'd hiked the peaks of Sioux Valley, but he hadn't told anyone where he was going this time. We had all agreed to enter into a thirty-day fast while he was gone to help him achieve greater commune with the Lord. We needed to help him find an answer, because the ground still wasn't responding.

Even Phil ate meat now. It was either that or starve, because no matter how hard we worked in the fields, our crops refused to cooperate. None of us knew anything about planting and growing vegetables in the wild, despite how organic we might have professed to be in our former lives. The only way to learn was by doing, and so far we'd destroyed more than what we'd created. Our supplies had dwindled down to almost nothing.

We'd all been counting the days until Ray came back, and today was the day. All we'd done while he was away was pray and meditate. No one had to voice what we all knew to be true—we couldn't live this way much longer. We had to find a way to survive or move on.

Darkness had settled around camp, and he still wasn't home yet. We all anxiously lifted our eyes to the hills around us, searching, all the while pretending like we weren't. For a second, the thought crossed my mind that he wasn't coming back, and I quickly admonished myself for living in such fear. The voice of fear was one of the hardest voices to squelch in my spiritual journey, rearing its ugly head whenever I thought I'd gotten rid of it for good.

Willow sought me out as soon as we had gathered around the fire. No matter what happened, each day ended with a fire gathering. "I'm so nervous. What if something happened to him?" she whispered, so nobody else would hear, since fear was contagious. "There are so many bears out in those woods. I just keep picturing him out there bleeding to death from being attacked. Did you ever see that Leonardo DiCaprio movie where he gets into a fight with that huge bear? What was it called?" She raised her arms and pretended to be a bear.

I giggled at how ridiculous she looked. "I don't know. I can't remember."

"Anyway, that's all I keep picturing."

The energy around the fire was nervous and tense, like it was whenever we were waiting for Ray to return. We were never the same when he wasn't with us. Beth was describing a way she'd found to decrease the flour we needed for bread when she stopped midsentence and yelled, "There he is!" as she pointed to a figure moving through the clearing.

You couldn't make out any of his features, but there was no mistaking Ray's gait, and nobody besides him would be traipsing out in the forest at this time of night. We jumped up. Someone took off running toward him, and before I knew what was happening I was being carried along with the group. We picked up speed as we went, laughing and giggling like schoolchildren being released at recess. We swarmed him and passed him around the group, hugging and kissing him and each other. Nervous chatter followed us back to the fire. We all took up the positions we'd been in before, eager to hear what he had to say, hoping he wouldn't wait until the morning to share it with us.

"Are you thirsty? Can I get you something to drink?" Bekah asked. Even though her belly swelled with pregnancy, she never tired of helping others. We had tried to get her to rest once it was clear what was going on with her, but she never would. The pregnancy had come as a huge surprise, since nobody knew she and Sam had been hooking up.

"I'm fine, thank you," he said. His face was solemn. I'd never seen him look so serious. Worry filled my insides. The others sensed it, too, as we waited for him to speak. The silence stretched on until it grew uncomfortable. He bowed his head and folded his hands. His hair had gotten so long it hung down past his fingers. When he lifted his head, the smile had returned to his face. "Family, you are all aware of the reason for my journey, and I felt your presence while I've been away. Thank you for your prayers, because we were in desperate need of revelation and light." He took a seat, folding his hands on his lap. "The ground around us only represents our inability to bring forth change and creation. It reflects what's happening inside our souls." He paused, giving his words a chance to sink in.

I'd had similar thoughts, because no matter how hard we toiled, nothing worked out. We'd arrived with a sense that we were going to create a new world, but so far we hadn't succeeded in creating much of anything. Anxiety and panic had started to creep in around us despite our best efforts. Our reaction to Ray's late arrival tonight was testimony to that. I eyed the circle, getting a feel for their emotional temperature, and it was the same as mine.

"The Lord has answered our desperate pleas and the petitions of our heart." He beamed. Gratitude swelled around us, lifting our spirits immediately. "We must be different if we are going to enter into the Lord's kingdom. Ray brought me this far, but he is not the man that is going to bring us into the Lord's perfect plan." He raised his arms and lifted his head to the sky. "Family, I had to put Ray to death so the Lord could establish a new covenant with us. I buried him in the banks of that creek." He motioned to the woods behind him. "I arose from my baptism in the dark waters and heard his voice as clearly as I did the day I received the vision for Love International. The Lord said, 'From this moment forward, you shall be called Abner. You are the Father of Light.'" He placed his hands in front of his chest and bowed before us. "I will guide us into the kingdom."

His words sent us into stunned silence. He didn't wait for us to recover before continuing. "I invite you to join me, but I must tell you, it will not be easy. There will be many trials and tribulations. Each time we advance to the next level, there are people who aren't ready, and there are those of you sitting here tonight who think you're not ready. You're disappointed that you've come all this way and given up so much of your life to have to return disenchanted and empty handed, but I encourage you to be open minded. To embrace what this moment has taught us and what it can continue to teach us." He shifted in his position. "Life is nothing but a series of births, deaths, and resurrections, and whoever chooses to advance must put to death the old so the Lord can raise up the new."

This was usually when he asked for questions, but he didn't seem interested in hearing our reaction.

"For those of you that choose to go to the next level with me, I want you to know that God revealed my deep responsibility for you. It will be my job to care for you and watch over you as the father of this light. Like any father, there will be times I will have to make decisions that might be unpopular. That hasn't always been the case. As you know from being with me all these years, I have always opted for the happiness of the group, even if I would've made a different choice. Going forward, I will not be as concerned for the happiness of the group as I am for their growth. If this is something you find uncomfortable or displeasing, then please do not follow us down this path. Anyone who doesn't want to go to the next level, I would ask that you please pack your things and leave by dawn."

———

People stumbled into the tent, bleary eyed and woozy from being up so late last night. We had all gone to bed wondering the same thing— would anyone leave? I hadn't even considered it. Where would I go? There was no home for me to return to. It'd probably been years since Scott or Abbi had given me a thought. So far everyone was here except for Will and Keith, but only because they were with Abner. We'd all talked about the name change and how tough it was going to be to remember not to call him Ray, but it'd been surprisingly easy. Even by the end of the conversations last night, we'd almost gotten used to it.

Someone had moved all the tables and chairs out of the tent. We stood in a huge mass, expectantly waiting for our next step. It wasn't long before Abner, Keith, and Will strode across camp and into the tent.

"I am so glad to see you all this morning, family. It fills my heart with such joy." Abner's love penetrated the makeshift room. "The word tells us that no one can enter the kingdom unless they are born again. I was reborn while away, and all of you must be reborn in the same way if you want to join me in the kingdom. If we are to be born again, then we must put to death our old identity." His hands never stopped moving, punctuating his words and accentuating his gestures. Will and Keith started bringing out the yoga mats we kept piled in the left corner underneath the blue canopy. "Today Will is ready to renounce his old, sinful life and be reborn into the kingdom." He started clapping, and we all joined in, even though we didn't know what was happening. The room reeked of nervous sweat. "Please clear a spot in the middle," Abner instructed. We moved to the sides, creating an opening within the circle. Abner and Keith rolled out the yoga mats next to each other. Abner motioned to Will when they'd finished, and he stepped onto the mats. I'd never seen him look scared. Even when Abner was barking orders and threatening punishment, Will remained calm, impassive. Not today. His face was white. He ground his teeth back and forth. His other hand twitched with nervous energy as he tried to be still and wait for whatever was going to happen next.

"The same rules will govern every ceremony." Abner spoke like a drill sergeant. "Unless one is born again, he cannot see the kingdom." He turned his attention to Will. "Are you ready?"

"I am."

"Then, as we discussed, you must stand naked in front of God."

Will pulled his shirt over his head and tossed it on the floor. He undid his pants and took them off until he stood in his underwear. He stepped out of his underwear next. I looked away out of respect for Margo.

"Jesus told Nicodemus it was impossible for a man to return to his mother's womb and be born again, but God has called us to return to the womb." Abner's gaze pierced the room while Will lay down on the mat. His body formed a T on it. He crossed his arms over his chest, his body glistening with sweat. Abner and Keith took a dark hood and threw it over Will's head before spreading one of our thick black sheets on top of him. They tucked it in around him before taking another sheet and rolling him on top of that one. They kept rolling him over until it was tightly wrapped around his body, with only his feet sticking out, and there was no way for him to move. They repositioned him on the mat so that his body stretched the length of it.

"Unless one is born again, they cannot see the kingdom." Abner nodded at Keith. Abner got on his knees and pressed his forearms onto Will. "The labor pains of this transformation are beginning. Behold, I make all things new!" he shouted. He moved around Will's body, pressing on different spots with his forearms. I couldn't hear what he was chanting underneath his breath. Keith joined Will on the floor next to Abner. Will's body writhed underneath them. How could he breathe?

"Everyone, come," Abner ordered. We swarmed Will's body—pushing, pressing, prodding. "Press harder. You're not pressing hard enough. Let him feel the labor pains. The struggle. Come, everyone. You have to work harder."

Everything moved quickly. Arms were everywhere. A sea of bodies moved around me.

"Renounce your old life," Abner called out, and we all followed.

"Renounce your old life!" we chanted louder.

Everyone pushed and moved like an angry mob at a rock concert. They pulled me along.

"Find the light. Move toward the opening. Leave your darkness behind." Margo's voice rose above all the others.

Willow gripped my hand. I looked down. Her face was pale, and her eyelashes were matted together with tears. I gripped her hand tightly and didn't let go.

"I can't breathe. I can't breathe," Will cried.

"You're almost there. This is the transition. Keep going. Keep going." Abner motioned to all of us again.

"You can do it!" we cheered.

His body twisted and flipped. Suddenly, his arm shot through the black sheet, tearing a hole in it. Everyone screamed and clapped like someone had just scored the winning touchdown at the Super Bowl.

Margo rushed forward to help get him out, but Abner shoved her away. "Stay back. He must do this alone."

His other arm came out. Then, like some kind of beast, he pulled his body through. The sheet tore. He flung off the other coverings. He got to his knees. Vomit covered him.

"Welcome to the kingdom," Abner announced.

TWENTY-FOUR

ABBI

NOW

My stomach jumped with nerves as I tapped on Mom's door. I was more nervous tonight than I'd been the first time I'd knocked on her door, because I'd brought my violin. She'd picked up the violin in high school, and she'd played through most of college. Dad said playing music made her happier than anything else, and he wasn't exaggerating. Watching her old recital tapes was one of my favorite things to do. Dad had put them on CDs for me after I'd almost worn out the old tapes. I loved watching her play. Her eyes danced along with the music, and she had a way of making the violin sound like it was weeping with joy.

It was a bold move to bring it. I had no idea how she'd react, but I was tired of things being so heavy and serious all the time. She rarely smiled, and when she did she grimaced like it hurt her, and it never reached her eyes. Hopefully, playing for her would cheer her up.

She opened the door. "Come in," she said.

"Thank you," I replied as I moved past her.

She immediately spotted the violin, and her eyes grew huge. "You play?"

"I do, but I'm not very good. I don't sound anything like you." It didn't matter how much I practiced; my playing would never match hers. Music required soul, and I didn't have it. Not like she did. Not even close. "Do you want to play?"

She didn't even think about it before shaking her head. "Will you play something for me?"

"Sure," I said, more nervous than I'd been at any of my recitals. I rubbed the locket around my neck out of habit, like I did whenever I performed. I smiled at the sudden realization that I wouldn't have to touch her picture to bring her presence with me into my next recital, because she would be in the audience.

Mom laid Shiloh at the top of the bed and put two pillows on each side of her so that she could give me her full attention. Maybe soon she'd let herself sleep in it too. She sat in the center cross-legged as I brought the violin up to my chin. I'd tuned it earlier today, so it was ready. I counted down the beat in my head, hoping I would make it through the piece without too many mistakes. The only reason I ever played was in remembrance of her, and it felt so strange to have her sitting on the bed in front of me. I shook out the nervous tension in my shoulders and stood straighter. I never looked at anyone when I played. It made me too anxious. I stared at my bow as I strummed the beginning measures of the new Taylor Swift song. My confidence grew as I went along, and I moved easily into the next song when I finished. It took me a second to look up, and when I did Mom was silently weeping. I didn't move to comfort her, like everyone else always did. Sometimes you just had to feel a moment, and this was one of those times. I kept playing, making my way through all the songs I knew, and started over at the beginning when I had finished.

"Wow," she said after my fingers were too tired to play anymore. "Thank you, Abbi. Thank you."

She was beaming with happiness, and I couldn't keep the cheesy grin off my face, but I didn't care.

"I haven't heard music in . . ." She was still having a hard time remembering what year it was, and it took her a second to remember and work out the math. "Eleven years."

"You haven't heard music in eleven years?"

She nodded. "Or taken a warm shower."

"What? Are you kidding me?" I set my violin on top of the dresser and raced over to the bed to take a seat next to her.

"We only used hot water to cook. Cold water for everything else."

"That's awful. You didn't have any electricity or what?"

"We heated our water to cook and had generators that we could've used to heat our bathwater, but we chose not to."

"Oh my gosh, why would you punish yourself like that?"

Mom giggled. This time she didn't slap her hand over her mouth quite so quickly. "It was part of our daily penance."

"Huh?"

"It was a way of reminding ourselves of our wicked nature and denying our bodies' appetites for pleasure," she explained.

"Like sleeping on the floor instead of the bed?"

"Yes, we do daily penance to prove our worthiness to the Lord." The recitation of the words did something to her as she spoke. Darkness clouded her face, and something about the memory snuffed out her light, like she was a candle being blown out.

"Mom?" I put my arm on her shoulder. "Are you okay?"

She wrapped her arms around herself, rubbing her hands up and down her arms like she was cold. She refused to return my stare. "I'm getting a headache. I think I better go to bed."

KATE

THEN

Today was my day. I'd volunteered to go next. We'd been doing a rebirthing ceremony every few days. We could only do one a day because we needed to rest in between them, since they drained so much from us. I stood in front of the tent while Abner made final preparations.

I didn't sleep at all last night, and my stomach was too twisted to eat anything for breakfast. I was drenched in sweat, and nothing had even happened yet. Vomit kept rising in my throat, and I swallowed it back down forcibly while I waited to begin. My head spun.

Breathe, Kate. Breathe.

I could do this. I had to do this.

Abner began reciting the familiar script, but his words didn't reach my ears, even though I was standing next to him. Fear had taken over, stripping every thought.

His voice broke in. "It's time to get naked before God."

My fingers shook as I removed my dress. I stared at the ground. I didn't want to see anyone's expression. Their fear would only increase mine. Soon the mat was in front of me, and I did what I was supposed to without being told. I laid my body across the mat and placed my arms at my sides. Every muscle twitched with the desire to move as they rolled me into the blanket. My ears rang. They flipped me around. Abner's face hovered above mine, his smile wide, eyes glinting.

"You'll be okay," he mouthed.

And then the black sheet was over my head. I stifled the urge to scream. The hard part hadn't even begun. My fingers curled into fists, nails digging into my palms.

"Today I declare—behold, I make all things new," Abner announced. "Unless someone is born again, they cannot see the kingdom."

My eyes throbbed. Red blotches filled my line of vision. The pressure started. It compressed my chest, making it harder to breathe. I tried to move away, but it was useless. The blanket bound me like I was tied with rope. My head pounded with panic, threatening to explode and shatter pieces of me against the sheet.

"The labor pains are beginning. Come, help her as she moves into this transition."

The pressure was everywhere. No part of my body was free. They pushed down. Harder and harder. A primal scream violently exploded from me. It did nothing. They kept pushing. They wouldn't stop.

"Renounce your old life! Renounce your old life!" Their chants filled my ears. "Prove your worthiness to the Lord!"

I kicked and flailed wildly, desperately trying to break free. My body writhed back and forth. There wasn't enough air. Every cell in my body screamed for oxygen.

"Find the light. Move toward the light." Abner's voice cut into my fear.

I wasn't strong enough. I felt myself departing, my brain detaching from my body, floating. Black seeped into the edge of my vision. All their sounds melded into a big blur in my head, ran together. They were right next to me, so close, but I couldn't hear them. I couldn't feel them anymore either. My body was light. I was floating above the black, watching myself as I struggled. Abner was there, too, standing next to me as he watched himself pushing on my body.

"Don't fight," he whispered in my ear before gently pushing me back into my body.

I forced myself to be calm inside the walls of my skin. And then I saw it. A pinprick of light, ever so small, but it was there in front of me, to the right. If I could just get my arm to it, I could stick my finger through.

"The light, Kate." The faint call of Willow's voice. I followed the sound, calmly turning and twisting until one arm was free. I moved toward the light and jabbed a finger through. Adrenaline shot through me. I pushed with every ounce of strength I had left in me.

And then there was a hole.

I made a hole!

Sobs shook me. I was so close. Almost there.

I heard their voices again. "You can do it! Come on—you can do it!"

I tore through the sheet, bursting into the light. I threw all of it off me, detangling myself. I laughed through my tears, hysterical.

Abner greeted me with a smile. "Welcome to the kingdom."

———

Abner's predictions about what would happen after we'd been reborn came true. We'd told the universe we were ready to change, and it had responded just like he'd said it would. Our plants and fields had started growing, row after row of green beans and corn springing up around us. Even our chicken had responded by laying more eggs. There'd been a shift in everything we touched. There had been no denying that, and we'd all felt it.

We only had two more ceremonies left until our transition was complete. Bekah couldn't go until after the baby was born, and we had no idea when he would show up. She still wasn't showing very much, but it was her first baby, and women were always small with their first. Willow was the other one who hadn't gone, and today was the day she'd agreed to try again.

Willow was struggling with the ceremony because she was terrified of closed spaces. She'd already backed out three different times. No one wanted to voice it, but we were all wondering what would happen if she couldn't go through with it. She was worried about it too. I could see it in her face. I'd suggested that we might be able to do something differ-ent for her to symbolize it in the same way, and Abner immediately shot me down. He hadn't been kidding about establishing a more dominant role. That part was taking some getting used to as well.

I hurried to get her from our room. We shared a cabin along with four of the other girls. There were three sets of cots in two rows. Willow sat on hers, nervously chewing her fingernails, something she hadn't done in months. She'd worked hard at breaking the habit, and it hadn't been easy, since she'd had it since she was a little girl. Abner had told her that nail biting was the same as eating away at herself. If he caught her doing it, there'd be a reckoning.

I sat down next to her and put my arm around her shoulders. "Look, you can do this. I know you can. You're one of the strongest people I know."

"Oh please," she said. "You're just saying that. Remember how you called me a spoiled hippy baby?"

I laughed. "Yeah, but that was before I knew you." I squeezed her tightly. "Come on—let's go. Don't think about it. The longer you sit here, the more worked up you'll get."

"Is it really that awful?"

"It is."

She slapped my thigh. "You're not supposed to say that. You're supposed to say that it's not going to be as bad as I think it'll be, and I'll be fine."

"Then I wouldn't love you like I love you." Her eyes filled with tears, and she leaned into me, resting her head on my shoulder. "It's pretty terrible. It's going to be as bad as you think it is—"

"Oh my God!" She giggled. "You're seriously not helping."

"Shut up; listen to me," I said through my laughter. "But you will get through it. Everybody does. It just feels like you won't, but you will." I stood, pulling her up with me. We headed out of the cabin and into the gathering place.

We were the last to arrive. Everyone stood waiting, eyes filled with encouragement. They started clapping when we got inside the large tent. She'd never made it this far. The family rushed to hug and embrace her. She turned to look at me before being engulfed by them, a big smile on her face. Her cheeks streamed with wet gratitude. I blew her a kiss as they carried her to the front of the room with Abner. Everything was set up just like it'd been two days earlier for Sol's.

"Which scripture governs this ceremony?" Abner asked in the same way he'd been doing for all the ceremonies. Hands went up. He called on my cabinmate, Lee.

"No one can see the kingdom unless they are born again." She recited it like a script.

He smiled. "Very good. We must get that step right." He scanned the room, making eye contact briefly with each of us so he could make sure we knew the seriousness of what was about to happen. The intensity was the same no matter how many times we'd done it.

Just like that, the ceremony began. Willow was wrapped up like me and everyone else who'd gone before. Same mat. Same blanket. Same everything. Her body looked so much smaller when it was wrapped up like a burrito. My heart ached for her. I forced myself not to move. She sobbed loudly as the sheet went over her head.

"Stop! Stop!" she cried. "I can't do this. I changed my mind. I changed my mind."

Abner ignored her and started pressing on her covered mound, which only made her cry harder. People moved around Abner despite her protests. They pushed on her body like they'd pushed on everyone's body, but her body was so small. How were they not crushing her?

"You're hurting me! You're hurting me! Please!" her tortured screams rang out.

Sol and I jerked our hands back. Abner shook his head and pointed to her covered body. "Keep going. You must keep going. Don't stop now." He grabbed my hand and shoved it back on her, pressing his hand down on mine. Her small body writhed underneath our hands. He let go and grabbed Sol next.

"I can't breathe. Please, I can't breathe."

It took everything in me to keep my hands in place.

"Fight for the light! Fight for the light!" we chanted. We were well versed in the routine. Transition was the hardest part, just like real labor. "Prove your worthiness to the Lord!"

"Help!" Her scream was so raw I felt it in my guts.

"Get away from her!" I screamed, pushing Daniel off her. He grabbed me and slammed me to the ground, pinning my arms behind my back. "They're hurting her. She wants them to stop. I've got to help her," I cried. "Please, I've got to help her."

"This is all part of her journey. She's looking into her awakening right now," Abner called.

Nobody stopped. I fought against Daniel, but he kept me pinned, forcing me to watch the scene in front of me with my face smashed to the floor. Willow's body thrashed around while everyone waited for her to break free. Her cries were silent. Just whimpers. This time, there was no hand. Time dragged. Everyone kept looking at Abner with hesitations in their movements, but he yelled at them to continue pushing. It kept going on and on.

She should've come out. Too much time had passed. Why wasn't she out?

"You must break free if you want to be free. Leave the darkness behind you." The determination in his voice was unwavering. Daniel slowly let me up. I stood with the others encircling her, hands at my sides. Her body stopped moving underneath the sheets. She wasn't making any more sounds. I clasped my hand over my mouth.

"You can step back," Abner said.

Relief washed over me so hard it made my knees buckle. It was finally over. Thank God.

We stepped back as Abner untangled the sheets from her body. She'd tied herself in knots. It seemed like it took forever to unwrap her, but when he finally did, Willow lay on her stomach. He turned her over, and she flopped on her back. Her lips were blue, her eyes wide open in terror, unblinking. He unwrapped the other blanket from around her. Her arm flopped to the ground. He put his face up to hers. Bekah and I rushed forward, pushing Abner and the others aside.

"Get off her!" I screamed.

Bekah knelt and put her head to her mouth, feeling for her breath. I squeezed Willow's hand. "Please be okay, please," I cried.

"I don't think she's breathing," Bekah said.

Ekon pushed through the crowd and shoved Bekah to the side, moving into CPR immediately. Time stood still while we watched him, waiting for any sign of life. He worked harder and faster. Bekah and I locked arms, willing her to breathe. Abner came up behind Ekon and placed his hand on his back.

"Enough," he said.

Ekon removed his hands from Willow's chest and sat back on his heels.

I lunged forward. "Don't stop! You have to keep going!"

Bekah pulled me back, hugging her arms tightly around me. I let out an involuntary sob. Ekon grabbed one of Willow's wrists and felt for a pulse. He looked up at Abner and shook his head before closing her eyes.

Abner laid his hand on her forehead. "The Lord giveth and the Lord taketh away."

I jumped up and pushed him away from her. "No, we can still save her. We have to save her!" Abner put his arms around me, and I flailed against him, pounding on his chest.

"She's gone, Kate. Willow is gone," he said before releasing me. I crumpled into a heap on the ground.

Chaos erupted. Everyone was screaming, trying to get close to her, crying.

"Enough!" Abner's scream cut through the noise. Everyone froze at the sound of his voice. "You must get yourselves together this instant," he said, disgusted with us. He knelt next to Willow and whispered something in her ear. The space erupted in collective sobs. He covered her lifeless body with one of the torn sheets. The sobs grew louder. Abner put his finger to his lips. "Hush, everyone. There is no reason to cry. How many times have I told you that there is a natural order to things? How many times?"

Nobody spoke.

"God weeds out those who are too weak to survive. We are not exempt from any of God's rules." His eyes scanned the room, but no one returned his stare. "Let this be a lesson to all of you."

TWENTY-FIVE

MEREDITH

NOW

Kate pushed open the glass doors of the police station and stepped outside. I'd waited in the car during her first appointment, because sitting in the police station for two hours sounded awful. I'd planned on going to Starbucks, but I'd never even put my keys in the ignition. As soon as I'd shut the door, all the questions I had kept buried just outside my awareness assaulted me, and I hadn't moved from my seat as they played themselves out.

As I watched her duck her head and cover Shiloh's like she did every time they were outside, I reminded myself to be quiet and let her do the talking. I'd acted like such an idiot on the way over. It was similar to how I'd felt driving Abbi to middle school by myself the first few times. The awkward tension between us had been so strong I hadn't been able to wait for her to get out of the car, even though I made sure not to let on that I felt that way. At least Kate's silences were different than Abbi's had been all those years ago. Distrust and preteen disdain had filled hers, and she had purposefully ignored me. Kate simply didn't need to fill up space with empty words, and something about it unsettled me, which only made me talk more. I'd ended up babbling the entire drive about nonsense.

She clasped Shiloh into her car seat before sliding into the passenger side. I turned the heat on for her. She was always shivering, no matter how warm it was.

"Hi," I said.

"Hi," she said without looking at me.

I pulled out of the parking lot and made a left, heading down to Highway 12. I kept glancing at her out of the corner of my eye. Her face was turned to the side as she stared out the window, so I couldn't see her expression. I was dying to know how her session had gone. But it felt too nosy and motherly. I wasn't trying to slide into that role with her. It was already strange enough driving her around.

She didn't speak the entire drive, and not talking made me break out in a cold sweat by the time we got inside. Our house felt so much bigger with everyone gone. Camille's team had packed up their last bit of gear this morning and had brought it down to the station. The expansiveness only magnified the quiet that had filled the rooms after their departure. She took off her shoes and scurried up the stairs with Shiloh. Her bedroom door clicked shut.

I quickly texted Scott that we were home. He had done everything he could to stall this morning before he left for his first day back at work, even though he had tried to act like that wasn't what he was doing. He had made a sandwich for lunch even though he always ate at work, because the company meals were better than anything either of us could have made. He had drawn out the process as long as possible and then had said he needed to check his email one more time before leaving. He'd already texted me three times asking for an update on how she was doing, and it wasn't even eleven o'clock.

None of his texts asked how I was doing. He hadn't stopped to consider that this morning might have been difficult for me too. And unlike him, who had a routine he could easily fit himself back into, I had no idea what I was supposed to do with a traumatized cult survivor who was also my husband's former wife. Dead wife, technically.

Like now. Was I supposed to go up there and ask if she was okay or leave her alone? And it'd be lunchtime in a little over an hour. Did I make lunch for myself or include her? If I made it for both of us, should I call her down to eat with me? Leave it out for her? What did I do for the rest of the day? Was I supposed to pretend she wasn't there?

Scott's inability to see how hard some of this was hurt. Obviously, what I was going through paled in comparison to what they were going through, but this wasn't easy. None of it had been. It didn't help that he'd barely touched me since she'd been back. Last night I'd made an effort to connect with him before we fell asleep, and he'd pushed my hand off him, mumbling something about being exhausted. It wasn't just that he didn't want to make love. He hadn't hooked my pinky with his like we did every night as we fell asleep, and that hurt more than his rejection.

TWENTY-SIX

ABBI

NOW

I stared out the passenger window as Dad drove me to school, wishing I was at home with Mom and Shiloh. It was my second day back, and I was dreading it. Going to school meant so much less time with them, since Mom was trying to get Shiloh on a regular schedule. She got her ready for bed around seven, and I didn't get home from school until after four, so that only left me three hours with them. I was barely going to be able to see them during the week. I crossed my arms on my chest.

"Can we talk about Mom?" I asked. I'd wanted to talk about her yesterday, but he'd spent the entire ride going over what I was supposed to say to any of the questions that I got from people about Mom. It wasn't that difficult—basically, say nothing—but he was so worried that I'd slip up and say something I wasn't supposed to. Thankfully, we didn't have to worry about the media, because they weren't allowed on school grounds.

He nodded, as eager to talk about it as me. It'd been almost three weeks since the knock on our door that changed everything, and we'd barely gotten to talk about things alone. There had always been somebody else in the room or someone nearby who might overhear. At least we'd be able to talk about things on our drives in the morning.

"What are the plans for her when she moves out?" I asked.

"Did she say she's moving out? When did she say that?"

"Dad, chill. No, Mom hasn't said anything to me about moving out, but I figured she must've talked to you about it."

He shook his head. "She hasn't said anything to me. Do you think she wants to move out?"

I shrugged. "I have no idea. I told you we haven't talked about it."

"Do you think she's thinking about it?"

"Dad, come on. Listen to me. That's not the reason I'm bringing it up." He could be so frustrating when he got fixated on one thing, and it was so annoying. "At some point, Mom is going to have to move out, and when she does I was thinking that I would go with her."

His face paled, and he gripped the wheel. "I don't know about that, kiddo. We would have to really think about it."

"But that's just it—I have thought about it." He knew me better than that. I didn't do anything without thinking about it, usually too much. That had always been my problem. "I only have two years before college, and I want to spend as much time as I can getting to know Mom and Shiloh before then." He wanted to object, but he knew I was right. College would be here in no time, and my heart had been set on Georgia Tech since I was in sixth grade, and, even if I didn't get in, I was committed to going to college somewhere out of state. Living with them would allow me to get to know them in a way that I wouldn't be able to do otherwise.

We rounded the corner past a Michaels craft store, and the school came into view.

"What does your mom think about it?" he asked.

"I haven't said anything to her about it yet. I wanted to see what you thought about it first."

He raised his eyebrows with surprise. "You did?"

"Of course." His opinion would always be first on my list. Nothing would change that.

"I'm going to have to run it by Meredith to see what she thinks," he said.

I rolled my eyes. "It's not that serious. Can you wait to say something to her? All I wanted to do was let you know that I wanted to do it when Mom was ready. I don't want to make a big deal about it until then." We made a left into the car pool lane. I grabbed my backpack from between my feet. "Please just think about it." I leaned over and kissed him on the cheek as he slid into line behind a blue minivan. "I love you, Dad."

KATE

THEN

We buried Willow—plain and simple. It didn't matter how many times Abner said we were returning her to the earth. We put her in the ground and shoveled dirt on top of her, chanting scriptures about ashes to ashes and dust to dust. My head swirled with what we'd done. We had suffocated her. That was what we had done, no matter how much they wanted to sugarcoat it or call it another name. We were responsible for another person's death. There was no moving past that, even though Abner acted like it was all meant to be as if it had been part of the master plan all along. Everyone agreed with him, like they always did. It sickened me. My insides had begun to bleed, anger and grief twisting knots into my guts every day.

My brain had been unplugged. Disconnected. I watched myself perform from somewhere above. Getting up each morning before the sun. Thirty minutes of meditation before heading out to the field.

Working in the fields all day. But I was gone. Willow had taken me with her into the earth.

———

Bekah's screams pierced through the night, traveling across camp. She writhed in agony on the mattress. She'd been that way for over twelve hours and couldn't take any more. Her pain had passed words a long time ago.

Margo crouched at the head of the bed while I knelt at her feet. She pressed cool washcloths on her forehead while I tried to help work the baby down. Nothing about her labor had been normal. I didn't need to be a doctor to know that blood at the onset of labor was not a good sign. She'd been in mind-numbing pain ever since.

The family had immediately gathered in the tent, and they'd been engaged in continual meditation ever since. It hadn't been that long since we'd lost Willow. The soil on top of her grave was still fresh. We couldn't lose anyone else. We'd hoped to have the baby here by sunset, but it had gone down hours ago, and there hadn't been any progress.

"We have to do something," I cried as Bekah arched her back and shuddered from the war going on inside her body.

"She needs a doctor," Margo said. She hadn't stopped saying it since two feet had peeked their way through Bekah's vaginal opening instead of a head.

"That's not going to happen, and you know that," I hissed at her. We'd begged Abner to let us take her to the hospital, but he'd refused.

"We cannot get in the way of God's will, no matter how difficult that might be," he had said. I'd been angry with him before, but I'd never hated him as much as I had in that moment.

Bekah moaned as another contraction seized her. She instinctively pushed like she'd been doing all day, unable to hold back, and the feet pressed through again. I had tried grabbing and pulling them once and the sounds that had come out of her weren't human. I wouldn't put her through that again.

"It's okay, Bekah. You're almost there," I said through my tears, but we both knew I was lying.

All the women had filed in to the birthing tent in the beginning, but they had started leaving almost immediately. Mothers were the only ones who stayed behind, since they'd been through it before, but they'd left as the intensity increased, until it was only me and Margo. There was no way I was leaving Margo alone. She was crying as hard as Bekah, her love for her as strong as mine for Willow.

I didn't touch Bekah's body during contractions. Touch only made it worse. We had learned that the hard way. I tried to breathe for her, willing my air into her lungs. Suddenly, her head rolled to the side and her eyes closed. Margo grabbed her head and lifted it up. "Bekah, don't you go to sleep on me, honey. Don't fall asleep."

She'd already passed out from the pain twice. The second time we'd had to slap her to wake her up. We didn't have any choice, because she was so unresponsive.

"Oh my God, Kate. She's out again."

I raced to the head of the bed and put my face against hers. She was barely breathing.

"Abner!" I screamed. "Abner!"

He flipped open the tent flap and rushed inside.

"She's really struggling. We have to do something." Margo and I talked on top of each other.

Abner knelt next to her just as Sam rushed in behind him.

"I don't care what you say, Abner. I'm not staying out there." His voice shook with anger. "I love her, and that's my baby. I deserve to be in here." Sam's eyes were lit with anger.

Abner sprang back up from Bekah's bed. "I told you to stay outside until it was finished."

Sam lifted his chin in defiance. "I don't care what you said."

Abner's eyes narrowed to slits. "I said go." He pointed to the exit. "And the Lord commands that today if you hear his voice, do not harden your heart in rebellion."

Sam stepped toward Abner until they stood chest to chest. "I'm staying in this room. Period. That's what my God would want me to do."

Abner shoved him, and he went flying backward. Sam sprang up and charged Abner. Margo and I jumped up.

"Stop it!" Margo screamed as we stretched our bodies between them. Sam's chest pounded against mine. "Stop acting like idiots and help Bekah."

The fight left Sam at the mention of her name, and he rushed to her bedside. I breathed a sigh of relief as Abner angrily stomped out of the tent. Sam would pay for it later—probably Margo too—but at least it was over for the moment.

Sam hovered over the bed. "What's happening?"

"The pain is too much for her. The baby is still twisted the wrong way inside her," I whispered. If Bekah could hear me in whatever space she was in, I didn't want her to hear me say it again. The last time I'd told her what was happening, she'd clung to me sobbing and begged me to let her go.

Pain filled his eyes. "Nothing has changed?"

I shook my head.

"Oh my God." He ran his hands through his hair. "What about the baby? Is the baby okay up there? I mean . . ."

Margo laid her hand on his shoulder. "I think we're losing them both."

"We have to save them, I mean, one of them. They can't both die. Jesus, Margo. They can't both die." He moved in anxious circles. "What was I thinking? What was I ever thinking?"

"Calm down, Sam," Margo said in her most soothing voice. "Just calm down. Maybe you should step outside to get some fresh air."

As if on cue, the tent opened, and Abner burst in, holding his gun and pointing it directly at Sam.

"What are you doing?" Margo shrieked.

"Inflaming fire and inflicting vengeance upon those who do not obey." Abner took a step closer to Sam. "It is my duty to obey the word."

Sam moved closer to him. "What are you going to do? Shoot me?" He gave him a cocky smile. "You're going to shoot me now, Abner?"

"The word says that 'whoever resists authority resists what God has appointed, and those who resist will incur judgment.'"

Sam shook his head in disbelief. "You're a crazy man. You know that?"

"I will ask you to leave this tent one more time, and then I will not ask you again." His hand never wavered from the gun.

"I'm not leaving." Sam took another step closer. "Go ahead. I'm not afraid of you."

The shot shattered the air. Margo and I let out bloodcurdling screams. Everything rushed forward. I flung myself on top of Bekah. Margo piled on me. Sam held his stomach, where he'd been shot, stumbling to his knees before falling to the ground, his eyes wide with disbelief and shock.

The family flooded the tent until no one else could fit inside. Abner stood rooted to his spot, staring down at Sam. "The word says that 'whoever resists authority resists what God has appointed, and those who resist will incur judgment.'"

Bekah's body was still underneath mine. "Please, Abner, we have to do something for Bekah." I couldn't let her die underneath me. I just couldn't. Abner didn't budge. "Abner!" I had never shouted at him before. He snapped to attention.

"Get him out of here," he barked, pointing to Sam's crumpled body.

For a second, nobody moved, but then Keith rushed to Sam's aid, and Sol quickly joined him. They threw an arm around each shoulder and lifted him off the ground. Sam yelped like a wounded animal. Blood stained the front of his shirt, leaving a trail behind him as they dragged him out the door. The others moved aside so they could get through and rushed to help once they were outside the tent.

"Let the Lord's will be done," Abner said to them, motioning everyone away with one swipe of his hand. They all scattered quickly, leaving us alone. He sealed the tent behind them.

Everything stilled. Margo and I peeled ourselves off Bekah and stood together holding hands, like little girls on the playground on their first day of school. We waited for Abner to speak as he strutted around the tent breathing heavily. His left hand still gripped the gun. Margo's fear chased mine. He walked to the head of the bed, stepping over Sam's blood like it was nothing. He leaned over the bed and felt Bekah's neck for a pulse, then her wrist.

"She's alive, but barely," he pronounced. He tucked the gun in the waistband of his pants, and I released the breath I was holding. "Let's see about this baby." He moved to the end of the bed and knelt between her legs, peering at her in the same way my obstetrician had done to me so many years ago. "Margo, bring me my knife."

A tremble passed through Margo's body. "I can't." Her voice was barely audible.

"Kate."

The way he said my name made my blood boil, but I didn't have a choice. I wouldn't be responsible for another person's death. I squeezed Margo's hand before letting go. Sam's blood pooled with Bekah's in the middle of the floor. I closed my eyes and forced myself to step over it. I fumbled with the tie and lurched into the night air, gasping for breath, head pounding.

They'd moved Sam to the gathering tent and were racing around camp trying to find medical supplies. I hurried to Abner's makeshift cabin. I'd never been inside, but he only had one knife—the one he used to skin all the animals with—so it couldn't be that hard to find. I swallowed the horror creeping up the back of my throat and focused on scanning the room. There wasn't much time. We might already be too late. No time to think. And then I spotted it on a hook above his bed. I grabbed it and rushed back to the birthing tent.

TWENTY-SEVEN

MEREDITH

NOW

I looked at the clock: 4:12. Ugh, only two minutes since the last time I'd checked. My head throbbed. I never should've had that second glass of wine at book club, but it had felt so good to be out of the house. Nobody had brought up our situation, even though they all knew about it, and it had been such a relief not to talk about it. I'd been up for over thirty minutes, and my body buzzed with restless energy. I eased out of bed, doing my best not to wake Scott, since he was such a light sleeper. I tiptoed into the bathroom, careful not to turn the light on or make any noise when I was finished. I crept out of our bedroom and headed downstairs. Maybe I would make a breakfast quiche for everyone, since I was up so early.

I rounded the corner into the kitchen. Kate stood beside the refrigerator, holding the phone up to her mouth. Shock stopped me in my tracks. She slapped the phone back on the wall at the sight of me. It took me a second to process what'd I'd just seen.

"Were you talking to someone?" I asked in disbelief.

Her eyes were wide, and she quickly turned around so her back was to me and whipped open the refrigerator door, disappearing behind it. "No." She laughed nervously.

I stayed rooted to my spot. "But you were holding the receiver when I walked into the kitchen? And I heard a voice when I came around the corner."

"Yeah, me too," she said. She closed the door. "Are you okay?"

I pointed to myself. "Me? Uh . . . yes, I um . . . I just woke up and couldn't fall back to sleep." My thoughts wouldn't come together.

"I just finished feeding Shiloh, so I got hungry." She flashed me the apple she'd gotten from the refrigerator. She moved by me and kept walking without looking back. "Good night, Meredith."

I stood there stunned as she hurried back up the stairs. Who was she talking to? I rushed upstairs and shook Scott awake.

"Is everything okay?" he asked, sitting up.

I put my finger up to my lips. "Shhh. Be quiet. I don't want her to hear us."

"Who?" he asked.

I pointed next door and mouthed, "*Kate.*"

He dropped his voice to a whisper. "What's going on?"

I kept my voice low too. "I woke up at three and couldn't go back to sleep. You know how I get sometimes when I drink. Anyway, I went downstairs around four, because I figured I'd make everyone a big breakfast, since I was up. I walked into the kitchen, and Kate was on the phone with someone. She played it off like she'd come downstairs to get a snack and denied being on the phone when I asked her about it." I still couldn't believe she was denying it after I'd caught her red handed.

"She was on the phone?" he asked, trying to clear the sleep from his brain.

"Yes, except she said she wasn't. Don't you think that's strange?"

"Maybe she wanted to talk in private."

"At four in the morning? Who is she having private conversations with at this time of the night?" He didn't have an answer for that. "Do you think she was talking to one of them?" I didn't have to let him know who I was referring to.

"I doubt it."

"What if she was, Scott? What if she's been making calls to them in the middle of the night this entire time? You have to call Dean."

"I will, but I don't think you need to worry about it. Either tonight is the first night she's done it, or she's been doing it the entire time, and they already know about it. If they already know about it and didn't say anything to us, then it's not something to be concerned about."

"Can you make sure to ask Dean about it tomorrow, please? At least I'd know they'd looked into it, and there was nothing to be paranoid about."

"Meredith, I just said that I would. I have to work in the morning." He was already moving back underneath the covers, willing to let the entire thing go that easily, but I wasn't.

TWENTY-EIGHT

ABBI

NOW

I stared at the blank screen in front of me like I'd been doing for the last hour, debating whether or not I should log on to the Vanished forums and update Mom's status. It'd been active again since word had gotten out about her return, but it was only speculation and stories. All the news outlets had interviewed the gas station attendant, but none of us had spoken to the press, and the police had only given scripted responses about the investigation and asked people to respect our privacy. Dad had said it would be a long time before they stopped hounding us for interviews. They still camped out at the end of our street. It was only the city ordinances that kept them off our yard and driveway.

I'd never posted anything before. Dad had never told me not to, but it was only because he trusted me not to be stupid enough to do it. But I wanted to tell her followers that she was doing okay, that she got better every day. They would be thrilled to talk about her progress, and so far her homecoming had only been depressing. I understood why, obviously, but I was happy she was home—no matter what the circumstances were—and wanted someone else to at least pretend to be excited about it too. Elziehunter, mindjam21, and crystalclear had been following her case since the beginning. You could feel how much they loved her in the things they said about her and how much time they spent on her case. They deserved to know how she was doing.

I logged on. When I'd first discovered the forums, I'd spent hours weeding through them. There'd been something comforting about it. Oddly enough, it still gave me the same feeling. I'd been on them every night since we found Mom, combing through them with different eyes. I clicked on the main page, browsing quickly to see if anything grabbed my attention before scrolling down to Mom's thread: *Arcata Mom Vanishes.* There'd been an update last night by someone named Gloria. I clicked her profile. Gloria had one post and had only been a member for two days. My gut churned.

I quickly scrolled down to the message and clicked it open on my screen:

Kate Bennett is a dead woman.

KATE

THEN

I hugged Bekah's baby boy close to my chest as the smell of smoke filled my lungs. The weight of my backpack pressed down on me, making it almost impossible to run. The home we'd worked so desperately to build burned behind us.

"We have no choice," Abner had screamed last night. Fury had lined his face and filled his voice. "This land is cursed. If you don't believe me, then look around at the bloodshed tonight." He waved his arm at our bloodstained paths. Sam's body lay covered in a sheet outside the gathering tent. Bekah's lay inside the birthing tent. Their baby was the only one who'd survived.

"Take him." Abner had shoved him into my arms shortly after he'd cut him out of Bekah, and I'd been holding him ever since. Images of his birth flashed through my mind unbidden, and I shoved them down. I would push them down as far as they would go, and, when they couldn't go any further, I would find another way to make them disappear. I kept telling myself over and over again that at least Bekah was dead when it happened, but it didn't matter how many times I said it. Her body was still warm when we cut into her.

The baby stirred against me. He was starving. I stuck my finger into his mouth, hoping it would pacify him. Without Bekah's milk, I didn't know how we'd feed him. I'd given him small sips of water with a few sprinkles of sugar in it, but that hadn't been enough. He had cried all night and into this morning. He was only quiet now because he was too exhausted and hungry to cry.

Margo sobbed behind me, a steady stream of tears as we walked. Will was holding her up while they went, and she plodded along as if each step hurt. I knew that feeling. The pain of being alive when someone you loved dearly was gone. It hadn't lessened.

She wasn't the only one crying. Intermittent sobs broke into the early morning as we stumbled along in shock. We'd failed God miserably. Abner had made that clear last night when he was the only one who'd remained calm and sought God's help while the rest of us flailed around hysterically. It had been utter chaos. Everyone had been fighting. Screaming—some for help, others for deliverance. He had had to fire the gun again just to get us to stop and settle down. He had ordered us to build a fire, and we had immediately moved into action, grateful to have a voice to listen to. We had stood around the fire when we'd finished.

"Don't look back when we leave this place. It will be just like the days of Sodom and Gomorrah when we leave camp." The fire in his eyes matched the flames of the ones the others had set this morning. "The Lord ordered them not to look back, but what happened?" He didn't wait for us to respond. "Sarah was turned to a pillar of salt on the spot." He snapped his fingers. "Just like that. Because when you leave, you leave it all behind. You burn your bridges and your ships."

And that was what we had done. We'd loaded ourselves up with as much as we could carry and run through camp, setting things ablaze.

"Burn it down to the ground," Abner had ordered.

I choked on the fear working its way up my throat. It left a bitter taste. I could barely make out Abner and Will at the front of the pack, leading the way through the snarled forest, the only ones who'd been back to the vans since we set up camp. He was wrong about everything. This wasn't the beginning. It was the end.

TWENTY-NINE
MEREDITH

NOW

I was having a hard time remembering Scott's password, since I rarely used the computer in our bedroom and stress made me forgetful. I still hadn't calmed down from this morning. Abbi had come into our bedroom before breakfast and told us that someone had posted a death threat to Kate on the forums. She was completely freaked out about it, and even though Scott assured her it was probably just another troll, she'd begged him to let her stay home from school. I was glad he'd made her go, though. There'd been so many nutjobs over the years who'd posted that I didn't blame Scott for staying away from anything written about Kate online. But the threat, stacked on top of Kate's phone call last night, had my nerves on edge, and Scott's conversation with Dean hadn't helped at all.

He'd called Dean after he'd dropped Abbi off at school, and we'd been texting about it ever since. His password popped into my head, and I quickly typed it in before I lost it again. Scott had asked him about the forum thread, and he'd said the same thing as Scott—don't worry about it. Dean hadn't been all that concerned about the phone call either. He'd told Scott that Kate had gotten up at night and walked around the house quite often, but that she'd never made a phone call. He'd also said that she'd seemed confused and disoriented about the time of day whenever anyone had tried to talk to her and was sure that was what had happened last night. Scott had agreed with his reasoning.

I would've, too, if she hadn't lied about it when I'd asked her what she was doing, but I wasn't going to fight with the two of them. I logged on to our wireless service provider. They provided our home phone service too. I scrolled to the current billing cycle and opened it up. It was too early for the calls in the last twelve hours to post, but there was one other phone call made from our home phone this month: two nights ago, 2:30 a.m., number unknown.

I scrolled backward through the months, but the last call from the home phone had been four months ago, when Abbi had called asking me to call her cell phone because she'd lost it somewhere in the house. I printed out the last four months so that I could show Scott when he got home. I'd never mistrusted his judgment before, but suddenly I found myself looking at Kate like she was a total stranger. Someone none of us knew who was living in our house. I tried to tell myself I was exaggerating, but I couldn't shake the feeling. How could I?

She'd lied to my face.

KATE

THEN

"Kate, why don't you ride with me?" Abner had asked when we'd stopped for gas.

He had phrased it like a question, but there had been no way to decline without making a scene, so I'd reluctantly climbed into the passenger seat of the van carrying our supplies. It was almost three days into our trip, and we still hadn't spoken. Nobody was saying much of anything, though. I had expected a big scene once we got to the vans, but there hadn't been a pause in our steps. We had just started throwing our stuff in the vans without any kind of discussion except where to store things. I was pressed up against the passenger-side door, as far away from him as I could get.

We'd been driving for over an hour without saying anything. The smell of smoke still filled my nose. We'd never get it out of our clothes, no matter how hard we scrubbed them. What we'd done was attached to us like a malignant tumor.

Three bodies.

That was how many people we were leaving behind. People had screamed at Abner about what he had done, but that hadn't stopped them from digging their graves. They'd buried Sam's and Bekah's bodies next to each other. We'd forgone the ceremony this time. Abner had moved everyone quickly into setting the fires, yelling wildly that the ground we stood on was cursed.

"It won't always feel like this," Abner finally spoke, breaking into my thoughts.

"Nobody is ever going to forget." Especially not me, I wanted to add, but bit my tongue. The sound of the gun going off hadn't stopped ricocheting through me, making me cringe each time, the intensity never lessening. "And they shouldn't." I spat out the last part, unable to help myself.

"Good," he said. "I don't want anyone to forget. I want everything that happened here to be seared into our memories in a way that no amount of time can erase. We have utterly failed each other, God, and ourselves. I knew things were going to be difficult when God called us to separate ourselves, but I never imagined they would be this tragic." His voice thickened with emotion. "This is a test, and it's the hardest one we've had to endure on our journey. There will be many more until we reach the kingdom, but all of this fits perfectly with prophecy. The death in childbirth. The obstinate rebellion. The confusion. The warring among us. It's all part of it. This is getting us prepared. You have to trust me."

I turned away, gazing out the window at the rolling hills and wishing I could jump out. I would never trust him again. Willow's and Bekah's deaths might have been accidents, but he'd shot Sam in cold blood. I flinched as he put his hand on my knee.

"Do you trust me, Kate?"

I brushed his hand off. "That's not what we're talking about. It's not about trust. It's about what you did. How you—"

He interrupted me. "Just answer the question—do you trust me?"

"I don't want to answer your question."

"You trust me. I know you do, as much as you don't want to trust me." He put his hand back on my knee, pointedly. "You're special. I've always told you that. Since the first week you spent in the cellar, when I was so disappointed because I thought you were leaving. Remember that? We're alike in so many ways. I feel a connection with you that I don't feel with the others, and it's because our relationship is built on trust. You passed the highest loyalty test—you left your family."

We rarely talked about those days. They were a different lifetime ago.

"That was because I believed in everything you were doing."

"But don't you see, Kate? None of that has changed. Nothing is any different today than it was three days ago."

"How can you even say that? Two people are dead!"

"Bekah died from complications during childbirth. There was nothing that could have been done about that, and you know it."

"And Sam?"

"God struck down those he loved all the time for disobedience. He wept each time in the same way I weep over Sam's death, but remember that Sam is rejoicing with the Lord in eternity. And if he should decide to journey to earth once again, he will have another chance to learn what he didn't learn this time around and expand his consciousness." He quickly glanced at me before putting his eyes back on the road.

"I'm not asking if you understand any of this or even agree with it. You don't have to agree with me. Again, the question is, Do you trust me?"

I nodded not because it was true but because I wanted him to leave me alone.

"You know we speak truths out loud."

"Yes, I trust you," I said, crossing my arms on my chest.

"That's my girl."

I wasn't his girl. Not anymore.

———

We gathered around the fire in our new space, except nothing about it felt new or fresh. Abner had led us down backcountry roads that wound their way through the mountains until we ended up at an abandoned RV campground. The concrete slabs were broken, weeds and stubble growing through the cracks. Every smooth surface was spray-painted with graffiti. The space was old and decrepit, cluttered with pieces of other people's lives. We'd quickly set up camp and built a fire, collapsing around it exhausted and emotionally spent. I cringed when Abner got up to speak. I was hoping he'd stay quiet tonight.

"It's unfortunate that Bekah's body was unable to sustain the complications of labor. It was tragic and unbelievable. Our grief will last a long time. It will affect all of us differently, and I ask that we treat each other kindly, no matter how one's grief chooses to express itself."

Sol caught my attention from across the fire and frowned. He'd been furious when Abner came out of the birthing tent, and he'd come at him swinging. It took three guys to pull him off. I shrugged and quickly looked away before Abner saw me. I might be angry with him, but I wasn't stupid.

Abner walked over to where Jane stood holding Bekah's baby. We'd all been taking turns caring for him. He wasn't adapting to the formula yet, spitting most of it up within minutes of finishing the bottle, but hopefully some of it was getting into his system before he rejected it. Abner scooped the baby from her arms and lifted him up, cupping his neck to support his head. "Bekah left us with the most precious gift. I was there when she died, and she begged me to take care of her baby."

The hairs on the back of my neck bristled. That wasn't exactly true. She'd been dead by the time he had laid a hand on her. She'd begged me and Margo to save her baby and let her die after she'd given up on going to the hospital. I forced myself to listen to what he had to say next.

"She entrusted her baby into our care and family. Despite all the ugliness going on and swirling about us right now, we are responsible for this baby." He cuddled him against his chest. "How many times have I said we are all one?" He stopped talking, and silence reigned for a few seconds, but he didn't expect an answer. It went without saying, since he'd said it hundreds of times over the years. It was part of our core, the thing that made us who we were. "I belong to you, and you belong to me. We are still bound by that agreement. We made it before the Lord and each other. Family, we are bound to care for this life." I shifted uncomfortably in my seat. Margo sat up straighter. "Jesus said, 'Let the little children come out to me.' Children were given to us by God, and they belong to all of us. They are our responsibility. This child?" His voice rose. "He is our future. We must all work together to train him up in the way he should go. The responsibility was never meant to be for just one or two. It was always meant to be shared." He paused a moment before continuing. "Who is with me?"

Margo surprised all of us by raising her hand first. Will followed quickly after her, and before long hands shot up all around the fire. Mine was there too. I didn't want to get called out for not joining in.

Abner's eyes filled with tears. "I want the rest of the children to come stand next to me," he said. He walked around the fire and held out his hand to each of the children in our group. The children came out and joined him, never taking their eyes off their parents. There were six, but I barely paid them any attention. They were more like cats swirling around my feet as I went about my days.

Anne clung to Michael's arm. She nudged him forward as if to say, "Do something." They had three kids in the circle—Chad, Shane, and Ben. Their boys held hands in the middle of the group. Nervous laughter filled the night as he positioned them and stood behind them with his arms spread out like they were going to take a picture.

"These children will be the first soldiers in the army for the Lord's kingdom. Where we have failed, they will succeed. In the areas where we have missed the mark, they will surpass it far greater than we could ask or imagine. Just like the word says. The Lord has sent us that same prophecy." Sweat dripped down his face as the spirit moved him. "Family, we have failed, but we are not failures. We are beaten down but not forgotten. He has given us this gift. An opportunity to right all the wrongs through this new offspring. Do you feel his presence here tonight? Don't try to pretend you don't. I know you do. Let go of your anger. Let go of your rage, the bitterness. It will destroy you. Don't hold on to it. These children will save the world. They will do what we couldn't, but you have to let go. Family, do you hear me? Can you feel me?"

Within seconds, people were on their feet, roaring and clapping. It wasn't long before someone broke into dance. Jane's melodic voice rang out. Someone chanted behind it, their voice a desperate plea to God to forgive us and give us another chance.

But I couldn't get up. I had forced myself to raise my hand, but I couldn't make myself celebrate or pretend to be excited about his words. I wasn't the only one who'd stayed seated. Were they asking the same question as me? We'd stood by and let people die—why did we think we deserved forgiveness or another chance?

THIRTY
MEREDITH

NOW

Neither of us had spoken since we'd stepped outside. It'd been almost a month since Kate had returned, and it was the first time Scott and I had been alone together outside the house. He'd asked if I wanted to go for a walk after dinner, and I had jumped at the opportunity. One of our favorite things to do was to fill our to-go mugs with coffee and stroll through the neighborhood. Our street was so pretty it'd been featured in *Woman's Day* magazine twice. He'd taken my hand as we'd walked down the sidewalk, like he'd done so many times in the past, and the simple gesture almost brought me to tears.

"I missed us," I said after a few more blocks had passed.

"Me too." He squeezed my hand. "Are you feeling better about things than you were this morning?"

I tried to hide my annoyance that he'd brought it up so quickly. Obviously, we'd talk about things, but I'd been hoping to enjoy a brief break from it all. I was never worried about the forum post. That was all Abbi. My concern was the phone calls, and it'd only grown larger since the call from this morning had updated on the log around noon.

The number was unknown, just like the other one. But I didn't want to bring it up and spoil the moment.

"I am," I lied.

"You've got to trust the investigators to do their job," Scott said as we walked down the sidewalk.

"Like you trusted them?" I said without thinking. His hand went limp in mine. "I wasn't trying to be mean. Honestly. But how many times over the years have I listened to you say how they mishandled Kate's case?"

He picked up speed while we walked. "This is a completely different situation. Before they focused on me as a suspect and ignored other important leads. Everyone has been on top of things since the beginning this time." His voice had an edge. "Believe me, we're not in any kind of danger. Dean never would've pulled all the security back if we were."

"And the fact that she lied to me about being on the phone?"

His body tightened next to mine. "Please don't be mad, Meredith, but, honestly, it's her business if she wants to be on the phone."

I jerked my hand out of his. "Are you kidding me right now?"

He raised his palms up. "I mean, we're not her parents. She can talk to people."

"And lie to me about it? That's acceptable?"

"No, of course not, but we've just got to keep giving her the safe space to get through whatever process she has to go through."

"Is Dean going to tell Camille and the rest of the team about the phone calls?"

"I'm not sure."

"You didn't ask?" He didn't have to answer for me to know he hadn't. "Why didn't you make sure that he was going to?" His ability to bury his head in the sand over this was infuriating. If she was lying about being on the phone, then what other things was she lying about?

The telltale sound of the guest door squeaked, and I sat up straight, instantly alert. I'd been up for the last three nights listening for Kate. This was the first I'd heard anything. I held my breath, as if hearing me breathe might signal that I was awake, and she'd chicken out and go back to her room. Old houses were unforgiving, no matter how sneaky you were, and there was almost no way to keep the second-to-the-last stair from making noise. As if on cue, I heard it, which was my signal to get out of bed.

I stood by our bedroom door for a few minutes, forcing myself to give her enough time to start making her call. Hopefully she would be listening harder to whoever was on the other end of the line than she would be for me. I opened the door and slid along the wall, where it was the quietest. I made my way to the top of the stairs and inched down them, holding my breath again. There was no mistaking the sound of hushed and frantic whispering coming from the kitchen. I skipped the squeaky step and walked into the kitchen to see Kate standing in the same spot she'd been before, with the phone up to her ear.

"I—" Kate froze midsentence, then quickly slammed the receiver back into its place. "Meredith, hi."

"I knew you were talking to someone," I said. There was no denying she was caught this time.

She shook her head and tried to feign innocence. "I wasn't talking to anyone."

"Are you kidding me?" I pointed to the phone. "I just walked in on you hanging it up."

"I wasn't. I don't know what you thought you saw." She tried to shuffle past me, but I blocked her path with my body, putting my hands on my hips.

"I know exactly what I saw." She wasn't getting off that easy.

She quickly reached out and pushed me aside before stepping around me. She turned to look at me over her shoulder as she walked away. "And even if I was talking on the phone, it would be none of your business."

I hurried after her and grabbed her arm as she was about to put her foot on the step. "We're not done with this conversation," I said as she turned around. There was no mistaking the anger in her face. People only got angry when they were caught doing something wrong. I waved the phone records in front of her. "You see this? It's a list of calls made from the phone in the kitchen during the last month, and guess what? There hadn't been a call made in the middle of the night until you moved in with us."

She jerked away from me. "Leave me alone. You don't know what you're talking about."

"Then why don't you fill me in?" Everyone tiptoed around her, but maybe it was time to see what she'd do if she was pushed a little bit.

"Please." She lowered her voice. "You're going to wake up Shiloh."

"She'll go back to sleep."

"Why are you doing this?" she asked. Her eyes filled with tears.

I refused to be moved by them, just like I'd done when my boys were toddlers and throwing fits. "Tell me what's going on."

She opened her mouth to speak, then quickly shut it like she'd changed her mind. "I don't have to tell you anything." She put her head down and jerked her arm away, moving past me. "Please leave me alone." She ran up the last few steps and down the hallway into her bedroom, shutting the door tightly behind her.

I raced behind her and into our bedroom, almost smacking into Scott as he knelt on the floor, digging through the laundry basket for something clean to wear. "What the heck is going on out there?" he asked as he pulled a sweatshirt over his head.

I shut the door and leaned over in front of it, trying to catch my breath. "I wasn't going to say anything until I had proof, so I don't want you to think I was purposefully keeping anything from you. Anyway, I started setting my alarm and getting up at different times to see if Kate would get on the phone again. Well, tonight I caught her. For sure. And she lied to me when I confronted her about it, just like before, but that wasn't the weirdest part. She asked me not to do this to her. I don't even know what she's talking about. I just wanted her to tell us the truth."

"So you're creeping around the house spying on her?"

The world tilted and shifted like I'd just slammed into a wall. "I'm spying on her?"

"I mean, getting up in the middle of the night and trying to bust her sounds a bit like spying to me. Did you forget we're trying to earn her trust, not break it?" He worked his jaw before continuing. "How is she ever going to open up if she doesn't trust us? And not just open up—get better. That's what we're trying to help her do. Remember?"

My pulse throbbed in my temples. Anger inched its way up my chest. My fingers balled into fists at my sides. "I thought it was pretty important to find out if she was talking to someone in the middle of the night and why she was lying about it. I didn't think there was any better way than catching her again."

"Why are you so obsessed with this?"

"Why aren't you?" His naivete about her was maddening. "What if she's talking to someone from Love International?"

He shook his head.

"What if she's still in contact with them?" I refused to let it go, especially if there was any potential that any of us were in danger.

"She's not," he said with conviction.

"How can you just blindly trust someone who left you for eleven years?" He recoiled like I'd slapped him. "I'm sorry. I shouldn't have said that. I wasn't thinking."

"Move," he said.

It slowly dawned on me that he thought I was blocking the door, because I was standing in front of it. "Where are you going?" I asked, even though I knew the answer.

"I'm going to see if she's okay."

THIRTY-ONE

ABBI

NOW

I pulled the pillow over my head. I would be so glad when I got to sleep like a regular person again. It was almost five, and I hoped I'd be able to fall back to sleep. Something next door had woken me, and then I'd heard Dad and Meredith's whispered yelling. I didn't even want to know what had happened.

I grabbed my phone from the nightstand and opened Vanished. I'd been obsessively refreshing it since Gloria's threatening post about Mom two nights ago. Who was she? I'd spent hours staring at the line, unable to move, just reading it over and over again. Of course Dad hadn't taken it seriously. He never did. This wouldn't be the first time someone had hijacked her thread with nonsense. Once someone had pretended to be her. A couple of other times someone had written something similar about her being alive.

Except Mom was alive for real, and the post just happened to have been made within weeks of her coming home. And I was supposed to believe that was all coincidence? If no one was going to take it seriously, then I would. Besides, Dean had said that he was going to be closely monitoring the forums, so what did I really have to worry about?

I looked around like Dad could see through the walls and into my bedroom and would come barreling in to stop me at any second. I created an account as fast as I could and registered to use the discussion boards. My heart thumped in my chest with each tap on the keypad. I was a registered user within seconds.

Why do you want her dead?

I quickly hit "Submit" before I changed my mind.

KATE

THEN

I shucked the beans, filling up the bowls before passing them to Margo as Abner walked past us. He was too busy communing with the spirits and muttering prayers underneath his breath to pay us any attention. Bekah's son, Miles, toddled behind him, doing his best to keep up. Even though Abner tried to pretend like all the children were equal in his eyes, he had a special spot in his heart for Miles. He favored him so much that he allowed him to sleep with him at night, and Abner always slept alone. I watched as they disappeared into his tent, wondering what they did in there. Sometimes they didn't come out for hours.

Margo eyed me from across the table. "They make an interesting pair."

My cheeks flushed. I was embarrassed she'd caught me watching them so closely. "Yeah, they really do, and I just don't understand it."

"It's because she was his. That's the real reason she kept her relationship with Sam a secret."

"What do you mean?"

"She'd never been with anyone else besides Abner."

I almost dropped my bowl. "She was with Abner?"

"Yes." She raised her eyebrows. "You didn't know that? I thought everyone knew that."

I shook my head, unable to speak around the emotions working their way up my throat. Abner had told me years ago that he practiced sexual abstinence, and he must've preached on sexual purity hundreds of times. Every time I was starting to soften toward Abner, he did something horrendous again. He'd done much worse things in the past, but I'd never caught him in such a big lie. Something about his dishonesty was unsettling in a way that none of his actions had been before.

"Wow, you really had no idea, did you?" she asked after a few minutes had passed and I still hadn't regained my composure.

"How many other disciples has he been with?" I asked, finally finding my voice.

"There weren't any others—just Bekah. Like I said, she was his."

Was that the real reason he was so angry with Sam? Jealousy? My knees felt weak. I needed to sit down. How did I never see it?

"Were they in love?" I asked, steadying myself against the table.

Margo let out a bitter laugh. "Love? No. He wanted a virgin, so that's what he got."

My stomach rolled. "What are you talking about?"

"You think people get here by accident?"

How else would they get here? Was this some kind of weird test? Had Abner put her up to it? I stopped what I was doing and dried my hands on my shirt. "None of this is making sense."

Her eyes swept the area around us before she spoke, making sure we were alone. "Back in the beginning, Abner made exchanges for what we brought in—"

"What do you mean by what you brought in?"

"Discipleship and membership have always been separate. You know that. Membership is voluntary and open to everyone. Discipleship is reserved for a select few who can pass certain tests or are brought in as a form of loyalty test as part of someone else's discipleship."

Her words knocked the air from my lungs. "You tricked people?"

"We didn't trick anyone. That's not how it worked. Every person and situation was different. Bekah was Will's exchange for me."

"Exchange?" I couldn't wrap my brain around anything she was saying. None of it made sense. Discipleship was all about choice—free will. How did any of this fit with that?

"Abner wanted proof that Will was willing to give up the thing that was the most important to him for Love International, so he asked to lie with me for one night. But Will refused to share me even for a night." Her eyes filled with pride. "The problem was that Will had been with Abner long enough to know that he couldn't simply refuse his request. He needed something to offer him in return, and it had to be equal to what Abner was asking, or he'd never consider it. He told him he could do better than allowing him to experience me. He could have his own virgin. That's how Bekah came into play."

My eyes widened. "You were a virgin when you married Will?" She nodded. "But you were twenty-six."

"I was a committed Mormon before him."

That meant Will was still the only man she'd been with, since she'd told me during our mentorship that they practiced monogamy. I took a moment for it to sink in. "How did it work?"

"What do you mean?"

"You can't just put an ad in the newspaper asking for virgins. How'd Will find Bekah?"

"He didn't." Grief clouded her face. "I did."

Horror filled my insides. "You found Bekah?"

"In a women's devotional group on the south side of Atlanta." She hung her head in shame.

"But that was just Bekah, right? Nothing like that happened with me, did it?" Margo refused to lift her head. Her silence was more than my answer. "Look at me," I hissed. "Tell me what you did to get me here."

"Nothing. None of that matters. I was—"

I interrupted her. "Yes, it does. You owe me the truth after everything we've been through."

She cleared her throat, eyes still downcast. "I'm sorry, Kate. I really am. It was a long time ago. You need to remember that. A different lifetime ago, really."

I wanted to shake her. Yes, yes, it was, and it was a lifetime where I had a family. One with a husband who adored me, who never would dream of hurting another human being, and there was a possibility I'd been tricked into leaving him? And a daughter who used to follow me around the same way Miles followed Abner.

I tried to keep my voice calm. She'd shut down if I got hysterical and drew attention to us. "It might have been a different lifetime ago, but it was my life, and I want to know what happened."

She let out a sigh. "We wanted to see if someone would leave their earthly family for us."

"But people left their family for Love International all the time."

"Yes, but we wanted it to be an amazing family they left behind." She lowered her voice, like it would lessen the impact of her words. "We wanted to see if what we had was powerful enough to make someone give up the love they had for something greater."

I couldn't process the truth. It was too big. How could they do that? How could they justify toying with people's lives like that?

Margo's face reflected my pain. "I'm sorry, Kate. It still makes your experience real. Nothing changes that. Nothing. We were never allowed to do anything once they were in the door. Our only influence was on getting the chosen ones there."

Calling me a chosen one didn't make the betrayal any less real. Tears slid down my cheeks, and I quickly brushed them away with my sleeve. "So all of this has been a game to you guys?"

She reached into my bowl and took both my hands in hers. "No, Kate. Every decision you made from the moment you walked through Love International's door was your own."

But I never would've walked through the doors if they hadn't called my boss and requested the interview. It tainted everything that followed. I jerked my hands out of the bowl. "I don't feel well. Find someone else to cover for me," I said and hurried back to my tent before the sobs overtook me.

THIRTY-TWO

MEREDITH

NOW

Kate hadn't been in her room when Scott had gone to check on her. She'd gone back downstairs to make coffee, and I couldn't help but follow him down there. I hated myself for doing it, but I wanted to see what he would say to her.

"Morning, Kate. Where's Shiloh?" he asked when he noticed she was alone. It was rare for her not to be wearing Shiloh strapped to her chest in a wrap.

"Upstairs sleeping," Kate said while she poured creamer into her coffee. She'd told them coffee was one of the things she had missed the most while she was away.

"Meredith just filled me in on what happened this morning," Scott announced, surprising me with his directness.

She turned to Scott, her back to me. "Meredith thinks I'm making phone calls while all of you are asleep."

"It's no big deal if you have been, you know. I mean, you can talk to whoever you want. It's not like we're your parents or something. You're not going to get grounded." He let out a nervous laugh.

She smiled. "I know that, but I haven't been talking to anyone. I don't have anyone to call."

"I know. I just, well, you know . . ." He shrugged. "Trying to keep the peace."

"She's lying, Scott. I caught her twice," I said. "And even if I hadn't caught her, I have the phone records to prove it."

"The records don't say who made the call. Anyone could have been on the phone," Kate said.

"Yes, except that I caught you."

"I'm sorry, Meredith, but even if I was talking to somebody, it wouldn't be your business."

"It's called keeping secrets," I said. "And we don't keep secrets in this house."

"Are you sure about that?" she asked.

"Of course I'm sure about that."

"I'm not the only one in the room with secrets." She shot Scott a pointed look.

"What's she talking about?" I asked, turning to Scott.

"Kate, don't," he begged.

The room spun.

"What's she talking about?" I could barely breathe.

"Ask him what we argued about on the day I left," Kate said.

Scott had never said they'd argued. That wasn't how the story went. And then I remembered what he'd said the other night before bed—how he'd hinted that I didn't know the full story. Waves of fear rocked my insides.

KATE

THEN

Margo spotted me coming out of the outhouse and made a beeline for me. I'd been avoiding her since yesterday, but it was only a matter of time before she cornered me, since there was nowhere to hide. She grabbed my arm, fingers digging into me, and pulled me to the other side of the outhouse.

"Did you tell him what I told you?" Her eyes darted around, watching the camp at the same time she spoke.

I jerked my arm away. "Of course not."

Abner grew more unraveled every day, and there was no telling what he'd do if he found out she'd told me their secrets. I'd be rewarded for calling out a dissenter—that was what he labeled anyone who kept a secret or went against what he said—but there'd be a reckoning for Margo. I couldn't do that to her, even if she had hurt me.

"Please, Kate, you can't stay mad at me. You have to understand that I thought I was doing the right thing. You know what it's like. You have to. Don't pretend you don't understand what it's like in the beginning. I would've done anything." Her eyes pleaded with mine for understanding. "But things are different now. Everything's changed."

A twig snapped, making both of us jump. We quickly stepped in line back toward camp. Too much time away from camp was unacceptable. She held on to my arm as we walked. "I'm sorry, Kate—please forgive me. I'm so sorry I got you into this mess. I'm sorry I got everyone involved." She was seconds away from crying.

"Stop it, okay. We're fine. Just stop. We're almost back to camp, and everyone's back there waiting on the gathering," I whispered. Margo straightened up immediately.

Abner had announced at breakfast that he wanted to have a midafternoon gathering. We rarely had middle-of-the-day meetings, since afternoons were reserved for chores, so whatever it was had to be important. We hurried underneath the tent, where everyone was waiting on him, and we took seats next to each other on one of the blankets.

It wasn't long before Abner stepped out of his tent and made his way to us. He strutted to the center of the circle, wasting no time in getting started. "As the outsiders discover how broken their world is, they are going to come searching for ours. They are going to want to steal what we have and make it their own. We must be ready for that time." He grew more and more paranoid each day about people finding out where we were before we had our army assembled. "And family, we are not ready. Not even close."

Six children weren't enough for an army. All our discussions lately had focused on procreating, but nobody had been successful. I didn't know if I could stomach another lecture on how important it was to channel our sexual energy into a shared purpose, but I couldn't tolerate much of anything lately, and I didn't know how I'd manage to keep fooling everyone after Margo's disclosure. I'd had dark periods of my soul, but this one wasn't leaving.

Abner's voice interrupted my thoughts, and I forced myself to pay attention. "We've been living bound by the agreements we made while we lived in the fallen world. Marriage is a man-made construct and a tie binding us to our former identities. We haven't been successful in procreation because we are still holding on to those ties. It's time to break the chains and leave it all behind."

The married couples stood next to each other. Their children curled around their legs tighter, because, despite how hard we all worked with the children, they still ran to their parents at night.

"How does any of this work?" Malachi asked the question we'd all been thinking.

"However it chooses to. There are no rules. That's the point. No constraints. No boundaries. The lines of separation between us no longer exist. We are free to procreate as God intended. Whenever and with whomever we feel."

Malachi cleared his throat uncomfortably. "I mean, that would mean you could have sex with my wife if you wanted to."

Abner nodded. "If she chose to." He pointed to the other men in the group. "Or she might choose to have sex with one of them."

The color drained from Malachi's face.

"But we don't have to sleep with anyone else unless we want to, right?" his wife, Gilly, asked, gripping his arm and moving closer to him.

"Of course not. No one is ever forced to do anything they aren't called to do. From now on, people are free to couple with whomever they choose." Abner's face beamed with purpose and light. "I will do my part as well. I will begin lying with our maidens to see if my fruit might create a soldier. This is how we will build this army."

THIRTY-THREE

MEREDITH

NOW

"If you'll just excuse me, I'm going to head to my room," Kate said, inching her way past us and moving upstairs. Scott looked like he'd been sucker punched in the gut. He leaned against the kitchen counter for support.

"What happened the morning Kate left?" Her words had done what she'd intended them to do—flipped my world upside down.

"You have to look at it from my perspective before you jump to any conclusions."

Oh my God, so he had lied. Scott had lied. I couldn't believe it. "She's not lying?"

He shook his head. "You have to understand—"

I cut him off. "I don't have to understand anything. I just want to know the truth. You owe me that, at least. All this time you've been on me about how important it is to build trust and safety for her, and you've been lying." I tried to keep from sounding hysterical, but I was teetering on the edge. "What happened?"

"I knew I hadn't been involved in Kate's disappearance, but I wasn't an idiot. I knew I was going to be their number one suspect. The husband always is. You know that as well as I do, and if I had told them that we argued that morning, it would only have increased their suspicion. They would've spent even more time investigating me when the real bad guy was out there with Kate. So I made a decision to lie, but I also knew that in order for it to be effective, no one could ever know the truth. I never told anyone. Not even Abbi."

"Why didn't you tell me once you trusted me?"

"Once you've told a story so many times, it just becomes the truth."

"But you passed the polygraph . . ." My voice trailed off, thick with unspoken meaning. He had passed the polygraph with flying colors; only seasoned liars could pull that off.

"And I want you to know that it's not even all that horrible, what happened. Regular married stuff."

"That you lied about for eleven years?" My patience had reached its limit. "Tell me what happened, and I'll decide how horrible it is."

Red flooded his face. "I practically forced Kate to quit her job and stay home with Abbi. She was never really set on the idea, and part of the reason was because she didn't want to give up her income. I convinced her we'd be fine, and for a while we were, but then everything crashed in 2008. You remember what it was like. This is so embarrassing." He cracked his knuckles like he did whenever he got nervous. "Commercial real estate tanked."

I waited for him to go on and explain himself, but he just stood there without saying anything. "And?"

He refused to meet my eyes. "Things got pretty bad for us financially, and I never told her about any of it."

"That was all it was?"

"And I took out a loan and second mortgage on our house without telling her." His sheepish look reminded me of my boys whenever they got in trouble when they were young.

"Kate found out?"

"Yes, the night before she went missing. It was so weird because I'd expected her to be angry with me, but she just kept saying how disappointed she was in me. That made it worse. Instead of manning up and admitting what I'd done, I acted like a complete idiot instead. Total ego bullshit."

"Why couldn't you tell the police exactly what you told me?"

"Come on, Meredith. For someone who is always accusing me of being naive, that seems pretty naive to me. 'Hey, Officers, I just wanted you to know that my wife and I got into a fight on the morning she disappeared over me being in massive debt and lying to her about it.' Any version of the story that included an argument was a no-win situation."

"Still, you could've told me. You should've told me," I added for emphasis.

He raised his eyebrows. "Really? Like you told me everything about you and James?"

THIRTY-FOUR

ABBI

NOW

I hadn't been at Meaghan's since we found out about Mom. We'd been best friends since second grade, and this was the longest we'd ever been apart. Her room was as familiar to me as my own—the queen-size bed in the middle covered with the quilt her grandmother made for her when she was a baby; her favorite teddy bear tucked underneath her pillow, a secret I'd kept since middle school; the pink wall I helped her paint; and the closet filled with half my clothes, which she'd borrowed over the last few years. But it all felt unfamiliar and surreal. Even Meaghan looked different, younger somehow. Or maybe I'd grown up overnight, crossed over some line that once you were over, you didn't ever get to go back.

Dad had forced me to come even though I'd wanted to stay home. He had insisted that I get out of the house so I'd feel like a normal kid again, but I was pretty sure it was so he and Meredith could fight in private. Things were so tense between them ever since Meredith accused Mom of lying. I was doing my best to stay out of it. If Mom wanted to tell me who she was talking to, then she would. If not, then that was okay too. It was her choice.

"You wouldn't believe what Sophie said to Josiah after football practice today. So ridiculous." Meaghan had been prattling on for what felt like hours, and normally I would've joined in, but it seemed wrong to talk about football games and homecoming when there were so many other important things going on. "Have you picked out your dress for the dance yet?"

"I forgot all about it. Things have been pretty crazy around my house," I said.

"Yeah, I bet," she said, shifting in her spot on the couch and grabbing her phone off the coffee table in front of her. "Kayla texted they're on their way. Finally."

We'd been lounging in their rec room for the last hour waiting on Kayla and Brynn. We were going to give each other pedicures while we watched a movie. The hours stretched out endlessly in front of me. I'd been obsessively checking the forum, but no one had answered back. I didn't want to be here when they did. Not that I could do anything different at my house, but I really wanted to be there even if things were a mess.

"Can I talk to you for a second?" Meredith asked when I got home the next morning. I'd been the first one to go to sleep last night and had sneaked out early before anyone else got up, eager to get home and check on things with Mom.

"What's up?" I asked, setting my backpack down in the entryway.

"I just wanted to talk to you about everything that's been going on lately and see how you were feeling. Answer any questions you might have."

I peeked behind her, scanning the living room and kitchen. "Is Dad here?"

"No."

We didn't have heart-to-hearts without Dad. She'd tried that when they'd first started dating, because she had probably read it in one of her self-help books or her therapist had suggested it. Either way, she had been convinced we needed to go on individual dates to get to know each other. We had gone to the zoo a bunch of times, and we had walked through the botanical gardens over on Mulberry. Sometimes we had gone out for ice cream. But it had never mattered where we went or what we did; things had never stopped feeling like we were on an awkward first date. Dad had balanced us out in a way we couldn't do ourselves when he wasn't around. She had been more relieved than anything when we'd stopped doing them, even though she had pretended to be hurt.

"Is he coming home soon?" I asked.

She shrugged, trying to look nonchalant. "He should be here in a little while."

"Do you want to text me when he's here?" I asked, bending down to scoop up my backpack and head upstairs.

"I thought the two of us could talk. He doesn't need to be here for this."

Alarm bells went off inside me as I followed her into the kitchen. She sat down at the window seat. "Have you and your mother still been hanging out at night?"

I nodded.

"What do you guys do in there?"

I shrugged. "Hang out. Talk. Nothing really."

"What kinds of things do you talk about?"

She tried to ask it like she didn't care, but Meredith was a terrible liar. Where was this going? Why did I feel like I was on trial?

"Stuff," I said, feeling more uncomfortable every second. Did she know I let Mom on my phone at night? I couldn't say no to her after I'd already let her do it once, so I didn't have a choice when she asked. Besides, she'd only had that weird reaction once. Now she just scrolled through the pictures for a few minutes and then handed it back to me.

"Has your mom talked to you about what it was like when she was away?"

I cocked my head to the side. "Why are you asking so many questions?"

"Oh, no reason. I'm just trying to get a handle on things. See if there's anything I can do to help."

None of her questions seemed helpful, just nosy. Meredith grew more paranoid every day. I'd be acting the same way if I were her, though. I mean, Dad's old wife was back. Everyone knew what that meant. Dad would still be married to Mom if she hadn't disappeared. He'd still be pining over her if the rest of us, including myself, hadn't pushed him to move on. I was surprised Meredith was keeping it together at all. I'd be a mess. Still, I wanted her to leave me alone. I didn't like the way she'd asked the questions, like I was involved in some elaborate conspiracy with Mom. Conspiring to do what, I didn't know, but that was how it felt.

"I think we're good," I said. "Are we done now, Meredith?"

"Honey, I'm only trying to look out for you. I just want you to be careful." She moved to hug me, and I stepped aside.

"Be careful? I don't need to be careful—she's my mom."

KATE

THEN

I ducked my head and tried to sneak back to my tent without anyone seeing me, like the family didn't already know we were sleeping together.

None of Abner's maiden selections were a secret. He announced them each night after the fire gathering. I hadn't expected him to get to me so soon, and I'd almost thrown up the first night he'd picked me. The thought of him touching me curdled my insides, and my body trembled as we walked from the campfire to his tent. But then he showed me a side of himself I'd never seen, and I couldn't help but soften a little.

His voice was kind and gentle. We sat almost knee to knee, like we'd done in one of our first meetings together, slipping between silence and conversation. He never even tried to touch me, and there was a tiny part of me slightly insulted by it and wondering if there was something wrong with me. I was surprised when he kept calling my name, and then a few nights ago he asked if I wanted a massage, and I gave in despite myself. His touch was so tender I almost cried. I couldn't remember the last time anyone had touched me in a way that wasn't clinical or part of an exercise. The same thing happened the following night, but his touch changed at the end of the massage, and my pulse dropped in a way it hadn't in a long time. I'd forgotten what it felt like to feel like a woman.

And I hated myself for liking it, but my body had been awakened, and I had to have more. He was a different man in the tent at night. It was like nothing else existed. Not time. Not space. Just the two of us joined together as one in a celestial space unlike any I'd ever experienced.

But today was different. It wasn't nighttime. We weren't going to bed. It was two in the afternoon. That changed everything.

I tried to keep a straight face as I came out of the bathroom, but I had just thrown up all my oatmeal from breakfast, and the only other time I'd thrown up in the morning had been when I was pregnant with my daughter from my previous life. My body recognized the feelings immediately. I couldn't believe I was the first one.

I had no idea what year it was, so many years since we'd recognized time, but late forties and pregnant? How was that possible? You were supposed to be less fertile the older you were. I'd secretly wondered if Abner's fertility might be responsible for how long it was taking him to get anyone pregnant, but everything must have still worked fine.

I refused to make eye contact with Margo as I filed in to help clear away breakfast dishes with the others. She'd take one look at me and know something was going on. I had to tell Abner first. He had left before dawn with a few of the guys to clear a field over on the north side of the property, and they probably wouldn't be back until after it was dark. How was I going to keep something like this a secret all day?

Maybe this was exactly what we needed to help lift the spirits around camp. As Abner got more and more frustrated with the lack of new children, his intolerance for our failures grew every day. The spirit around camp grew heavier and darker with all these drills and exercises. He was convinced that the outsiders would come upon us unexpectedly, and we'd be unprepared for their attacks. It was this unpreparedness that drove him mad like none other.

I flexed the muscles in my arms instinctively and felt the tight string pull back. All his calisthenics were working. I was in the best shape of my life, but all that was about to change, because there was no way he'd make me still participate in all the physical activities and other drills. Everything was going to change with this new life inside me, and as proud as I should've been about being chosen to carry his seed, I couldn't shake the fear creeping in around the edges.

THIRTY-FIVE

ABBI

NOW

I waited to go back downstairs until Mom and Dad were down there, because I wasn't about to get cornered by Meredith again, but she was so busy cooking breakfast that she didn't notice me as I joined everyone in the kitchen.

"Oh, you're here," Mom said as I slid into the seat next to her. "Good." She cleared her throat. Then cleared it again. "Can I talk to everyone?"

Dad sat across from us and set his phone down to give her his full attention. Meredith stopped what she was doing and came to stand behind his chair, still holding the spatula. Mom's legs shook underneath the table. I found her hand and took it in mine, giving it a squeeze. Whatever it was, we'd get through it. That was what families did.

"Thank you for everything you've done for me. I am so grateful." She kept her eyes focused on the syrup in the middle of the table while she spoke. "The thing is—I'm such a burden. I don't want to do that to your family—"

I interrupted her. "What are you talking about, Mom? You're our family."

"Thank you." Her eyes misted, and she struggled to keep it together. "But I've been thinking it might be time to find my own place to live so that you can have your lives back."

Dad reached across the table and took her other hand in his. "Stop talking like that. You're not any kind of a burden to us. We've never thought of you that way."

Mom smiled. "You're so kind, Scott." She raised her head and eyed Meredith. "But I know this has been hard." She quickly averted her gaze. "I want to start looking for another place to live." Her lower lip trembled. "And if it's okay with you, I'd like Abbi to come with me when I move out."

I shoved my chair back and jumped up. "Really?" Mom smiled and nodded. I threw my arms around her and gave her a huge hug. We'd never even talked about me living with her. I couldn't believe we were on the same page.

Dad was trying not to cry. He probably hadn't expected this any more than I had. I wished he could come with us. Meredith stepped in after a few minutes had passed, and he still hadn't responded.

"I understand where you're coming from and agree that it's probably time to think about what happens next," she said, nodding in Dad's direction like she hoped he'd jump in at any time, but he was content to let her talk. "I'm open to helping you in whatever way I can. So is Scott, of course. But I'm not sure how we feel about Abbi living with you right now."

"She can't live with me, Scott?" Mom's voice sounded like a little girl's.

He rubbed his forehead, struggling to find the right words. "I . . . um, I think we would have to be confident of a few things before that happened."

"Are you serious?" I slapped my hands on the table. "You would actually say I couldn't go? You'd keep me away from Mom?"

"Of course not," he said.

Meredith piped up. "That's not what we're saying at all. I don't think we've had time to consider any of the practical things about how something like that would work."

She stood next to him, holding his hand in solidarity, like the family therapist had suggested. I didn't want to talk about this with her. This was between Dad, Mom, and me, anyway.

"There are lots of things you would need to think about before making such a huge decision. It's stuff you probably haven't even thought of, because you're so young, but living on your own can be very difficult," she said.

"I wouldn't be living on my own. I'd be living with Mom," I said in my snottiest voice.

She glanced at Dad, then back to me. "Right," she said slowly.

"It's okay, Abbi," Mom said, grabbing my arm and trying to get me to sit back down.

I refused. Meredith wouldn't ruin this for me because of whatever weird trust thing she had going on with Mom. "I'm not asking your permission, Meredith. I'm asking my dad."

"Abigail!" He only used my full name when he was really upset. "Apologize to Meredith immediately."

Meredith tugged on his arm. "No, honey, it's fine. Really it is."

"No, it isn't. That's unacceptable, and she knows it."

"I'm not trying to be mean. I'm just telling the truth, and you know it." Tears flowed down my face. I always cried when I was angry. I hated it. "This is between us. Why does she get a say in where I live? She's not my mom."

He pointed to the stairs. "Go to your room now."

I couldn't remember the last time he'd sent me to my room. I shook my head, refusing to go. "You can't treat me like I'm a kid. I'm sixteen years old, and I'm living with Mom when she moves out."

THIRTY-SIX

MEREDITH

NOW

The three of us sat unmoving in the kitchen after Abbi had stormed upstairs. My head was pounding with a headache, and it wasn't even seven o'clock yet. There was nothing that sounded better than hunkering down with Scott, but Kate wasn't stable enough to take care of Abbi, and the mother in me wouldn't do that to her, no matter how much it might serve me.

It wasn't a coincidence that she'd announced leaving the morning after I'd caught her in a lie again. She might be able to lie to everyone else, but she and I knew the truth, no matter how she played it off to the others. Besides the fact that you couldn't trust her, she was nowhere near being functional enough to be a single mom raising two kids.

"Kate, I really don't think you should leave," Scott said. He slid into Abbi's chair and pulled it up alongside her. "Things are weird right now, and it might be that way for a while, but eventually we're going to figure out how to do this thing. We should give it at least a few more months before we make any decisions, and if we still are having a hard time, then maybe we could even go see our family therapist." He turned to me as he spoke. "Think about how amazing Dr. Greer was when we were getting married, Meredith. She loves complicated blended families. This would be right up her alley."

"Live here? All of us?" Kate asked.

"Yes, sweetheart. We can figure this out," he said, pulling her close to him. She melted into his chest. He glanced up at me with a huge smile on his face, so proud at having worked it out.

I was too shocked to say anything—their bodies fit together seamlessly—so instead I just nodded at him and smiled back like I agreed, while my insides screamed at what he was suggesting. I didn't want to be married to Kate too. A sob worked its way up my throat, and I choked it back down. But then he'd have to choose, and there was no way I could compete with what I saw in front of me. Nobody could.

KATE

THEN

I cuddled her next to my naked chest, breathing in the smell of hair. We'd named her Shiloh. Her name meant *his gift* and fit her perfectly. She was perfect. Everything about her. I'd been so nervous for labor after what had happened with Bekah, but I had kept telling myself that my body would remember what to do, since it'd done it before. It had been the most excruciating pain of my life, but I couldn't even remember the feelings as she lay resting on top of me, exhausted from her trip to earth.

Margo threw back the canvas of the birthing tent and poked her head in. She tried to move through without getting stuck, but the awkwardness of her eight-month-old belly made it difficult, and we burst out laughing at how ridiculous she looked. Her turn was coming soon.

It had taken her a long time to adjust to her pregnancy, since she hadn't wanted to lie with Abner. She'd denied his initial requests three different times, committed to Will. But then one morning she surprised us all by announcing she'd changed her mind. She told me privately later that Will had asked her to, saying God had told him to allow it. They'd only done it that one time. But that was all it had taken. For a while, we had wondered if it might be Will's, but they had confessed to practicing abstinence within their partnership. They had said it helped them focus on the spiritual and not get distracted by the carnal pleasures of the flesh.

She'd been with me since the first pangs of labor and had held my other leg while I had pushed. Even though she'd never had a child of her own, she had been guided by unbelievable maternal intuition and our experience with Bekah. I'd focused on her and drawn from her inner strength to get me through. She'd only stepped out to go to the bathroom after she'd helped clean us up. Abner had followed her. He'd sat outside the tent while I labored, preferring to be in deep meditation. His face broke into a wide grin at the sight of us.

"There you are. My two beautiful brides," he said.

Margo spun around. "What did you say?" she asked, wide eyed.

He grinned again, the mischievous grin of a little boy in his eyes. "My brides." He pointed to her and then me. "That's the surprise I've been telling you about."

Nobody ever talked about marriage anymore. Besides Margo and Will, everyone was mixed up, and it was tough to remember who went with who. It didn't matter anymore. What was he suggesting?

Margo looked back at me, searching my eyes for answers, and I shrugged. He'd never said anything to me and clearly not to her either. She stepped back so he could come farther into the tent, coming to kneel next to my bed. She held her hand on her back. I could tell by the way her face was stretched thin that it'd been a difficult pain day for her. I turned my attention back to Abner. It didn't matter what he had to say—nothing could ruin this day for me.

Everything I'd gone through on this journey. All the toil and sweat. The sacrifices. They'd all been worth it after I laid eyes on Shiloh's sweet face.

I made myself focus on what he was saying as he rambled on about how we had created the first of the Lord's children. "My seed created these children because of the Lord's will. It is his life that came through me and into you, much like the way the Holy Spirit moved through the Virgin Mary. So I moved through you and will continue to move through you until our numbers are as vast as Abraham's." He spread his arms out wide, his face beaming with purpose and light. "After Margo has brought the next soldier into the world, we will have our ceremony. I will inform the family at the fire gathering tonight."

"Wonderful," I said as Shiloh stirred and searched for my breast, just like she'd done after she was born. I breathed a sigh of relief that she nursed easily.

"Margo?" Abner prompted.

"What about Will?" she asked.

"Will ceased being your husband a long time ago. You are aware of how we broke those earthly covenants."

I wished I could shield Shiloh from the negative energy shifting between them. She didn't need to be affected with any darkness so close to having left the light. I swore I could still see parts of it when I looked into her eyes as she nursed. She'd only opened them twice, but I'd been right there for each one.

"I just meant, you know, is he okay with this?"

"Margo, he is a servant of the Lord."

Neither of them spoke. The silence stretched out until Margo's voice finally cut into it. "That's wonderful, Abner. I'm very excited to be your wife."

I didn't need to look up to know he was smiling. "I'll be back again after fire gathering," he said.

Margo waited until he'd left the tent before she began crying softly.

THIRTY-SEVEN

MEREDITH

NOW

I'd barely been able to keep it together until after Thad's wife left us alone in the den and had been crying ever since. It'd been three days since Kate announced she was thinking about moving out, and so far Scott and I still weren't talking about his offer to let her stay indefinitely.

"Mom, you've got to talk to him. He can't start making permanent plans—especially ones that include his first wife becoming like a second wife—without knowing how you really feel about it."

"Am I overreacting?" I asked. Caleb would protect my feelings, but Thad would tell me the truth no matter what. He'd been a ruthless teenager.

"Absolutely not." He vehemently shook his head. "It's almost got a weird sister-wives feel to it."

Relief washed over me. "You have no idea how glad I am to hear you say that. I wish you could have seen how he looked at me while he was comforting her the other day. It wasn't like it was sexual or anything." I blushed despite thirty years of frankness about sex. "It was more like he was waiting for me to join them in the hug because we were truly one big happy family, or that's what he thinks we should try to be in the future." I grabbed the Kleenex he'd handed me earlier and blew my nose. "Maybe I should be the one to move out."

"What? No, Mom."

"When we got the call about Kate, we didn't have time to think or process anything. All we did was react. But if I had thought about it at all beforehand, I might have offered to leave while they worked things out. They deserve to have the time and space to figure things out as a family."

"Work things out as a family?" His brown eyes flashed with anger. "Mom, you're part of the family."

"I know that, honey, but it doesn't change the fact that they have a lot of stuff they need to figure out. It might make things easier for everyone if I go for a while." I said it with much more confidence and optimism than I felt. I couldn't help but remember how Scott had said something almost identical to Kate the other night, and he'd begged her to stay. Would he do the same for me if I said I wanted to leave?

Thad shifted gears, since we'd already been down this path more than once already. "What's it like having a baby around again after all these years?"

"Honestly, not that big of a difference, because nobody gets to interact with the baby except Kate and Abbi."

"At least she lets Abbi."

"Yeah, I guess, but I'm cooking her meals and shuttling her back and forth to appointments, so you'd think I'd at least be able to hold the baby every now and then." I quickly slapped my hand over my mouth as soon as I'd said it. "I'm sorry. All of this is making me ugly, and I don't like it."

Thad burst out laughing. "Oh my gosh, Mom. Give yourself a break. That's the worst thing you have to say about all this? Please." He waved his hand at me, and I couldn't help but smile. "How about Abbi? What does she think about all this?" he asked.

"Things are always bumpy with her. You know that. She's getting angry with me and siding with Kate more and more, but I think that would've happened no matter what the circumstances."

"Do you want me to talk to her?"

"You're so sweet, but no." There wasn't anything more to talk about with Abbi. She wasn't the one who made the final decision about our living arrangements. That conversation had to be with Scott, and I was dreading it, because there was no way to have it without looking like the evil stepmother.

———

Scott was mowing the front yard when I got home, which wasn't a good sign, since he only mowed when he was stressed. Usually he hated it, which was why we had a gardener. He stopped in his tracks as I came up the walk.

"How's Thad?" he asked.

"Good. He's swamped with work, but that's pretty much how it's going to be until he gets the promotion he wants," I said. Even our small talk felt forced. It was going to be that way until we cleared the air. "Do you think you could turn that thing off so we could talk?"

"Sure," he said, flicking off the switch and bringing the roaring to a stop. "What do you want to talk about?"

I did my best to sound loving and kind with my words. "Scott, Kate can't keep living with us. You know that, right?"

"Why not?"

"She's your . . . old wife? First wife? I don't even know what to call her." My heart sank. "You still think about her that way. And it's okay. I understand why. But I can't live in a situation where you have two wives, and that's what it'd be like if we all lived together in the same house."

"It's not about her being my wife." He let my hand go, his pleasant demeanor gone that quickly. "You always want to make it about her being my wife."

"You're the one who called her that, not me," I snapped. There wasn't any way to have this conversation without bringing up the night he called her his wife.

He started walking across the lawn, heading toward the sidewalk. "You're something, you know that?" he said.

I forced myself to calm down as I tried to keep up with him. One of us had to stay rational. "What's it about, then?"

"We're the only family she has. She's got nobody, Meredith."

I hated to be the one to come out and say it, but it was time—it had to be said. "Scott, she left you guys. No matter what the reason or how it's framed, she left you and Abbi. Take a minute and remember everything she put you through for all those years. I remember what it was like for you back then. And now she expects you to help put her life back together again because she's in trouble? That doesn't seem selfish to you at all? Not even a little?"

He stopped dead in his tracks. "I had no idea you could be this jealous."

I whirled around to face him. "I'm not jealous. All I'm doing is saying out loud what everyone else is afraid to tell you. Somebody has to. Thad and Caleb think it's horribly selfish too."

He snorted in disgust. "I'm sure they do. Your boys would say she had a horn growing out of her forehead if you told them to."

"Now you're just being a jerk," I said. "And for no reason. All I'm trying to do is have a conversation with you."

"Oh, is that what we're doing?" He smirked at me. "Well, then, in my case, this conversation is over." He turned around and headed back in the direction of the house. I didn't bother to catch up with him this time.

KATE

THEN

"Abner, no, please, you can't be serious. You can't." I fell on my knees at his feet, my face drenched in tears. Our marriage ceremony was complete. He'd draped Margo's head and mine with a dirty white veil and spoken scripture over us before slipping into his new prayer language. It was a secret language between him and God. The wedding wasn't bringing me to tears. It was what he'd told us after that shook me to my core—our babies would stay with us until they were weaned, at which point Abner planned to take them on a soul journey with him, where they would be surrounded by nothing but the light and administered to by the Lord. He wouldn't say how long he would have them or where he was going. He wouldn't even say when. Only that it was happening.

He nestled Shiloh against his chest, trying to comfort her, but she wailed like she did each time he held her. "We voted on it last night, and it was a unanimous decision by the family."

I couldn't remember the last time we'd voted on anything. Those days were long gone. I turned to Margo. She whimpered in the corner, her baby boy cuddled underneath her chest. Zed. Born four days after Shiloh.

"Why?" I'd give anything, do anything, to prove I was worthy of his covenant. But not my baby. I wouldn't give him my baby. Anything but that.

"We can't question his plans. You know that, dear." Shiloh's face was furiously red while she screamed in his arms.

My milk spilled out of me at the sound of her, drenching the front of my dress in no time. "Please give her back to me. Let me hold my baby," I begged him, beyond caring how desperate I sounded.

"She's not your baby. This is the Lord's baby." He stared at me pointedly.

I reached my hands out. "Please, she's hungry. I need to feed her."

He handed her back to me, and I couldn't help but weep. What would I have done if he hadn't given her back? I pulled her to my breast immediately. Three weeks old today, but it was like life never existed before her. I couldn't imagine a life without her in it.

Margo's eyes searched mine, her mind still twisted from her difficult labor. Hers hadn't gone well. Her pale face let me know she was still losing lots of blood. This would throw her off even more. She was too weak to handle this. I couldn't lose her. Not again.

"We knew God was going to require a sacrifice in order for my brides to wed me. Both of you were prepared." His words dropped like lead in our tent.

"Abner, please no." Margo begged from her spot in the corner. She was too exhausted to move.

"It is not up to me. You know that." He eyed both of us before exiting the tent.

"Please, we have to think of something. We have to," Margo cried as soon as we knew he was out of earshot.

"There's nothing we can do. You know that."

Shiloh startled on my chest, and I moved her to the other breast. The contact grounded me. She was my light, my love.

Margo frantically shook her head, her face wet with tears and contorted in pain. "What if we left?"

The world rolled underneath me.

THIRTY-EIGHT

ABBI

NOW

I trailed after Mom into one of the apartments on her list. Dean had helped her apply for something called a Sacred Heart grant, which paid the first month's deposit and rent for homeless people. It was weird hearing her referred to as a homeless person, but I guess it was true. I'd researched the organization, and it was a tough grant to get. Dean was probably going to have to pull some strings for her. Ever since she had announced that she was moving out, she'd spent almost all her time searching for apartments, and she'd made an appointment as soon as she'd gotten the list from him, like she couldn't get out of our house fast enough.

The apartment door opened into the living room. There was an area to the right of the living room that was supposed to be a bedroom, but it looked more like a large walk-in closet, and there was barely enough space for a bed. The living room was split into a small galley kitchen that led to the bathroom. There was only a shower—no tub.

"What do you think?" Mom asked.

"It's definitely got potential," I said, not wanting to hurt her feelings.

It was small—so much smaller than I'd expected. Most hotel rooms were bigger.

She pointed to the bedroom. "The bedroom is all yours. Every teenage girl needs their privacy." There wasn't even a door on the bedroom. We would have to hang a curtain or something. I had to remember to look on Pinterest for ideas.

Mom reached over and pulled me close to her, squeezing me tightly. "I'm so glad you're coming with me."

"Me too," I said, even though I had no idea how that was going to work. I hadn't talked to Dad about it since she'd brought it up, and they'd told me no. I had been thinking about bringing it up last night, but he and Meredith had gotten into a huge fight outside yesterday, and there had been no way I was going to do it when he was in a bad mood.

He didn't know we were here. I'd told him Mom and I were going to stop at the grocery store on our way back from her appointment with Camille. I hated lying to him, but I didn't want to risk him not letting me go. Still, it didn't feel right. Maybe they'd see Mom was responsible if she got this apartment and set everything up herself. It might help them change their minds about her being able to take care of me. That's what I kept telling myself to justify lying to Dad, anyway.

———

Angry voices from downstairs broke into my homework session. I pulled my earbuds out and rushed down to see what was happening. Mom, Dad, and Meredith were in the kitchen arguing again.

"That's going too far. You crossed a line," Mom was shouting at Meredith.

Mom had never raised her voice before. What was going on? I was getting really sick of all the fighting.

"I crossed a line?" Meredith pointed to a camera sitting on the dining room table. I'd never seen it before. "After everything you've been through, this is the thing that offends you?"

"Yes." Mom's lips were set in a straight line. "You never asked my permission."

"I wouldn't have had to ask you for anything if you'd told the truth when I asked you, but we all know you weren't telling the truth, were you?" Meredith stood unmoving next to the table, facing Mom head on. Dad looked back and forth between them, like he wasn't quite sure what he was supposed to do or whose side he was supposed to take.

"What's going on?" I demanded, interrupting them.

Everyone froze at the sight of me. Finally, Mom stepped back, and Meredith lowered her arm. Dad stayed rooted in his spot between them, his arms extended to hold them apart.

"Meredith has been recording us in the kitchen," Mom said.

I balked. "You've been recording us? How?" Meredith was one of the least tech-savvy people I knew.

Dad spoke without turning around to look at me. "Abbi, honey, I know this must look really confusing, but I'm going to ask you to just go back upstairs and try to get some work done. We can talk about this later."

I put my hands on my hips. "I'm not going anywhere. Not until I know what's going on."

Meredith took a step in my direction. "I think your dad is right. It's probably best that you let us talk this one out alone." She glanced in the direction of the stairs behind me. "Besides, if Shiloh wakes up, you can take care of her for your mom."

I shook my head. There was no way I was leaving.

Mom spoke up. "I'm okay if she stays."

Meredith whipped around to face her again. "You're okay if she stays?" She couldn't hide her annoyance.

"I don't keep secrets from Abbi." She gave me a tentative smile. I smiled back. I wanted our relationship to be built on the truth too. No lies.

"So two against two unless you've changed your mind, Dad?" I asked.

"Fine," he said, but he didn't look happy.

"What's going on?" I asked, giving him all my attention and blocking out the others.

He refused to look at Meredith while he spoke. "You know the arguments that your mom and Meredith have been having over the phone calls, right?"

Was that what this was about? Why couldn't Meredith just leave it alone? I nodded.

"Meredith decided that she would record your mom talking on the phone, and your mom just discovered the camera."

"I stand by what I did," Meredith said. "She didn't give me any choice."

"How'd you record it?" I asked.

"I ordered the camera I use for the birds in the backyard and hooked it up the same way." She pointed to the top of the refrigerator. "Then I put it up there."

"You've been recording all of us?" I asked. My mind flitted through anything that had happened in the kitchen in the last few days. I had nothing to hide, but I felt slightly violated at the idea of Meredith watching me when I didn't know. There was definitely something wrong about it.

Meredith turned to Dad, bypassing me altogether this time. "It's been up there for two days, and I just reviewed the video from last night, and guess who snuck down to the kitchen to make another midnight phone call?"

"I can't believe you would invade my privacy like that," Mom cried.

"Your privacy? You're in our house. We have a right to know what is going on underneath our roof."

I turned to Dad. Every part of his body tensed with anger.

"I don't even recognize you anymore," he said to Meredith, shaking his head in disgust.

"Me?" Meredith yelled. "Why is everyone mad at me for this? She's a liar!"

Dad stepped closer to her. The veins in his neck popped out, and his voice shook with anger. "We are supposed—"

"No. No. No." Mom moved around Meredith and stepped between them. "Look, stop. Just stop." She held her hands up in front of Dad, just like he'd done a few seconds ago to her and Meredith. "We're not going to do this. Not this. I'll go. It's time."

"What? No, you can't do that," Dad said. His anger was immediately gone and replaced with concern.

"It's what's best for everyone." Her eyes filled with tears.

Dad's voice cracked. "Where will you go?"

"I'll stay in a hotel until an apartment opens. I—"

I jumped up before she finished her sentence and raced upstairs as fast as I could. I flung open my closet door and dug around for my duffel bag. I found it stuffed underneath a pile of empty shoeboxes. I flung it over my shoulder and headed back into my room, where I tossed in clothes before hurrying to the bathroom for my toothbrush and deodorant. I heard sounds in Mom's bedroom and hurried in there.

She was stuffing things in Shiloh's diaper bag, like I'd done with my things. She'd already folded the towels they'd used in the bathroom and placed them in a neat stack at the end of the bed.

"Where will you go? How are you going to get there?" Dad was circling around her as she packed. He kept reaching out his arms like he wanted to stop her and then quickly pulling them back.

"I'll find something," she said. There was no fight left in her voice.

"At least let me give you some money," Dad said. He turned to leave so he could go back downstairs to get his wallet and noticed me standing in the doorway with my bag slung over my shoulder. "Where do you think you're going?" he demanded.

"I'm going with Mom."

"Absolutely not," he said, shaking his head.

"I'm not asking your permission." I reached down and grabbed one of her bags lying on the floor. "Come on, Mom. Let's go."

THIRTY-NINE
MEREDITH

NOW

It'd been over two hours, and Scott still wasn't back. He'd insisted on driving the girls to their hotel and checking them in, but it couldn't have taken him this long. Not unless he'd driven them to another city, but there was no way he'd do that. He would never let Abbi stay so far away from him. I couldn't believe he'd let her go with Kate. Her heart was set on it, but he should have put his foot down.

He was probably driving around trying to calm down. He might not be so upset if he'd watched the video, but he had refused to look at the screen even when I shoved my phone in his face. I'd gotten the idea to record her when Dean had mentioned something about the videos they'd reviewed earlier that day, and I had planned to analyze her phone calls in the same way they'd analyzed the footage of her mumbled pacing. I cared about what she was doing at night, even if nobody else did. The audio was terrible and the video fuzzy—nothing like the high-tech gear the FBI had used—but she had unmistakably been talking to someone.

I kept thinking Scott would change his mind about blindly trusting her if he saw it with his own eyes. He needed to see how Kate had sneaked downstairs twice to make sure I wasn't following her before making her call. The second time she'd hidden behind the wall in the living room for over thirty minutes, staring at the foot of the stairs. There was no doubt that she had been waiting to see if I would come downstairs behind her. It wasn't until she was convinced she hadn't been followed that she had tiptoed into the kitchen and picked up the receiver. She had quickly punched in the number and had spoken with her hand cupping the receiver in hurried whispers for several minutes, her eyes never leaving the doorway to the kitchen.

Who was I kidding? It wouldn't matter what was on the video. Nothing would change how he felt about her. It'd been almost a month, and we had never had a conversation about how this would affect our relationship. Not once. He hadn't asked how I was doing or what I was feeling. Not a single compassionate comment hinting that he'd thought of how difficult it might be for me during all this. If proving that she was lying and sneaking around our house at night wouldn't change his perception of her, then nothing would. That much I knew for sure.

I was the replacement wife, and, like any good replacement wife, my time had come to an end. I had never stood a chance once Kate came back into the picture. My services were no longer needed. I wanted to collapse into a heap of tears on the kitchen floor, but I forced myself to get up. I couldn't be a mess when he got home. I had to hold on to my last shred of dignity.

I let out a deep breath and wiped away the mascara smeared underneath my eyes. What would I do without Scott? I willed my body to move. I'd been through crisis before. The key was to focus on what was directly in front of you at the time and do it. All I needed to do at the moment was pack a bag. I'd figure out the rest from my hotel room.

My luggage was in the garage, stacked next to the plastic containers of Christmas decorations and boxes of old photo albums. I grabbed a suitcase and headed back inside. I didn't notice Scott's car in the driveway and almost ran into him on the landing of the stairs.

"What are you doing?" he demanded, with his hands on his hips.

"What does it look like I'm doing?" I hadn't meant to sound mean. It just came out that way. I moved past him and into our bedroom.

"You've got to be kidding me. You can't leave." He reached for my bag, and I twisted away from him.

"You won't even notice that I'm gone." The sadness of the moment seeped into me.

"That's not true, and you know it," he said.

I turned my back on him and started opening my dresser drawers, trying to keep my emotions at bay so I could think straight. I needed to pack enough things so that I wouldn't have to come back to the house for at least a week. I needed time to think, and I couldn't do that here. Not when I had to see him every day or watch how he interacted with Kate. He placed his hand on my back.

"Meredith, please stop," he said tenderly. "Will you just turn around and look at me? For a second, please?"

I couldn't turn around because I might stay if I looked in his eyes, and I couldn't stay when I knew how he felt, despite whatever he was about to say to me. Whatever he wanted to say, he would only be saying it because he was a good guy, and that was what good guys did. There wasn't any doubt in my mind that he'd honor his commitment to me, but that was all he'd be doing—honoring a commitment. His heart would always be with her.

It always had been.

KATE

THEN

"Is this a phone?" I asked Abner as he handed it to me. We didn't use phones. They were one of the ways that the darkness had taken over the rest of the world. I couldn't remember the last time I'd seen one.

"It is, and now it's yours. Feel better now?"

He searched my face for approval as I took it from him, but I didn't understand. I didn't need a phone. Or want one. Its presence had already brought heaviness into the tent.

"It's for when I'm away with the children. I have one too. Do not use it unless it is an emergency. I do not want to be interrupted during this critical period," he said. "If something should happen to one of the children, then I will call you. Write both of these numbers down."

I scurried to the corner, searching through my backpack for my notebook. My movement woke Shiloh, and she immediately started crying. She always went from dead asleep to ear-piercing shrieks in two seconds. I paused, torn between finding the paper and comforting her before her cries irritated Abner.

"Give her to me," Abner ordered, as if he could read my mind.

"It's okay. I've got her. This will only take a second," I said, willing her to quiet herself. He found her crying intolerable.

"I said give her to me." There was no room for argument.

I stood and unwrapped her. Her tiny body was curled into a ball, face scrunched up beet red. He took her from me in one swift swoop. I hurried back to my backpack and found my notebook.

"422-3876."

I scrawled down each digit. "Can you say it one more time?" It was hard to hear over her cries.

He repeated himself, and I double-checked each one. Shiloh had worked herself up to the point where she was going to be too frustrated to eat. Abner was circling the room with her. "Quiet, now, child. You be quiet," he said in the same voice he used to command us all.

"Abner, she's just a baby. She doesn't understand what you're saying to her," I said.

"Nonsense. She knows exactly what's going on. She's willfully disobeying."

A knot of anxiety balled in my stomach.

"I said, be quiet, child," he told her another time, but her cries didn't relent. Before I could stop him, he slapped his hand over her mouth, so big it covered her tiny nose and mouth. She quieted instantly. Her body writhed underneath his. "Quiet now. There you go. Quiet."

"Give her to me!" I screamed, ripping her from his hands.

His hand smacked me across the face. My skin stung as my teeth cut through my lower lip. He grabbed me by my hair and yanked me up, tightening his grip. "You do as the Lord commands. Do you understand me?"

Blood pooled in my mouth. "I understand, I understand," I said as the blood drained down my throat. It wasn't the first time he'd hit me, just the first time it'd been in the face. He released me, and I staggered backward, clutching Shiloh. I dropped my head down. "I'm sorry, Abner. I'm sorry. Please forgive me."

He pointed to the tent entrance. "Get out."

———

Margo and I had emerged from the birthing tent a few days ago, and so far neither of us had put our babies down. We wore them at all times. Each minute counted. Margo had pleaded our case to Will, but he'd barely let her speak before making it clear he sided with Abner. The children were the Lord's—not ours—and giving them over to Abner to work with their souls so young would have a huge impact on the kingdom.

"You should hear Will. He's just like, 'I don't see what the big deal is; they'll be back.' Uh, they're babies?" She rolled her eyes. "He would've let Abner get him pregnant if he could have."

I twisted toward her in shock. "Margo!"

"You know it's true."

Normally one of us would've laughed, but nothing about this was funny. How could one person take care of two infants in the middle of nowhere? Even the most skilled child expert couldn't do it alone. And where would they be? They didn't have a shelter or supplies. Would he take them someplace? Where would he take them? How would they get there? My brain spun with constant thoughts, and I hadn't expected to sleep at all last night, but I did despite my worries. My sleep was fitful, continually interrupted with images of Abner returning from the woods empty handed, saying he'd lost our babies. It was awful.

We watched him as he made his way across camp with Miles. Our eyes had been glued to them whenever they were around, studying Abner's interactions with Miles. I had noticed things I'd never seen before, like how he flinched every time Abner moved fast and the way he was never more than a certain distance from him, as if an invisible cord was tied to him, but not in a good way. He cowered in fear whenever Abner raised his voice. Margo had seen it all too. We didn't need to talk about what it meant. We'd had to pull Abner off adults when his punishments went too far. What would happen if he lost control with the children and no one was there to stop him?

I double-checked to make sure no one was around before quickly filling Margo in on what had happened last night. "I thought he was going to smother her," I whispered out of the corner of my mouth, keeping my eyes straight ahead.

Margo instinctively kissed the top of Zed's head. "What will he do when he can't quiet them?"

"What about what we were talking about before?"

"Leaving?"

I nodded, looking behind us again.

"I'd never make it. I lose pieces of blood every time I walk." Her hands were still buried in the bubbles of the dish soap. We'd been relegated to light dish duty until further notice.

"You're still bleeding like that?"

261

"Yes, and I'm scared. It's been a week. That's too long. Sometimes I feel like I'm going to pass out just from standing up." She dropped her voice even lower. "I think I'm going to die here."

"Don't say that," I hissed. "You can't talk like that."

"It's okay. I've accepted it," she said. There was no fight in her voice. "My baby is going to die, and so am I."

"Stop it." I pulled her hands out of the water and dried them on a towel. "Your baby isn't dying, and neither are you."

Her eyes rolled slowly as she tried to focus on me. "Save your baby, Kate."

I pointed to the tree stump behind her. "Sit. You need to drink water. You're dehydrated."

She started laughing, but within seconds her laughter had moved into tears. I grabbed my water and brought it up to her lips. "Drink this."

She took a sip. "I still love him, you know. Even after everything that's happened. All this time."

I assumed she was talking about Abner, because I shared the same conflict, but I followed her eyes to the gathering area and found them centered on Will.

FORTY

ABBI

NOW

How's it going?

Dad had been texting me pretty much nonstop since he had
dropped us off. I quickly tapped out a response, telling him I was going
to take a shower, so he would at least lay off it for a little while. We were
staying at Extended Stay America, one of those places you could book
by the month, so it was more like a small apartment than a hotel room.
It was nicer than the apartments we'd seen. There was a queen-size bed
and pullout couch. Mom offered to sleep on the couch right away.

She still seemed nervous even though it'd been over two hours since
we'd checked in. Shiloh had fallen asleep thirty minutes ago, but Mom
was too keyed up to sit down.

"I'm so sorry for all of this," she said as she paced the hotel room,
wringing her hands together.

"Please stop saying that," I said. She'd been apologizing over and
over again, but she couldn't help that Meredith had freaked out and
gotten all superspy on everyone. Nobody would've predicted she'd act
that way. I hadn't told her that Meredith left tonight too. She would

really feel bad then, and there was no way I was going to do that to her. Besides, Meredith would probably be home in the morning. She'd stormed off one other time when they'd gotten into a fight. Spent the night at Caleb's, I think, or maybe it was Thad's. Anyway, she'd been back by lunch the following day.

"Are you sure I can't make you any soup or tea?" I asked her.

We'd walked down to the 7-Eleven on the corner to pick up a few supplies. I put everything on my debit card. Dad had given me permission to use it however I wanted. He'd never given me free rein on it before.

"I'm okay. I'm really not hungry," she said, but she'd barely eaten all day.

And then I remembered she was used to going days without food, and this was probably nothing for her. Maybe she was intentionally fasting. She prayed underneath her breath while she walked. It was oddly soothing, and it wasn't long before my eyelids grew heavy with exhaustion. How was she still standing? Let alone walking around? I kicked off my shoes and collapsed on the bed. It was hard, and the pillow felt scratchy against my cheeks, but I didn't care. That was how tired I was. I could've slept on anything. I fell asleep before I had a chance to say good night.

KATE

THEN

My heartbeat exploded in my ears. The darkness pressed in on me. My body screamed to run, twitching as I forced myself to be still and wait. Where was Margo? This was the spot. We'd been over it at least ten times—follow the deer trail to the tree with all its bark stripped away. I had barely convinced Abner to let me sleep alone tonight. He hadn't wasted any time trying to create the next soldier and planned to have me pregnant again by the time he left with Shiloh. I'd pretended to have the stomach flu tonight, and even then he'd tried to talk himself into staying in my tent. Gagging in front of him had finally made him leave me alone and pick someone else.

I scanned the forest line for her, terrified his voice would call my name out at any moment, summoning me back to him. What was taking her so long? We were counting on the lengthy discussions that followed his lovemaking sessions to give us a far enough lead before anyone realized we were gone, but they didn't go on forever.

A twig snapped behind me. I whirled around to see Margo hurrying through the trees. Zed was pressed tightly against her chest, and she clutched her stomach with her other arm as she shuffled along. I raced toward her and hugged her like it'd been years since we'd seen each other.

"Thank God. I was getting so nervous, and every sound is magnified out here, which only made it worse." I put my arm around her waist and tried to help her walk. "Come on, we have to hurry." I tried to pull her along.

But she wasn't moving. She stood still.

"No, Margo, no. Don't." The clouds made it impossible for the moonlight to penetrate the dense canopy above us, making it almost pitch black, but I didn't need to see her face to know she was crying.

"I can't leave him. I just can't do it," she sobbed. She held Zed out to me. "Take him."

"I'm not taking him. That's ridiculous. You're just scared, but we have each other. We can do this together. I'm scared too. Come on, we have to go."

She stayed rooted to her spot. I grabbed her and shoved her forward. She'd be grateful once we were gone. She pushed me back.

"Get off me!" she yelled.

We froze. She put her hand over her mouth, recoiling in horror. "Oh my God, I'm so sorry. I'm so sorry." She tried to hand Zed to me again, but I shook my head. We both knew she was dead if she went back without him.

Tears streamed down my cheeks. "I can't leave you."

"Go. You have to." Her voice shook. "Run."

"Come with me, please," I sobbed. "I can't do this alone."

"They're going to be coming any minute. You have to go now. You can't wait." She took a step backward, ready to bolt. "Remember what Abner always says—when you go, you don't look back. Go, Kate."

My sobs shook me. "Margo, no." But she had already turned her back and started running to camp. For a second, I almost followed her, but Shiloh's breath against my chest gave me the courage I needed to turn and run into the night.

FORTY-ONE

ABBI

NOW

A hand over my mouth startled me awake. My entire body tensed. Mom's face came into view as she hovered over me. She held her finger up to her lips and motioned for me to get out of bed. The shape of the hotel room formed around me as my eyes slowly adjusted to the dark. She wore Shiloh in a tight wrap across her chest and anxiously jiggled her as she threw the covers off me. What was going on? Why were we being quiet?

"Hurry. We have to hurry," she mouthed as I stumbled out of bed, scanning the floor for my clothes.

"Where are we going?" I mouthed back.

She frantically shook her head and pointed to my Nikes in front of the bathroom door. I threw on the jeans and T-shirt I'd been wearing earlier and knelt down to pull on my shoes while she peeked out the front window. I started shoving things into my bag, but she grabbed me and pulled me to my feet.

"There's no time," she whispered in my ear.

She pressed her face against the peephole before opening the door and stepping outside onto the patio. She grabbed my arm and hurried us down the cement corridor, never taking her eyes off the parking lot below us. She rounded the corner past the ice machine, where the staircase led down to the ground floor.

"Mom, what's going on? You're totally freaking me out," I said as soon as we hit the stairs. Her nails dug into me. She acted like she hadn't heard me. Was she having one of her posttraumatic episodes or whatever they called it?

We reached the parking lot and darted through the lines of cars until we reached the street. She pulled me to a stop. She furtively looked in each direction. "Where are we going?" I asked.

"I'll explain it all as soon as we get there," she said breathlessly.

"I need to call Dad." I fumbled in my pocket for my phone. Where was it?

Mom glanced behind us, then took off running down the left side of the street. She stopped as soon as she saw I hadn't moved from my spot on the curb and raced back across.

"Abbi, we have to go. Come on." Something was wrong with her face. Why did she look so strange?

"I can't find my phone." I tried to keep the hysteria out of my voice. I had to call Dad. He'd know what to do.

"We don't have time." She grabbed my arm again and pulled me forward along with her. Shiloh's head popped out of her wrap, and she let out a wail. Mom slapped her hand over her mouth. "Shh, be quiet."

She was losing it. Nobody could hear us.

We hit the street, and she broke into a run, gripping my hand as we moved down the pavement just as a black van sped around the corner. It came to a screeching halt in front of us. We froze. The front doors flung open, and two men jumped out of the cab. Terror filled my insides as they moved toward us. Mom put her arm around my waist, gripping me tightly.

"Mom?" I whimpered.

"The Lord is with us. Don't be afraid," she said.

They were on us within seconds.

I let out a bloodcurdling scream when one of them grabbed me by the wrist and twisted my arm behind my back.

"Shut up, kid," he hissed within inches of my face. His eyes were wild. Dirt crusted his face; his hair was bushy and uncombed. His skin was tanned and leathered, peeling in parts.

"Help! Somebody help! H—"

His hand smacked my face, snapping my jaw shut. My heartbeat exploded in my ears. I shoved him away and took off running in blind terror, screaming wildly. He pummeled me from behind, smashing me onto the concrete. I flailed against him, biting and clawing at him, trying to jab my finger in his eyes, kick between his legs. It was no use. He was too strong.

"Scream again and I'll hurt you." His breath was hot on my neck. He smelled like rotten cheese. I fought the urge to pull away again. My entire body trembled.

"Please, what do you want? Just tell me what you want," I cried. He ignored me. He yanked both arms behind me, and something sharp cut into my wrists as he tied them together. He worked in silence. "Please let us go. Please don't hurt us." What did they say in class? Appeal to their humanity. Make yourself human if you can't make yourself repulsive. He lifted me up like I weighed nothing and spun me around. "Do you have kids?" I blurted out.

Sweat dripped down his chin. He ignored me and pulled me back in the direction of Mom. His partner had his arm around her waist. He was whispering something in her ear, touching her. I squeezed my eyes shut. I didn't want to see it, couldn't.

"Please go away. Leave us alone," I begged, dragging my feet as he pulled me along.

The man with Mom turned around. A scruffy layer of facial hair covered his face. "Hurry up." He peered at me with beady blue eyes.

Why wasn't she running? How come she was just standing there? And then I spotted it—the gun slung on his hip. The two of them surrounded me. My captor shoved me toward the scruffy man, and he grabbed me, his fingernails digging into my arms. I let my body go slack. I couldn't take my eyes off his gun. The one with the dark beard opened the back door of the van.

"Please, God, no, please." I was sobbing so hard I could barely talk as they shoved me inside.

They paid me no attention. One of them slapped tape over my mouth, while the other wrapped my ankles together. Paralyzing fear shot through me. My eyes searched for Mom. She slowly crept closer. My pulse pounded in my temples. I forced myself to be still and pretend like I didn't see her. What would she hit them with? She was so close. Right behind them. Every muscle tensed.

She stepped between them. Everything moved in slow motion as she unwrapped Shiloh and handed her to the man on the left, the one with the gun. And that was when it happened. My brain stopped. Took them in—really took them in—long, scraggly beards, beige T-shirts, and khaki pants, dirty and worn. Mom's eyes caught mine, and she saw the realization hit. She didn't blink as she reached out and slammed the van door, sealing me inside.

I screamed *No!* so hard behind my tape it felt like my eyes would burst.

"Hurry—we've got to move, Abner," Mom said.

I froze. It was the same voice she'd used in her home videos.

"I told you I could do it," she said. "I made the Lord proud. You know I did."

He laughed. "I missed you, my love."

I couldn't make out what she said next as their muffled whispers made their way to the front of the van. The doors opened and then slammed shut. The van lurched forward. I tried to grab for something—anything—to steady myself, but there was nothing. The back was stripped bare. I dropped to the floor and scooted against the wall, curling myself into a ball. The ties cut into my wrists. My head throbbed.

Where were they taking me? The realization that she'd brought me to them on purpose hit me again and again, hardening my stomach into knots. I shook so hard my teeth chattered. Her betrayal hurt too much for tears. Why were they doing this to me?

The van slammed to a stop, sending me flying to the other side of the vehicle. I smacked my head against the metal. Waves of panic shot up my spine. There was wetness between my legs, like I'd peed myself. Did I pee? I tried to scream, but it wouldn't come out. Tears trickled out of the corners of my eyes. The van lurched forward again. Then stalled. Dizziness washed over me. Tires squealed. Stopped.

"Freeze! Police!" A man's voice shattered the air.

Wailing up front. Like an animal. Was that Mom? Did he hurt her? I scooted over and threw myself at the back wall, beating my bound feet against it.

"Stay away from her!" I tried to scream, but the words were trapped behind the tape covering my mouth. I kicked the wall a final time before scooting back to the corner. The police wouldn't hurt her, would they?

More screaming. So many screams. A gunshot rang out. My insides froze; I was too scared to breathe. The door clicked, then was flung open. Dean plunged into the van. He knelt in front of me, carefully taking the tape from my mouth. "Are you okay?" I wanted to talk, but all the sounds stayed stuck inside me. "Are you hurt?" he asked again, peering at me within inches of my face. He didn't wait for a response. He quickly untied me before scooping me up and lifting me off the floor like I weighed nothing.

I clung to him and buried my face in his chest. He carried me through the van, stepping over the blankets spread out on the floor, and outside into the commotion. Flashing lights were everywhere. The helicopter above us roared in my ears. My eyes searched for Mom's.

"Close your eyes," Dean shouted. "Just close your eyes and hold on to me."

Too late. A body lay covered with a blanket in the center of the road.

"Is that . . ."

I couldn't finish.

"It's not your mom," Dean said.

I closed my eyes, shaking with sobs as he carried me. I didn't open them until we were in the ambulance. Medical personnel swirled around me. There were so many lights. Why were there so many lights? They were too bright. I felt like I was going to throw up. Too late. Just that quickly the liquid was gone, swiped off my face.

"Abbi?" A woman's face in mine. "You're safe now. Your parents will meet you at the hospital. Okay? Do you understand?"

I turned my head away, the movement sending shooting pain down my neck. The scene moved in front of me, liquid and warm.

Mom? Where was she?

I closed my eyes again so the world would stop spinning.

FORTY-TWO
MEREDITH

NOW

"Scott, slow down. What are you talking about? I don't understand." I sat up, rubbing the sleep from my eyes, instantly awake. I brought my phone to my other ear, sliding my glasses on so that I could see in the dark. "I'm here, but I don't understand a word you're saying. You have to slow down."

"They tried to kidnap Abbi. Oh my God. I can't even believe this. How could I be such an idiot?" he sputtered.

"Are you driving? It sounds like you're driving. Why don't you pull over and talk to me?" I flicked on the light above the nightstand.

"I can't pull over. I have to get down to the hospital. How did I not see this? You were right, Meredith. You were always right."

"What are you talking about? You're not making any sense."

"Okay. God, I just can't believe this—"

"Scott, focus. Either that or pull over, because you can't be driving like a crazy man, or someone is going to get hurt." I slipped a gray hoodie over my head and searched for where I'd thrown my sweatpants before getting into bed last night. "Take me through what happened. One step at a time. It will help you calm down."

"I kept texting Abbi after you left, but she stopped responding after a while. Probably because I was annoying her. Anyway, I fell asleep watching TV, and my phone woke me up. I knew it was bad as soon as I saw that it was Dean. I jumped off the couch, and I'm like, tell me what's going on. He said he couldn't talk about it over the phone but that Abbi was in the hospital, and Kate was in custody at the police station because of a kidnapping sting. He was going on and on about how Ray and one of his men showed up near the girls' hotel and grabbed them. They tied Abbi up and threw her in the back of a van. He kept saying 'they,' and it took me a while to realize he meant Kate too. She was in on it."

I stopped midstride. "Wait? What are you saying? That she helped kidnap Abbi?"

"Yes." His voice cracked, thick with emotion. "How could I have been so stupid? I should've listened to you."

"Has she been in contact with him this entire time? Are we sure we're okay?" My heart jumped as I tried not to run. I searched for my car in the unfamiliar hotel parking lot. I waved my fob, listening for the sound of the beep.

"I have no clue. Our conversation lasted all of two minutes. I'm not kidding. He said he'd fill me in on the details once I got down to the hospital." He wasn't any less choked up, falling to pieces still. "I need you there. You have to meet me down there. I can't do this without you."

I slid my key into the lock. "I'm on the way." No matter what had happened, they were still my family, and Abbi would need me as much as he did right now. She'd been too young to feel the devastation of her mom leaving before, but she'd feel the impact of this hit, and she would need me to help her through it, even if she didn't know that yet.

Scott rushed down the hospital corridor at the sight of me. His clothes were wrinkled and rumpled, and he wore two different tennis shoes—one navy, the other black. His eyes were watery and bloodshot as he leaned in, giving me a tentative kiss on my cheek.

"I can't believe I let this happen." He struggled to control his emotions.

"You didn't let this happen." I opened my arms, and he fell into them, but his body was rigid, stiff with unspent worry and grief. I rubbed his back in circles, hoping it'd help him calm down. "Where is she?" I asked.

He pulled away. "She's still not back from her CAT scan." His eyes filled with tears. "How did I not see this?"

He'd be asking himself that question for a long time. We didn't have time for his guilt now. "How badly is she hurt?" I asked.

"Pretty banged up. It looks like she put up a fight. Just like they taught her." His voice caught. Dean had insisted Abbi take a self-defense class when she was thirteen. She'd loved it.

"And Kate?"

His entire body stiffened. "She's fine. In a holding cell at the moment. They didn't touch her."

"I don't understand any of this. How did they know where they were? Who was involved?"

Just then the double doors opened, and Dean burst through them. Scott and I rushed to him, trying not to talk on top of each other with our questions. He held his hand up and motioned to the chairs lining the hallway. "Why don't you take a seat so we can talk?"

Scott shook his head, so I stayed standing next to him. "Just tell me what happened," he said. "Everything."

"Sure. Absolutely." Dean nodded a few times in rapid succession. "We left the wiretap on your phone lines after we removed the surveillance equipment, just in case someone from Love International contacted Kate. We never expected her to be the one to contact them," he said. "We were in complete shock the first time she reached out."

I stopped him. "I thought they were these remote outcasts. How'd they have phones, let alone service?"

"We don't know about any of the others, but Ray has been in San Francisco, and he's the one she's been talking to." Dean paused, taking a deep breath before continuing. The bags underneath his eyes suggested he'd been up for days. "There's a few things you need to know about Ray. First, he's also who Kate refers to as Abner. We've always operated under the theory that Abner was some kind of divine being they believed in as part of their whacked-out theology. Early on we considered the possibility that he might be a person, but we ruled it out fairly quickly, because of the way she spoke about him. Basically, we thought he was their god." He cleared his throat uncomfortably. "Turns out, he is, in a way, just not how we imagined. Kate says he's Shiloh's father. We put a rush on the DNA, but she has no reason to lie about that, so it's a pretty safe bet to assume that he is. Also, you should know she's been referring to herself as his wife since they brought her in."

I felt Scott's sharp intake of breath beside me. I'd always suspected Ray was Shiloh's father. Hadn't he? I'd always assumed it was why we hadn't talked about it. Everything was awkward enough without addressing that part of the equation.

"Is that why she came home?" The color drained from his face. "To bring Abbi back to him?"

I placed my hand on his arm. "Let's try and sit, okay?" I led him to the chairs Dean had motioned to earlier, and he reluctantly took a seat in the one next to me. I tucked my purse underneath my feet.

Dean leaned against the hallway wall and crossed his arms on his chest. "Something legitimately spooked Kate enough to leave Love International. Her terror in the beginning was real, so it had to be pretty bad. But that's the thing with domestic violence victims—the fear never keeps them away. They go back. She was the one who made initial contact, and her voice changed as soon as she heard his. She was under his spell almost immediately, talking in this weird submissive tone I'd never heard her use. By the end of their first phone call, she was begging him to come back. In the beginning, he refused to take her back. He—"

Scott interrupted. "Why did she contact him the first time? Did she ever say?"

"She did, but I don't want either of you to ever tell Abbi what I'm about to tell you." His eyes were serious.

Scott and I exchanged a glance before nodding our agreement. What could he possibly have to tell us that we couldn't share with Abbi?

"Abbi and Kate looked at Ray's pictures on social media together at night. Seeing his picture set her off, and it was enough of a pull for her to reach out to him. Then, once she heard his voice, it was over."

We'd told Abbi so many times to stay away from social media on the case, but how could I be mad at her about it when I'd done the same thing? There was no way she'd considered how it might trigger Kate. I hoped she would never make the connection, for her sake.

"Because she saw a picture? That's all it took?" Scott asked.

I couldn't tell if he was disgusted or hurt. Maybe a combination of both.

"It's not that simple. You have to think of her as a domestic violence victim. Most women never leave their abusers, or if they do, it takes them an average of seven times before they're successful," Dean explained.

Scott didn't look convinced. I shared his skepticism. She couldn't leave her abuser, but she could plan her daughter's kidnapping?

"So what happened?" I asked.

"She wanted to come back, but he refused to take her. She'd betrayed him by leaving, but Kate kept begging for his forgiveness and saying she was willing to do anything. That's when everything turned. He started toying with her, asking her to do little things to prove herself to him, and she did."

Scott interrupted again. "Like what kinds of things?"

For a brief second, embarrassment flashed across his expression before he quickly erased it.

"Things of a sexual nature and others of a punishing nature. She's covered in self-inflicted wounds running down her legs that she's been carving into herself as a form of penance. She'll show them to you if you ask her. She's quite proud of them."

Scott gripped both sides of his chair. I was grateful we'd sat down. He looked almost as wrecked as he'd been the day we found out she had returned.

"Kate kept coming up with ways to prove her loyalty, and eventually they agreed she could come back, on the condition that she brought Abbi with her. We—"

"Why did you let them kidnap her?" Scott interrupted him. "If you knew that was what they were going to do, why'd you let them go through with it?"

It was Dean's turn to look uncomfortable. He shifted in his position. "We knew this case would be huge as soon as we found out she'd been with Love International. One of the first things we did was investigate any former complaints or charges against them, and we didn't have to look far. Cases popped up everywhere, especially the one of a twenty-four-year-old girl named Willow. Her parents always suspected Love International had something to do with her disappearance, and they'd never given up looking for her. They were extremely helpful with our investigation." He cleared his throat. Cleared it again. "The good thing about guys like Ray is that they think they're smarter than everybody else and above the law, so their conversations were gold mines of information, because they never expected anyone to be listening. It wasn't long before we were connecting dots everywhere. Unfortunately, the dots led to three bodies in Oregon that our teams found in unmarked graves."

Scott narrowed his eyes to slits. "You're still not answering my question. Why let them kidnap Abbi?"

"We needed to get them on kidnapping charges so that we had something that would stick. We hope one of them flips on the other, but we needed to hold them long enough to build our case against them. And this case is going to be huge. Believe me, Scott, so many families are going to get answers once this is all said and done."

Scott leaped up from his chair and shook his finger at Dean. "You used her as bait! That's what you're saying, isn't it? How could you?"

Dean lifted his hands in surrender. "Please, Scott. I'm sorry, but just listen to me. Each step of the way was carefully monitored, and, believe me, Scott, I wouldn't have done it if there was any other way."

"Carefully monitored?" Scott shrieked. "I just heard on the news before Meredith got here that someone died at the scene."

I jumped up next to him. "What?" I wanted to hit Dean too.

"Calm down, please. Calm down. We do things like this all the time. It's what we're trained to do."

I didn't care how many times he'd done it. This was Abbi we were talking about.

"Ray's partner, Will, fired at the police officers, and they had no choice but to use deadly force to protect themselves," Dean said, like that excused his behavior.

"And if he would've chosen to shoot Abbi instead?" Scott asked what I was thinking.

Dean didn't have a response. I'd never seen him speechless before. I couldn't help but wonder what Abbi knew about all of this. "Can we see Abbi now?" I asked.

"Abbi says Kate is the one who locked her inside the van. She heard them talking while she was inside about how much they'd missed each other and how proud the Lord must be of them. It makes me sick," Scott said.

I reached out and took his hand. "She's delusional, Scott. That's what you've never understood. I'm sure she used to be a rational and logical human being, but she's been warped. But right now, we can't focus on that. We need to go to Abbi. She needs us."

FORTY-THREE

ABBI

NOW

The police station resembled my doctor's office. It even had stands filled with old magazines. The only telltale sign was the receptionist's desk shrouded in Plexiglas. The room was practically empty except for a woman in the corner frantically tapping away on her phone. Dad gripped my arm while the receptionist pressed the button requesting an officer to take us back to Mom. They'd kept me in the hospital overnight for observation, and I'd begged Dad to take me to the police station before he brought me home. He didn't like the idea, but Meredith encouraged him to take me, and he'd finally relented. Meredith had opted out of the meeting, saying she was exhausted and needed to lie down, but she didn't want to see Mom any more than he did.

The doors buzzed, and an officer walked through, scanning us up and down on the spot. I'd expected him to be in his uniform, but he was wearing a collared shirt tucked into formal pants. "Scott Bennett?" he asked. A clear formality since there wasn't another man in the room.

Dad stepped forward, and I fell in line next to him.

"This way," the officer said.

Dad and I didn't speak as we followed him down the corridor. A series of identical metal doors lined each side. My head throbbed with a headache that hadn't left since they'd thrown me in the van. I didn't like how the pain medication made me feel, so I hadn't taken any this morning, but I was starting to regret it. Dad kept turning around to make sure I was okay. He wasn't going to let me out of his sight for a long time, but I was okay with that. All I wanted to do was curl up in a blanket on the couch at home and watch movies once this was over with.

The officer stopped at one of the doors and scanned his keycard to open it. He held the door for us, and we hurried inside. The room was square with almost perfect lines. A table stood in the center with two chairs on either side. An old-fashioned water dispenser, the kind we used in elementary school with coned cups, stood in the corner. Dad and I took a seat next to each other on the chairs. The door clicked shut behind the officer.

"How are you doing?" Dad asked.

"I'm okay," I lied. What did people do after their mother kidnapped them? Her arraignment was tomorrow, and they were charging her with kidnapping and obstructing justice, both felonies. They'd offered her a plea bargain for any information she gave them on Ray, but she had refused. No surprise.

"You should be at home resting," he said.

"Dad, I'm fine." He acted like I had some terminal illness. "Are you okay?"

He hadn't seen Mom since it had happened, and he had sworn the only time he ever wanted to see her again was in court. But then I had asked to visit, and he hadn't had a choice, since there was no way he'd let me go by myself.

"I just want to get this over as quickly as possible," he said. The red light from the camera blinked above his head. The room was probably wired for sound too. But this wasn't about getting information.

Mom shuffled into the room with her hands in front of her in cuffs. The legs of her pale-blue jumpsuit were too long and dragged on the floor as she walked. Her hair was matted in a big ball behind her, like she hadn't brushed it for weeks, even though she'd only been here overnight. She rushed forward like she was going to hug me.

"No touching." The officer jerked her back and nudged her to the other side of the table. "Sit," he ordered.

Mom sat on command, stretching her hands in front of her. The officer unlatched Mom's cuffs. She twirled her wrists in circles, like they needed to stretch, then clasped them in her lap.

"Oh Abbi, thank God you're here. Are you okay?" she asked. New wrinkles lined her face. Dark bags circled her eyes.

Was her concern real? Did she care? "I'm fine," I said, setting my jaw. It hurt, but I wouldn't cry. I would do what I'd come here to do. I needed her to look me in the eye and tell me what she'd done—what would've happened if Dean and his men hadn't jumped out to stop them.

"The police took Shiloh. Just ripped her away from me like savage beasts. Can you believe that? She's breastfeeding." She jiggled her legs while she spoke. "How's she going to eat, Abbi? She doesn't have teeth. She's never eaten any food. What if they give her that poison?" Her words dripped with hysteria. "Will you help me? Please? There has to be a law against this. Mothers can't be separated from their babies. Please help."

"I don't know anything about the law and babies," I said. How could she have a baby with that monster? What did that make her? At least Shiloh was going to be with a family that would keep her away from them. Dean said there was a list a mile long of people who wanted to adopt babies.

Dad stiffened next to me, staring at her with anger radiating off him. She'd never felt permanent to me, and I'd been collecting memories of my own as we went along, because I wasn't getting stuck without any this time. I'd kept pieces of her—the towel she'd used on her hair, a corner of the ratty shirt she'd slept in every night, and the toothbrush she'd used at the hospital. Were they all tainted with her lies now? Part of me wanted to gather them all together and burn them in a big pile in the front yard.

"Can you imagine?" She broke down in tears in the same way she had during her first few days with us. Wrecked. Pitiful. So much that you felt sorry for her and wanted to help her. Even now her tears pulled at me. "Poor Shiloh."

Had she never thought about getting caught? Or was she that sure of their plan?

"You said once that you wanted us to have an honest relationship. Did you mean that?" I asked.

She nodded through her tears. "I meant everything, Abbi. Everything." Snot dripped onto her upper lip, unapologetically.

"Where were we going that night?" I asked like I didn't already know. I'd spent the last twenty-four hours being questioned by police and investigators and was well versed in their plan. Ray had wanted Mom to bring me to him as some bizarre loyalty test to show her repentance for leaving. I refused to listen to the FBI recordings of her phone conversations with him. I wanted her to say it to me. It didn't matter how many times Dad walked me through it. None of it would feel real unless it came from her.

Her eyes darted around the room, and she lowered her voice. "We can talk about that later. It was all part of the Lord's plan. His plans are not always easy. Sometimes they are very difficult." She choked on a sob.

Which part was difficult? I wanted to ask. Giving me up to your psycho leader? Was that hard? Or had that been easy? Was she talking about how hard it had been for her to be away from them all this time?

"I thought about backing out, Abbi. I did."

Except she didn't. As if thinking about it meant anything. It wasn't even a cheap consolation prize. "Please, Mom, just tell me where we were going?"

"It doesn't matter." She straightened in her seat, twisting her hands in her lap.

She had no grasp on reality if she thought it didn't matter. It meant everything. "Why were you going back to them?" I asked, trying not to cry.

She stood, then quickly sat again. "None of this is important. Where's Abner?"

And then it hit me—she wasn't going back to them; she was going back to him. Had it always been about him? Was Love International just the excuse to make it okay to leave us? I leaned into Dad. He put a supportive arm around me. Maybe he was right. Maybe this wasn't such a good idea.

"Have you seen him?" she asked.

I saw his beady eyes every time I closed my eyes to sleep. I hadn't slept since the attack. Dean told me it was normal and would pass over time. He said he'd get me help if it didn't.

I shook my head.

Mom laid her hands on her chest and closed her eyes. She took a deep breath, followed by another. Some of the tension left her face. "Oh thank God, he's here. I can feel him. As long as we're still together, we can get through anything." She took another deep breath, as if she tasted him in the air. She let him fill her before blowing him back out.

"Actually, you're wrong," I blurted out. "He's not here."

Her eyes snapped open. "Where is he?" She leaned across the table. "I thought you didn't know where he was."

"I don't know where he is, but I do know who he's with," I said. I hadn't planned on saying anything about Ray—or whatever his name was—but it hurt that all she cared about was him.

She practically leaped across the table, every muscle in her neck strained forward. "Where is he?" she asked again, scanning the room like I might be hiding him.

"His mom bailed him out last night," I said.

Mom's face contorted into the same shocked expression as Dad's face had last night when they'd told him the news. She jerked her head back and forth. "What? No. That's not possible. His mom died when he was sixteen."

"His mom is alive and well. Always has been. A mighty rich lady too. So was Ray. Turns out that's where he got all his money. Still has it. He's worth millions. He never actually worked a day in his life."

She jerked her head harder and faster. "No, no, no. You're lying. That's not true. Why would you lie? I don't understand. This must be a test. What kind of a test is this?" She raked her fingers up and down her forearms. "I'll figure it out. I will. I'll pass this one. I pass all of them."

"His name isn't even Ray." I let the final bomb drop. "It's Harold Allen Fitzgerald."

She jumped up from her chair and leaped across the table at me. "Liar!" she screamed.

Dad shoved the table into her, and she flew back. The officer in the doorway rushed into the room and grabbed her from behind. Mom flailed against him.

"This visit is over," the officer said, twisting Mom's arms behind her back and cuffing her again.

"Stop lying! Why are you lying? How dare you fill me with such lies?" She shook her head like a mad dog. "You're evil."

Dad stood. "Don't you ever come near her again. If you—"

I grabbed his arm. "It's okay, Dad. I'm done." I stood next to him and pushed in my chair. I reached up and undid the locket around my neck—the one with her picture that I'd been wearing since I was five. I set it on the table in front of her.

"Goodbye, Mom."

ABOUT THE AUTHOR

Photo © 2017

Dr. Lucinda Berry is a trauma psychologist and leading researcher in childhood trauma. She uses her clinical experience to create disturbing psychological thrillers, blurring the line between fiction and nonfiction. She enjoys taking her readers on journeys through the dark recesses of the human psyche.

If Berry isn't chasing after her ten-year-old son, you can find her running through Los Angeles, prepping for her next marathon. To hear about her upcoming releases, visit her on Facebook or sign up for her newsletter at https://lucindaberry.com/.

Made in the USA
Middletown, DE
29 August 2022